# "If I lose any more people, the Iraqis won't reach the States."

The colonel's stance was threatening, belligerent.

Mack Bolan's icy gaze locked on Watkins for a stretched second. He was aware that the colonel was poised to turn the raid into a personal vengeance hunt. Suddenly the Executioner knew he was on his own and decided he would have to watch his back.

"I want Condor One off the roof and our evac vehicles out back in two minutes," Bolan ordered. "And raise those Apaches. I want them on standby and ready to nail anything that tries to keep us from getting to the LZ."

After drilling a piercing stare into Bolan, Watkins got on the radio.

With the stench of battle behind him, the Executioner headed into the tunnel, feeling an itch between his shoulder blades.

*Other titles available in
this series:*

# DON PENDLETON's
# MACK BOLAN®

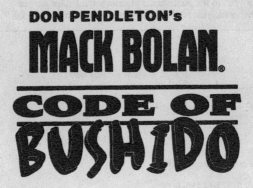

# CODE OF
# BUSHIDO

## A GOLD EAGLE BOOK FROM
# WORLDWIDE®

TORONTO • NEW YORK • LONDON
AMSTERDAM • PARIS • SYDNEY • HAMBURG
STOCKHOLM • ATHENS • TOKYO • MILAN
MADRID • WARSAW • BUDAPEST • AUCKLAND

First edition August 1997

ISBN 0-373-61455-1

Special thanks and acknowledgment to
Dan Schmidt for his contribution to this work.

CODE OF BUSHIDO

...War, he sung, is foil and trouble,
Honor but an empty bubble,
Never ending, still beginning,
Fighting still, and still destroying.

—John Dryden
1631-1700


Vengeance is mine; I will repay, saith the Lord.

—The Holy Bible
Romans 12:19


There is no honor in seeking vengeance, no honor in killing innocents to correct a perceived wrong.

—Mack Bolan

# CHAPTER ONE

*Beirut, Lebanon*

Mack Bolan steeled himself to greet the new day in Beirut with a silent message of doom. Once the raid on the terrorists' armed haven started, it couldn't stop. Hesitation or the mere hint of retreat meant failure. To fail now meant certain and sudden death.

Shedding his kaffiyeh and robe, which revealed his combat blacksuit and weapons of war, the Executioner crouched beside the jagged teeth of an alley. It was clear to him his position had recently taken the brunt of gunfire and rocket bombardment during one of the countless savage battles between rival Muslim factions that raged with eternal and unrelenting fury in the southern part of the city.

For the past several weeks, though, the street fighting in Beirut seemed to have taken on a greater and bolder ferocity. Various factions of Arab terrorists seemed to be competing for turf, notoriety and weapons. Evidence of the bloodbath covered the street and alleyways like a mad painter's depiction of Armageddon. Corpses were left where they fell in the street, or in gutters, doorways and alleys. Several vehicles lay in smoldering ruins at the far end of the street, where black smoke drifted in thick, coiling tendrils to blot out the distant buildings of neighborhoods to the north. Clearly, as Mossad undercover agents in Beirut had indicated during briefings at the Hotel Saint-Georges, not even the Lebanese or Syrian army patrols wanted to venture into that part of town, where everyone was fighting and killing.

The stench of blood and bloated corpses stretched out behind him, and the acrid smoke wafting from the wreckage of a nearby smoldering vehicle clawed into Bolan's senses. The Executioner moved the strap of the Uzi submachine gun higher up on his shoulder, conscious of the weight of the .44 Magnum Desert Eagle in shoulder leather. There was also a radio handset on his webbing for contact with the evacuation team, plus six pairs of handcuffs for the prisoners. Prime target—Mahmud Abriz.

Two months earlier Abriz and his Iraqi brother terrorists had set off a series of bombs and suicide attacks in Chicago that had left more than two hundred innocents dead and countless others seriously wounded. Eleven other Iraqi terrorists had been caught via an Arab FBI informant who got cold feet and wanted immunity. Abriz, mastermind of the terrorist attacks and leader of the group known as the Death Brigade, had somehow fled American soil along with ten other terrorists. Combined intelligence from both the Israeli Mossad and the Americans had tracked, then pinpointed, the exact whereabouts of Abriz in Beirut.

To snare Abriz and the other targets for extradition to the United States to stand trial, Hal Brognola had gone directly through the White House and had Bolan put in charge as Colonel Rance Pollock. The Executioner was heading up a Special Forces commando unit called Strike Force Grim Reaper. In charge of the unofficial commando unit, but second-in-command to Bolan, was Colonel Ray Watkins. Already the two men had danced through some tense moments of testing wills. But the Executioner was in charge, and that came straight from the top brass at the Pentagon, thanks to Brognola.

Using cover as journalists, Bolan and Watkins had gone to Beirut only twenty-four hours earlier. Weapons had been smuggled to a safehouse in northern Beirut by the CIA after the arrival of the "journalists." Two hours before dawn, the rest of the team had been dropped off by helicopter with four AH-64 Apache gunships making sure the commando unit safety hit the Mediterranean shoreline of Beirut. If needed, Bolan knew those Apache gunships would provide air cover to get the team and its prisoners out of Beirut.

As he prepared to be the first one through the door and into the viper's nest, adrenaline cleared the soldier's head. Unleathering then lifting the sound-suppressed Beretta 93-R, he fixed his sights on another sentry who had just stepped out of the doorway of the targeted apartment building to replace the guard on duty. Bolan quickly surveyed his surroundings.

Across the street three hunched shadows with custom-silenced M-16s fanned out over the rooftop of another apartment complex. Bolan glimpsed the sentry, who had an AK-47 slung across a shoulder. The terrorist was busy firing up a cigarette, unaware of the danger closing in on him and his Death Brigade comrades.

Combat senses on full alert, Bolan looked at the rooftop, peering through the gloomy curtain of dawn, turned dark by the smoke of flaming wreckage. A moment later he saw the three snipers of the U.S. Special Forces commando team vanish. Then he glimpsed their muzzles stab the murk as the commandos waited for the doomsday numbers to tick down. Bolan knew three other Special Forces snipers were in position, with a two-man team in place in the street behind the complex in case the rats fled their hole.

After one last hard sweep of the quiet street, Bolan checked his chronometer. Watkins and his six-man hit team would be moving in from the north end of the street at that very moment. And they all had less than two hours to get out of Beirut and link up with the C-130 that would be landing on a stretch of isolated beach between Sidon and Tyre.

When the numbers counted down, the Executioner

wheeled around the corner, drawing target acquisition on the sentry. In the next moment the terrorist was alerted to Bolan's sudden presence by his own combat instincts, turning toward the Executioner but freezing with the cigarette poised to touch his lips. Bolan caressed the Beretta's trigger, chugging out a 9 mm round that cored through the terrorist's skull and kicked him off his feet.

Tucking the Beretta away and plucking a grenade off his webbing, Bolan headed toward the steel door to the target building. The soldier pulled the pin just as he spotted Colonel Watkins and his team rolling like wraiths out of the gloom to hug the facade of the building some twenty yards from Bolan. Through the murk the Executioner locked gazes with Watkins. There would be no mistaking friendly forces here. Each member of Strike Force Grim Reaper wore a combat blacksuit with a black beret that had an emblem of a viper wrapped around a death's-head. Aside from Bolan, who had an Uzi, they all toted M-16s with attached M-203 grenade launchers.

Bolan dropped the armed grenade in front of the door, then hustled back to the corner of the alley. A second later he heard a muffled voice from behind the entryway.

"Kabir?" Then more urgent. "Kabir!"

Peering around the corner, Bolan saw the door open. A man's head appeared, then the grenade erupted at his feet. Steel fragments, ripping through the air in a fifteen-yard radius, all but vaporized the terrorist. Bolan was up and racing toward the smoking entrance. Just as the Executioner bounded up the short flight of steps, autofire rang out from somewhere across the street. A hurricane force of lead peppered the doorway beside Bolan, but the Executioner was already plunging inside the target building, his Uzi subgun tracking for enemy blood.

# CHAPTER TWO

Even as he burst through the swirling dust, a sustained burst blowing two AK-47-toting terrorists off their feet, Bolan was grimly aware the hit was about to throw death back in his face. The American shock troops had only moments to seize back the initiative, or the terrorist safehouse would become their graveyard. There was no time to wonder about or curse the sudden counterattack out on the street.

Enemy chaos had erupted throughout the first floor of the building, but heavy footsteps sounded like rolling thunder beside, above and below the Executioner. Moving on, he caught sight of three more gunmen surging through the beaded curtains of archways down the hall.

No sooner did they show themselves than Bolan dropped them with controlled bursts of 9 mm lead even as the tracking line of return fire tattooed the wall above him. Having seen enough intelligence photos of Abriz and the other terrorists, the soldier knew none of the enemy at that point was his prime target.

No mistake, their faces were branded in his mind.

Scuffling sounds to his flank caught Bolan's attention. As he hit a combat crouch beside a beaded curtain, autofire chewed the archway. Not missing a beat, even with stone chips spitting past his face, the Executioner armed, then hurled, a grenade into what appeared to be a living room. More enemy gunfire was silenced moments later when the bomb scythed through three armed shadows scurrying across the room.

Watkins hurried to Bolan's side. "They knew we were coming."

The colonel, who was referring to Mossad's Arab informant, clearly felt betrayed. Bolan detected the same bitter resentment Watkins had displayed since he had been ordered subordinate to the Executioner. Only now the colonel looked ready to explode with rage.

"I don't think so," Bolan said.

Watkins kept his voice tight with controlled fury. "*You* don't think so, Colonel? Well, take a look at that. I just lost a good man."

He jerked a nod behind him, and Bolan followed his gaze through the cloud of smoke. A Grim Reaper commando was being dragged through the doorway, then dumped on the hallway floor. Blood poured down the man's face. His skull was shattered, his eyes wide in death.

Only sporadic bursts of autofire erupted from beyond the doorway. A distant scream told Bolan the silent cross fire from Reaper snipers had retaken the street. Their rear might be recovered, he knew, but the worst was dead ahead—and below in the cellar, which was, according to the informant, a labyrinth that bunkered even more terrorists than had been taken out in the opening moments of the raid.

Watkins put his face close to Bolan's. "Being the first one through the door made you one lucky son of a bitch, Colonel."

"If you have a problem, Colonel, I suggest we address it later," the Executioner growled as he pulled a grenade off his webbing.

Three more terrorists appeared out of nowhere at the top of the steps that led to the second story. One-handed, Bolan triggered the Uzi, pumping out a burst of 9 mm death that stitched the lead terrorist's chest in a scarlet figure eight.

Behind Bolan, Watkins and his commandos cut loose with combined M-16 autofire and two 40 mm grenades. More enemy screams pierced the air for a heartbeat before the ear-shattering blast silenced their cries forever. As more fresh dead piled up, Bolan searched the hall and upstairs landing for any more lurking terrorists. No takers, but the soldier made out the distinct sounds of men scrambling below the floor. According to the informant, there was a hole in the floor at the end of the hall. Apparently Abriz hid there and was surrounded around-the-clock by his brothers-in-blood.

Long strides took Bolan to the rug at the end of

the hall. With the commandos on his heels, the Executioner pulled back the rug, exposing a steel door with a metal ring. He gave Watkins the nod, then armed the grenade. The colonel threw open the door.

Just as Bolan anticipated, a lead hellstorm erupted from the hole, fiery streaks stabbing through the murk below. Watkins and his commandos bolted out of the line of fire as slugs whined off the ceiling and walls in a screaming wave.

The Executioner counted down three seconds, then pitched the grenade into the gloom.

A flash of light and the thunder of an explosion were followed by screams. Bolan plunged into the roiling smoke, hearing Watkins order two of his commandos to cover their rear from the hall. He bounded down the steps and over rubble and bodies, the Uzi up and searching for fresh targets in the dim light cast by a single intact lightbulb.

Hugging the edge of the wall at the foot of the steps, Bolan peered around the corner, taking in the underground haven. Soviet and Czech-made weapons were scattered across the large bunker or leaned against the stone walls. Crates of ammunition and explosives were piled in a far corner. Strings of smashed lightbulbs hung from wire stretched across the ceiling, swaying now from the soldier's explosive entry. Wavering light caught shadows scurrying across the room, heading for the mouth of what Bolan had been informed was a tunnel that led to a back street. A mere dozen feet away, Bolan heard and then saw a terrorist bellowing into the headset of a radio console in Arabic. The terrorist was so busy speaking into the headset that he didn't see Bolan until it was too late.

As he pushed off the wall and sprinted for the cover of a thick wooden pillar in the middle of the room, the soldier drilled a furious barrage into the man. The mortally wounded terrorist collapsed to the floor, followed by the flaming and smoking radio console. Once again the Mossad informant had been right—the Death Brigade was in contact with Lebanese army patrols in the vicinity. And Bolan knew that if the Lebanese army showed up, their problems had only just begun. Intelligence reports from both the CIA and Mossad had the Lebanese army in possession of a small fleet of recently purchased Russian attack helicopters, notably the fearsome Mil Mi-24 Hind.

At the moment, as autofire opened up from the mouth of the tunnel and from a room to his right flank, another battle for survival seized the Executioner's immediate attention.

Watkins loosed a burst from his M-16, covering two of his commandos as they broke from behind their colonel and raced for a large divan, rounds from their M-16s turning two terrorists downrange into whirling bloody sieves.

Bolan decided to turn up the heat before they were pinned down any longer. He pulled two incendiary grenades from his military webbing. The crates of explosives were in the far corner to his left flank, and the bunker looked large and sturdy enough to contain the thirty-five-yard radius of the hellbomb without bringing down the ceiling, or setting off an explosion that could kill all of them. It was risky, but he knew he had to act fast, or a stray bullet might be enough to ignite the crates.

Crouched low, with wood shrapnel flying over his head, the Executioner sent the first bomb flying into the room, then lobbed the second toward the mouth of the tunnel. The enemy tried to scramble clear of the grenades, but was a fraction of a second too slow. Twin balls of brilliant fire erupted, igniting a half-dozen gunmen into shrieking demons. White phosphorus, burning at 2700 degrees centigrade, clung to its victims like glue. It was the shock effect Bolan was looking for. If any of the terrorists had been having doubts about resisting the invasion of their lair, then flight now certainly looked better than fight.

Dealing the screaming terrorists quick mercy rounds, Bolan raced for the mouth of the tunnel. Primed to drop anything that moved, the soldier reached the escapeway moments later. He caught the pounding of boot steps in the distance and risked a look around the corner. Another naked bulb glowed down the tunnel. The corridor was long and narrow, bending away some ten yards from Bolan's position. Just as the footfalls of running men began to fade, Bolan glimpsed the warhead attached to an RPG-7 a moment before the terrorist vanished around the bend. A detonated grenade or warhead launched from either side in the close confines of the tunnel could bring an avalanche of rubble down on all of them. The danger ahead looked worse now than when they'd first stormed through the front door. Islamic extremists had time and again proved themselves suicidal in their belief that dying for their cause would whisk them away to Paradise. Reckless assaults, and certainly suicide, were never part of Bolan's game plan.

A quick check of the bunker told Bolan the commandos were toeing the dead to make sure they were just that, while other shock troops burst into rooms, prepared to mow down any surviving terrorists. But judging by the footfalls he'd heard, the Executioner knew the rest of the Iraqis were fleeing for the back street.

As Watkins closed on his rear, Bolan said, "Tell your men out back our pigeons are flying. And tell them I want Abriz taken alive."

"Tiger Teeth to Tiger Tail, come in." The radio crackled in the colonel's hand with an affirmative response. "Our cockroaches are fleeing the light. Take them down breathing." Watkins hesitated, and Bolan caught a sadistic glint in the colonel's eyes. "If at all possible."

Bolan clenched his jaw at the obvious attempt at insubordination. "Tell your men to stay well back of anything that looks like an exit. I saw an RPG. Our targets just might blow their way out the back.''

The look died in the colonel's eyes as he radioed back his commandos. ''Stay back from anything that looks like an exit. Roger that.'' Once his commandos affirmed the order, Watkins said, ''Some pencil-pusher inside the Beltway may have somehow gotten you in charge, whoever the hell you are, but these are still my men. If I lose any more of my people, none of these Iraqis are going back to the States. You understand, Colonel?''

Bolan gave the man a graveyard smile. ''Six feet deep.'' The cold grin vanished, and the Executioner slapped a fresh magazine into his Uzi as the commandos filed in behind Watkins or took up positions on the other side of the tunnel entrance. His icy gaze locked on Watkins for another stretched second, knowing the colonel was poised to turn the raid into a personal vengeance hunt. Suddenly Bolan believed he was on his own and decided he would have to watch his own back. But what Watkins had neglected to mention, Bolan thought, was that if their informant was right about Lebanese army patrols protecting the Death Brigade, then none of them might ever see American soil again.

''I want Condor One off the roof and our evac vehicles out back in two minutes,'' Bolan stated. ''And raise those Apaches. I want them on standby and ready to nail anything that tries to keep us from getting to the LZ.''

After drilling a piercing stare into Bolan, the colonel got on the radio.

The stench of roasting flesh in his nose, Bolan headed into the tunnel.

MAHMUD ABRIZ WAS AFRAID.

As he led a dozen of his comrades down the tunnel and toward the thick double wooden doors, Abriz was wondering who could be attacking him. Certainly the last thing he wanted to believe was that their attackers were American commandos. That was the most frightening scenario of them all.

Despite the fact he was a hero in the Islamic world, he was still in hiding like some wild and hunted animal. The American and Jew infidels had let it be known across the four corners of the earth that he was a wanted criminal.

Silently Abriz cursed this bad fortune. Why now, when he was but a mere twenty-four hours away from being reunited with his Iraqi brothers who had pledged to come and see him safely back to his homeland? In Baghdad he would undoubtedly receive the justified welcome and worship due a conquering warrior, bask in the public praise Saddam was sure to bestow on him. Indeed, how many brothers in the jihad could boast they had successfully invaded the soil of the Great Satan, slain many of the enemy and escaped to become a legend?

At the moment, though, visions of glory were

nothing more than a fool's dream, he knew, unless he got out of Beirut in one piece.

Clutching a Vz61 Skorpion machine pistol to his chest, the short, lean Iraqi stopped, checking his rear. It was suddenly too quiet behind them. With the echoes of the hideous shrieking of men in agony still in his ears, Abriz realized more than ever that he didn't want to die like some cornered rat in a hole. He then caught a sickly sweet whiff of burned flesh. What weapon was the enemy using? Incendiary explosives? Flamethrowers? Somehow he fought off a shudder of terror, shoved the image of himself being torched alive out of his mind. Yes, Abriz was all too familiar with the shrill bansheelike screams of someone being burned alive; he'd personally set off one of three incendiary explosives that had torched dozens of people in Chicago.

Beneath his checkered kaffiyeh, Abriz felt the sweat run cold down his neck, plastering his long, curly black hair to his skin. He swore out loud, his dark eyes burning with hate, rage and fear, his face slick with sweat. The entire block was supposed to have been secured. He had bought off soldiers in the Lebanese army, and they were supposed to keep him informed of any suspicious movements near Death Brigade turf. Now this sudden attack. It was all on the verge of falling apart, Abriz feared. He had no desire to commit suicide in some last-ditch stand against an unknown enemy. Secretly he had always believed martyrdom was for other soldiers of the jihad. No, today wasn't a good day to die. Not when he was slated for a hero's return home. And not when he was on the verge of personally delivering the Suitcase from God to Saddam.

Abriz became aware of his brothers, searching him out through the dim light, awaiting orders.

"Mahmud? What do we do now?" One of his fighters demanded. "They are sure to have the back street covered. We are trapped. If we fire the rocket or they set off more grenades, this tunnel will not be strong enough to hold up. We will be crushed like insects."

Abriz indulged a fleeting moment of anger. Since he wasn't one for martyrdom, he had declined mining the safehouse or booby-trapping the entrances to the bunker with enough C-4 to turn half the block into a smoking crater. He also questioned his refusal to have surveillance equipment monitor the streets of the neighborhood, relying instead on his sentries and army patrols who had now obviously proved they weren't worth the money he had paid for protection. Worse still, perhaps, was his show of benevolence and understanding where the hash smoking among some of his brothers was concerned. It wasn't for him, and it was considered sacrilege to Islamic law, but he had tolerated the use of the drug as long as it was recreational and didn't get out of control. It was a bad mistake. He was sure the reaction time of many of his now dead brothers had been dulled by hash, allowing the enemy precious seconds to overtake them.

Abriz pinned Habib Ayube, who was lugging the RPG-7, with a fierce eye. "If they are waiting for us, then they will be burning in hell in a matter of moments. You can be sure our brothers in the neighborhood have heard all the noise. They will be ready to fight when we hit the street. Obey me and we will live to see tomorrow. Destroy the door."

As Ayube hefted the rocket launcher to his shoulder, Abriz squatted. Just as he caught the sound of movement down the tunnel, the warhead streaked past him. When the deafening explosion obliterated the doors, Abriz dashed into the smoke. With his machine pistol sweeping the jagged edges of the blasted hole, he didn't know what to expect, nor was he all that certain how he would react to the sight of an overwhelming force. Before now, he had always killed and maimed when the odds were stacked in his favor. Being attacked was a new and terrifying experience.

What Abriz didn't expect was to feel the cold muzzle of a weapon sticking in his ear as soon as he hit the sidewalk. He heard a man bellow in English, over and over, "Drop the weapons!"

Then Abriz saw a black-clad commando appear in front of him. When the M-16 was thrust into his face, he knew he was poised at the edge of extinction and that any sudden move would prove to be his last. There was something about staring down the business end of his own death that caused Abriz to let the machine pistol slip from his fingers. "Do as he says!" he barked. "Drop the guns!"

Quaking with terror, Abriz thrust his hands above his head, hoping against hope his brothers didn't choose this moment to become sacrificial lambs.

No, martyrdom was definitely not for Mahmud Abriz.

WITH WATKINS RUNNING by his side, Bolan braced himself for the worst. He charged into the churning smoke, the roar of the blast fading in his ears. Ahead he saw most of the terrorists drop their weapons, then raise their arms in surrender. Two of the Iraqis decided to become martyrs, so Bolan paved their way to Paradise with a burst from the Uzi as soon as they wheeled toward him with their AK-47s.

"We surrender! We surrender!" Abriz shouted.

"Get on your knees! Get down!" Bolan ordered. As he closed on the group, something began to feel terribly wrong to the Executioner. They were giving up too easily.

"You heard the man!" one of the commandos shouted, clipping a terrorist over the head with the butt of his M-16, dropping him to the rubble.

Bolan swept past the clustered group, scanning the narrow, dark street. Above, the three snipers of Condor Two were rappeling down the side of the target building. Pouring onto the sidewalk, commandos fanned out on both sides of the Executioner, M-16s probing the murk. It was too quiet on the street for Bolan's liking, and he could feel the eyes of armed enemy gunners boring into him from somewhere in the dark, squat buildings up and down the street.

A burst of autofire sounded, and Bolan whirled. Three of the Iraqis were spread-eagled into the rubble as Watkins loomed over them, drilling long bursts from his M-16 into their bodies. The other terrorists turned wide-eyed stares on the colonel, who showed Bolan a challenging smile. For just a second, the soldier couldn't believe what he'd just seen. Then again, he'd suspected all along that a moment like this would expose Watkins's true sadistic nature—not to mention the man seemed determined to usurp Bolan's authority.

Watkins inched the M-16 around, his burning stare locked on Bolan. "For every man I lose, I'll personally send three of these murdering scumbags straight to hell where they belong. I hope you don't have a problem with that, Colonel."

The situation was set to erupt. Watkins's commandos had one eye on the street with half their attention torn between the terrorists and the budding confrontation. No matter what, the Executioner intended to see that his prisoners reached the United States unharmed. However, this was no time to go head-to-head with Watkins. And cold-blooded murder never failed to strike anger in the Executioner. Later he would let actions speak louder than any words he could say right then.

Bolan pitched a set of handcuffs at Watkins, who caught them without taking his eyes off the Executioner.

Bolan strode for Abriz, cuffed his hands behind his back and hauled him to his feet. "You want to give me a hand cuffing our prisoners, Colonel?"

"Colonel Watkins, I've got movement down the south end of the street," a commando called out. "It's going to hit the fan."

South, Bolan spotted the armed shadows sliding through the gloom, darting behind a line of parked vehicles. Checking the north end of the street, the Executioner found their evac vehicles rolling toward them. The Super Hummer and the custom-made black van were angling toward them when autofire shattered the air.

Bolan and several commandos cut loose on the men firing at them from the south end of the block.

Then the entire street seemed split asunder by the roar of one simultaneous eruption of autofire. Windows everywhere flared to life with barking weapons.

The Executioner roughly hustled the prisoners toward the evac vehicles when a volley of rounds drilled into commandos around him. He heard sharp grunts of pain, then blood sprayed into his face. Two, then three, commandos pitched to the gutter.

## CHAPTER THREE

An unwitting Iraqi shield became the only thing that stood between Bolan and sudden death during the opening round of the onslaught. There was a brief cry of pain, and Bolan found the prisoner tumbling away behind a shower of blood, leaving the Executioner exposed to the barrage of bullets washing over the sidewalk.

They were hemmed in by enemy cross fire with the definite prospect of death staring them in the face, but Bolan and the surviving commandos didn't flinch or waver. Instead, they returned fire at the shadows in the windows of the target building. Long sweeping bursts from Bolan's Uzi were followed up by streaking 40 mm grenades, which instantly punched gaping holes in the wall above. The rain of lead momentarily ceased—at least from that direction.

From the back of the Hummer, an MK 20 heavy machine gun started to pound out 20 mm rounds. Instant decimation ripped across the buildings on the other side of the street, producing screams and silencing more than a few of the guns in the drab stone dwellings.

Out of the corner of his eye, Bolan saw Watkins take some rounds, high and low. Judging by the amount of blood soaking him and the snarl of rage and agony twisting the man's face, Bolan suspected the colonel had taken a few hits during the opening round before attempting to join the counterattack. He took yet another round, this time in the leg. His cry of pain was mingled with a vicious curse before he toppled. Blood spurted freely from several holes in the man's upper chest, stomach and lower back. Two commandos began to drag him toward the cover of the vehicles, but their attention became fixed in the next instant on survival as blood exploded from their upper torsos. Still, they triggered their M-16s with the tenacity of men determined to take out as many of the enemy with them as they could.

As more bullets careened off the sidewalk around him, Bolan shouldered Abriz to the street. Wheeling, he dropped a figure who rushed through the blasted opening, then jacked Abriz to his feet and pushed him into the van. Forced once more to rivet undivided attention on their attackers, Bolan expended one clip after another. The Executioner struck some lethal paydirt, but as he felled two or three of the enemy, another four or five gunmen seemed to pop up out of nowhere.

Ignoring the swarm of steel-jacketed hornets peppering the armored hull or skidding off the bullet-proof glass of the van and Hummer, Bolan kept the terrorists toward the southern end of the street pinned down, ordering the commandos to get the rest of the prisoners cuffed and inside the van. Once again, though, the Executioner was forced to turn his fire on the target building behind him, as muzzle-flashes winked from the darkness of the windows. He drilled a grenade through a second-story window, watching as the ensuing blast sent torn figures hurtling out into the street.

Suddenly Bolan felt slugs whizzing past his ear, biting at his shoulder and side. He angled for the deeper cover of the van as fire raced through his body and he realized he'd been hit. Bolan didn't know how bad the wounds were, but he went on firing his Uzi, determined to get them out of there.

But some of the commandos, the warrior knew, weren't going to leave Lebanon alive. He covered the soldiers piling the prisoners and their wounded and dead into the van with more relentless Uzi fire. Somehow Watkins had struggled to a knee. Drenched in blood, yelling curses at the top of his lungs, the colonel began to fire a series of projectiles from his M-203 launcher before he went down again with ragged crimson holes marching up his side.

The danger, Bolan knew, was far from over. Getting to the LZ would prove a road to hell for somebody, but Bolan intended to raise the C-130 and bump the evac site in closer. It was too hot to go with the original game plan. First they had to get out of Beirut.

So far the enemy had opted not to display any rocket firepower, not wanting to risk killing their own. Bolan believed once they were rolling out of the hellzone, that would change.

Catching sight of Watkins crawling through his own blood toward the Hummer, Bolan rushed to the colonel to help him into the vehicle. As he bent toward him, the colonel shot clawed hands for Bolan's throat. Eyes of pure hate and rage stared up at the Executioner, who grappled with bloody hands dug into his throat like talons. As stray bullets zinged off the pavement beside him, Bolan wrenched the hands from his throat, indulging a moment of disbelief over the colonel's dying show of raw, ugly emotion.

"You...are one lucky bastard...get my people home..." Watkins croaked.

Just like that, the angry light faded for good from Watkins's eyes. Even in death his face was carved in bitter anger.

"Colonel Pollock, we've got to go!"

Bolan found the commando he knew as Lance behind the Hummer, directing autofire at a target across the street. "Lance" was a code name. It had already been determined that none of the American commandos would be left behind if they fell in death. The Arab world would be outraged over this invasion and the snatching of a so-called Islamic revolutionary hero from under the protective umbrella of a terrorist state. Not to mention there would be no doubt who had stormed the city. But Bolan wasn't even going to imagine the atrocious image of the bodies of American soldiers desecrated and dragged through the streets of Beirut. Not even the sadistic late colonel.

Draping Watkins over a shoulder, Bolan angled for the van. "Take the wheel of the Hummer," he told Lance. "You know the way, soldier."

"Yeah," Lance roared between twin bursts of weapons fire. "South. Let's just get the hell out of Dodge, Colonel!"

"Goliath," Bolan growled at a giant black commando over the endless stutter of autofire, "take the van. Take the lead. Anything that moves, get it out of the way and don't look back. I'll have our rear covered."

Nodding, the commando hopped into the van. Bolan knew that anything standing between them and evacuation would wish they had run like hell instead. Both vehicles were actually war wagons. Beneath the frames on both sides of the van and Super Hummer, M-60 machine guns and rocket pods were ready to unleash massive firepower at the electronic touch of twin gunsticks beside the driver of the war machines. They would prove themselves to be hell on wheels before they reached the LZ, the Executioner knew. The easy part was over.

As Bolan placed the colonel's body at the feet of the prisoners, he was momentarily surprised at the lack of anger or sympathy over Watkins's death in the faces of the commandos. It made Bolan wonder just how much loyalty these men would have shown Watkins, or maybe, he thought, they'd pegged the man long ago for what he was—a borderline sociopath with authority and the will to flex deadly muscle, even against his own.

"You will never get out of Lebanon alive, American! You will all end up like this murdering infidel!" Abriz stated, kicking Watkins.

"Let me tell you something, Abriz. If it looks like we're not going to make it, I'd find some prayer beads and start praying to God, who's got a nice little hot seat reserved all for you." Bolan waited a couple of heartbeats to let that sink in, then closed the door on that stark face of fear.

Under fire, Bolan raced for the back of the Hummer. The MK 20 was strangely silent, but as he leaped into the rear, he discovered the gunner he had known as Wolfman had taken a bullet right between the eyes. Three unscathed commandos the warrior knew as Bonebreaker, Lion and Blitzkrieg were hunched around three other dead commandos and one seriously wounded soldier who had passed out. The commandos fed fresh clips into their weapons and eyed Bolan with iron determination.

After giving the order to Lance to move out, radio the Apaches they were en route and provide them with air cover, Bolan manned the big gun. There was enough space in the vehicle for the commandos to

crowd around him to provide additional rear firepower.

With the Hummer rolling out and rocking under
enemy bullets, Bolan took charge of the street with
deadly precise machine-gun fire, the commandos
flanking him adding chattering streams of autofire.
Shadows, some of them now shouldering RPGs,
were scrambling after the vehicle. Tracking on, the
Executioner and the commandos began to drop dark
figures like human bowling pins with lead thunder
and lightning. Spent casings pinging off the hull
around him, the Executioner raked the tripod-
mounted weapon back and forth until he was satis-
fied their rear was secured.

But the respite was brief. Bolan spotted a military
jeep at the north end of the street. A machine gun
cut loose from the vehicle, which flew the Lebanese
flag, and three soldiers with AK-47s opened up on
the Hummer.

Return enemy fire was short-lived.

Bolan blew that vehicle into a searing ball of
flames behind a chugging wave of armor-piercing
rounds. Then, just as the Hummer started to round
the corner, Bolan glimpsed the gun barrel of a tank
swivel into view, then poke through the flames to
draw target acquisition. It was a monster, a T-54, if
Bolan guessed right. A heartbeat before the Hummer
plowed through debris and angled around the corner,
the tank belched its doomsday payload.

The titanic explosion blew a gale-force concussive

wind over the Hummer. Jarred, Bolan and the commandos hit the deck as rubble slammed into the vehicle. Then the warrior discovered the shell had taken out the entire front wall of the last building on the street. The Hummer swung out of the T-54's gun sights, safe for the time being but far from clear.

Bolan checked the way ahead, his vision obscured with flying grit.

At the moment it looked like an easy run out of the terrorist-controlled neighorhood.

All that was going to change, the Executioner knew, just as soon as they found the road to the ancient port city of Sidon.

The odds, he would bet, were going to be stacked against them.

TWENTY-FIVE MINUTES LATER they began to reach the outer limits of Beirut. The sun was now up, casting a shimmering golden light over the tiered houses in the southern suburbs of the city.

Bolan had already checked his wounds. Bullets had grazed and nicked him in a few places, gouging out furrows of skin, and his blacksuit was sticky with blood and sweat. The wounds were uncomfortable and burning, but they were superficial.

With adrenaline pumping through him, Bolan maintained hard vigilance as the Hummer rumbled through the narrow streets. Congestion now became a problem, donkeys and sheep meandering alongside the people strolling through the area.

South. That was all that mattered.

"So far, so good, Colonel," Lance said, one hand on the wheel with the other on the gunstick.

"Too good," Bolan said, his voice cryptic.

Reading the grim looks of the commandos loud and clear, Bolan knew they were braced for what he already suspected. A trap was being laid. The only questions left unanswered were where, when and how many they would be facing down. And Bolan wouldn't even entertain the ultimate question. Too much was at stake and too many lives had been lost to fail now. But most importantly Bolan believed getting home with their human cargo would save countless innocent lives in the long run.

"Those Apaches are locked onto our homer, sir," Lance said. "We should be seeing them anytime."

"Just be ready." After checking the sky for any sign of friendly or enemy aircraft, Bolan belted the MK 20 with high-explosive rounds. The German-made weapon could pound out a mix of armor-piercing and HE rounds up to one thousand 20 mm annihilators a minute. And it could certainly blow any low-flying aircraft out of the sky in the time it took to blink.

A few minutes later they hit a clear patch of unpaved road leading south. Another thirty-minute stretch then dragged on with agonizing tension. At worst, the roads in Lebanon were proving merely dirt tracks to nowhere, pocked with ruts and stone, and at best, the main seashore highway would be paved but narrow. The roads might be primitive by Western standards but were good enough, the Executioner knew, to accommodate a military convoy. Once they hit the open road for Sidon, they would be fair and defined game for predatory warbirds.

Still no sign of their Apaches.

Ever alert to any sign of danger, Bolan took in his surroundings. This was ancient land, torn between the old and the modern, ripped more often than not by distorted political and religious ideology. To this day, many Lebanese still considered themselves Phoenicians or direct blood of the seafaring conquerors who had so long ago made Lebanon the financial and commercial mecca of the world. Indeed, this was land that had been invaded, conquered and occupied for thousands of years. Romans, Greeks, Persians, Assyrians, French and British—all had scarred this country with war and brutality. The country was torn, troubled and soaked with the blood of the guilty, as well as the innocent.

East, Bolan spotted the tents and hovels of what he guessed was a Palestinian refugee camp. Countless figures were shuffling among the dust of this Lebanese purgatory. Scratching out another day of survival, hungry, angry and dying, these displaced outsiders were both the homeless and the scourge of the Middle East. No bleeding heart by any stretch, Bolan knew many of them, especially the young boys, would be recruited out of that camp by Syrian soldiers or the older leaders of terrorist groups to become cannon fodder for the Islamic revolution.

No, their plight wasn't beyond Bolan. In fact he understood it all too well. In every corner of the world there was oppression and injustice due to the savage nature of animal man. The once innocent could be turned into savages if the seed was planted just right, if they were told the enemy was anyone who wasn't like them or didn't believe what they did, if they were made to think their suffering was due to evil circumstances beyond their control. Unless, of course, they took up arms. All of the factions in this country, Christian and Muslim alike, might proclaim to be warring under the banner of their faith, but no righteous God, Bolan knew, wanted the blood of his children on his hands in his name. No, men fought, killed and imposed their will on one another for themselves. In Lebanon, Bolan had witnessed firsthand that there was no clear and definable justice on any side, which made everyone wrong.

"Colonel, I'd just like to say something, and I'm sure I speak for the rest of us."

Bolan fixed a steady gaze on Lance, who was staring at him in the rearview.

The commando cleared his throat. "The colonel was neither a good man nor was he all that bad a man. This is a righteous mission, and all of us knew we could get killed going in. Those bastards who stepped on American soil and slaughtered unarmed and innocent civilians *will* be going back to stand trial.''

Bolan gave them all a brief nod, then locked eyes with Lance. "What you're saying is that I don't have to watch my back."

"I'm saying, Colonel, that we pledge complete allegiance to whoever is put in charge of us. You don't have to watch your back, because we'd just as soon take a bullet for you if it came down to that. We're not Watkins. Watkins won't be missed. Sir."

Bolan believed him.

"Colonel, it might be roughly fifty miles to the LZ, but it could seem like an eternity, if you know what I'm saying."

As they hit the coastal highway, Bolan looked at Lance and nodded. What the man said was all too true and grim. Lebanon is about fifty miles east to west and about 120 miles north to south. It was a small country, but there was plenty of room to bury them.

Bolan got on the radio to raise the Apaches. "Striker to Condor's Nest, come in." Contacting the pilot-in-charge, the Executioner gave their position and was informed the Apaches were moving up the coastline, four miles south and closing fast on their position.

Giving the skies a hard search, Bolan spotted them. He told the pilot to stand by.

Northeast, fanning out and growing quickly in view, the Executioner counted six Hinds. Another sweep of their rear revealed a convoy rolling hard down the highway, coming fast at their tail, cutting the gap. Grabbing a pair of binoculars and adjusting the vision, the Executioner counted six jeeps and a transport truck, all of the vehicles bearing the Lebanese flag. At a distance of approximately two hundred yards and closing, he saw assault rifles, mounted machine guns in the beds of the jeeps and several rocket launchers.

Things were about to get real serious. For a moment Bolan was slightly amazed at how quickly the Death Brigade's allies had mobilized. But from the very moment he'd dropped the radioman in the bunker, the soldier strongly suspected this moment would come. How the soldiers would play it was anybody's guess. Some of them would be hard-core militants, others with shaky allegiance to a faction they were supposed to be protecting, or maybe a number of them even completely ignorant of the payoffs by Abriz to keep the Death Brigade entrenched in Beirut. And maybe the soldiers were now simply under orders to make a clean sweeping kill to dispose of both the commandos and Abriz, sparing guilty officials the embarrassment of admitting to taking bribes.

Bolan informed the Apache pilot of their predicament. "Get in touch with Dragonship. Find a stretch of beach somewhere close to our present position."

"I'm way ahead of you, Colonel," the pilot responded. "It's already been taken care of. We've got a nice strip of sand already picked out. Dragonship ETA is ten minutes. And don't worry about those Hinds. We'll take care of business, then we'll bring you in for the home stretch."

Signing off, Bolan decided more than a pat on the back was due to the pilots. Air support was on the way, but the top guns had already been briefed of contingency plans if things went sour.

Combat senses on full alert, Bolan peered through the windshield. There was a bend in the highway, roughly 250 yards ahead. There the final touches of the trap lay waiting.

Bonebreaker whistled softly at the sight of twenty jeeps and armored trooper carriers, as well as dozens of armed Lebanese soldiers strung out across the highway.

Goliath raised Bolan. "Colonel, guess you see what I'm looking at."

"Here's the game plan, Goliath. We've got more heat on our rear. Slow it down, we'll take the point but stay to our starboard. Air support will be here in about three minutes, but we don't have time to wait. Once we cut loose, you follow our lead."

"Understood, Colonel. Guess this is where we earn our keep."

"And then some." Bolan told Bonebreaker to man the gunsticks, gave Lance the order to plow through the barricade and not look back.

The Executioner manned the big gun as the Hum-

mer picked up speed, sliding beside the van to take
the point. Lance kept the vehicle ahead of but to the
right of the van, giving the second war wagon a field
of fire at the barricade's left flank.

Bolan swung the machine gun toward the Hinds
as the warbirds kicked up a duststorm to the east,
flying in low and hard for a strafing run at the highway. Lion and Blitzkrieg took up Bolan's flank. It
was all or nothing.

"Maybe seventy yards and closing, Colonel!"
Lance shouted. "Ready when you are!"

Miniguns flamed on the noses of the warbirds. The
Lebanese were playing for keeps, and it told the warrior everything he needed to know.

"Give it everything you've got, soldier," Bolan
ordered, then cut loose on the Hinds.

The Hummer shuddered with the tremendous
opening rounds of fire, with Bolan directing a raking
line of 20 mm doom skyward, sweeping the machine
gun flank to flank on the warbirds. Flashes of autofire
from the far rear of the Hummer caught Bolan's eye
as bullets from all directions tore into the war wagon,
rocking the vehicle with the relentless pounding of
a man-made hurricane.

Two of the Hinds, engulfed in flames, plunged for
the earth, victims of the Executioner's relentless barrage. As fiery wreckage hammered the ground, the
other warbirds suddenly veered north. Gone, Bolan
assumed, to reassess the situation.

"Everybody grab their balls!" Lance shouted a moment later.

Bolan looked past the commando, bracing himself a heartbeat before his bulldozer earned every dime of his pay. Ahead uniformed figures were firing wildly at the Hummer with assault rifles and submachine guns. Some of the soldiers raced out of the war machine's path in the split second before the vehicle exploded through the barricade like a runaway train through a shanty. Bolan caught a glimpse of a face of agony slamming off the windshield before the earthquake force of the collision sent him and the commandos on his flank crashing off the armored walls of the bed. Senses jarred, his ears ringing with the deafening rain of lead, from both friend and foe, he took in the carnage in their wake.

Behind them many of the soldiers began to chase the war wagons down the highway on foot. Twisted wreckage hammered the road, and a wall of fire started lapping with unforgiving hunger through the obliterated barricade to touch off a roaring wall of fire. But razoring steel, scorching flames and screaming balls of fire became the least of the Lebanese soldiers' worries. With the rocket pods and machine guns swiveling to once more turn up the heat, Bolan ripped a long fusillade of 20 mm pulverizers through the barricade.

In their wake still more men died, and many more guns went silent forever.

They might have been clear of any effective fire

from the barricade, but Bolan saw the convoy on their tail quickly split the flames and hurl debris out of its rampaging path.

Worse, seconds later the four remaining Hinds loomed in the distance beyond the billowing smoke and towering flames.

Where the hell were his Apaches?

The Executioner's silent question was answered as soon as he began unleashing the MK 20 at the convoy. Beyond their blanket of lead and streaking rockets, the sky was suddenly peppered with mushrooming fire clouds. Three of the Hinds were vaporized instantly, with the fourth banking away from the Apaches that had come in on their rear from out of nowhere. A grim smile ghosted Bolan's lips as he watched the Apaches sweep past the showering and flaming hulls of the warbirds to begin a savage mop-up on the convoy. A slow but deadly run over the convoy sent man and machine flying off the highway in all directions with the earth-ripping combination of Minigun and rocket fire.

Bolan gave the troops around him a quick check, and found that the few survivors were still breathing. His radio crackled with the voice of his top gun. As the Apaches soared overhead, the pilot told Bolan to follow them. Before signing off, the Executioner told the pilot to watch his rear for the lone Hind.

Turning toward the barricade, Bolan saw a good number of vehicles burst through the wall of smoke down the highway. The hellhounds were going to chase them clear to the seashore. They were far from being home free.

With the commandos ramming fresh clips into their weapons, Bolan scoured the blue sky over the glistening emerald waters of the Mediterranean to the west, searching in vain for the C-130 Hercules. Maybe half a mile later the Hummer was bounding off the highway, rolling down a tortuous path cut between mammoth black cliffs. They rumbled downhill for the wide mouth at the bottom of the trail, beyond which stretched the deserted beach of their LZ. Bolan was informed by his top gun that the C-130 was coming in for a landing from the south.

While the Apaches soared over the long and narrow strip of white sand, Bolan then spotted the C-130 touch down to begin its lumbering taxi along the shoreline. Beyond the giant bird, blue sky and turquoise waters seemed to mesh in the distance, the white sand gleaming under the fiery eye of the rising sun. Under normal circumstances it would have been a picture-postcard heaven of tranquillity. Normal, right.

The Executioner braced himself for death to come lapping at their heels again.

It did.

Just as soon as they plunged onto the beach, he saw the line of jeeps and armored vehicles race down the seaside trail, uniformed soldiers triggering warheads from RPG-7s.

Bolan was feeding the MK 20 with a fresh belt,

the Hummer zigzagging their pursuit and leading the van across the beach, when a deafening blast suddenly rocked the war wagon. Cutting loose with the machine gun, the warrior turned a pursuing jeep into flaming scrap as soon as it barreled off the trail. Still more jeeps, machine guns blazing, bulled through the wreckage in grim chase.

Then it sounded as if the sky were split asunder. One of the Apaches took a hit, turned into a fireball and plummeted toward the sea.

Evacuation was poised to become doomsday.

In the distance the C-130 slowed, stopped near a jagged wall of rock and swung around.

Out of nowhere the surviving Hind swooped in from the ocean, Miniguns flaming. Water geysered under the tracking storm of lead, with sand spraying in all directions. The hellstorm of bullets was marching right for the C-130 when the air war abruptly ended. Bolan directed fire at the Hind but found the Apaches had already locked on, blowing the enemy warbird out of the sky.

Bolan's top gun, his voice edged with anger, told him they'd cover their rear.

"Just get the hell in that Herc!" the pilot growled.

Like predatory birds swooping for the kill, the Apaches unloaded Armageddon on the enemy vehicles swarming onto the beach. Smoke, rock and human body parts were hurtled into the sky.

The blue sky over the beach went black with

smoke, and daylight was threatened with the twilight of war.

Then, before he knew it, adrenaline racing like wildfire through him, Bolan felt the sudden uphill jolting. Turning, he found the Hummer rolling into the belly of the C-130, slipping into the darkness seconds later.

A tracking line of fire followed the van up the ramp.

When the ramp started to close, muffled thunderclaps and Minigun fire hit the hull of the transport aircraft as it started to roll forward.

Just before the ramp shut, the warrior turned to check the troops. A crimson stickiness clung to his face like a second skin, but sixth sense told Bolan it wasn't his blood.

Looking down, he found the unseeing eyes of the commando named Lion staring up at him. Bolan clenched his teeth, trying not to think about the enormous cost of life expended in the name of justice. In the corner of his eye, he caught the anguished look on Blitzkrieg's face as he stared at his fellow commando.

Sucking in a deep breath that seemed to burn right to the core of his soul, feeling the C-130 lift off, the Executioner raised a hand and brushed the young commando's eyes shut.

THEY WERE THIRTY MINUTES out to sea when another commando died from his wounds. Gently the Executioner shut Anvil's eyelids. A lot of bad men and more than a few good men had died to bring a horde of savages to justice. A number of the dead commandos couldn't have been more than thirty years old, Bolan figured, gazing sadly at the bodies of the young soldiers stretched out beside him. The toll was indeed heavy, and would reach even further than their own deaths. Some of them had wives who would grieve their loss, maybe children who would grow up without their fathers. Certainly they were sons who would be buried by weeping parents. The price tag for justice was enormous. Though he hadn't known them personally, he knew them as well as he did his own soul. They were all soldiers who had given their final blood for their country, so that justice could be served, honor upheld and wrong righted.

But their mission was accomplished. Or was it? As he drilled a cold eye into the prisoners, something began to pick at the back of Bolan's mind. He couldn't put a finger on it, but the longer he looked at the terrorists the more troubled he felt. Nine members of the Death Brigade were chained together, hand and foot, aft, bathed in the soft glow of the overheads. There was something about the way they sat, Bolan thought, smug to the point of arrogant, staring ahead at nothing. But something glinted in their eyes. It was as if they knew it wasn't over, as if it had only just begun. But what could possibly go wrong now? Bolan wondered. They would be covered by six F-16s all the way to the Rhine Main Air Base in Germany. Any MiGs on their tail would be blown out of the sky. In a few short hours there would be a debriefing at Rhine Main, the dead and wounded would be off-loaded, then the transatlantic flight to Andrews Air Force Base. There the FBI and United States marshal would step in to take over.

What could go wrong? Anything. The trial of the century lay ahead, Bolan knew. A band of international terrorists had been snatched by a secret American commando unit and whisked back to the scene of their atrocities. If convicted, the Iraqis could face the death penalty. The United States government would spare no expense, wouldn't cave in to plea bargaining from Iraq. Make no mistake, justice was going to be swift and severe. But the unanswered question now nagging at Bolan locked onto his thoughts with some ominous foreboding. Would the other side sit idle and watch their own feel the wrath of American justice?

Standing amidships, Bolan turned brief attention to the team of Special Forces medics working on the wounded. Groans were silenced by morphine, IVs hooked up and fresh blood pumped into wounded commandos. Quietly the warrior declined to have his wounds tended to. He would live.

Lance informed Bolan he had a call from the States. Walking with heavy legs and heavier heart to the stern, the Executioner picked up the headset of the radio console. Hal Brognola was on the other end.

"I just heard," the big Fed said. "The mission was a success?"

"Costly success," Bolan said, his tone grim. The abrupt silence on the other end was hard. Brognola knew the score.

"I'll be there when you reach Andrews, Striker. Catch your breath on the flight home. We need to talk."

After some solemn words of congratulations mixed with sympathy for the dead, Brognola signed off.

Turning toward the source of his silent grief and rage, Bolan found Abriz watching him closely. As he met those quietly laughing eyes of the terrorist, a haunting weight settled on the Executioner. Four words from the Justice man rang like doom through his head: *We need to talk.*

No, some instinct warned Bolan that this was far from being over.

# CHAPTER FOUR

*Tokyo, Japan*

Takio Ashiba knew it was a dog's way out, but he had left himself no choice. Still, even though he was considered in certain circles *shinjinrui,* the post–World War II generation of little or no discipline who chased the empty gods of Western materialism, Ashiba endured a burning shame over what he had done and what he was about to do.

With trembling fingers he rifled his wall safe, emptying its contents into two large leather briefcases on his desk. The first briefcase would go to the source of his betrayal, the second was stuffed with a million dollars in U.S. currency. Everything was set. Once he reached New Tokyo International Airport and boarded the flight for Honolulu, he was home free. And he could forget about the past two years, which had led to this night, where he stood, alone on the thirteenth floor of his office of Osaka Enterprises Worldwide, running scared, hiding in the dark, fleeing the light.

Or would he ever forget?

Already the ghosts of dishonor haunted him.

A mighty clap of thunder and a blinding flash of lightning made Ashiba jump. He thought he heard movement from somewhere, but the building would be empty now, except for security and cleaning crews. His belly coiled tight with fear, Ashiba stared into the soft yellow light spilling through his open doorway from the tight cubicles in the bay of the Osaka accounting firm where he had worked as chief accountant for the past year. He thought he saw a shadow, just beyond the door.

"Hello? Is anybody there?" Ashiba called out.

Silence.

Trying to force a calm he didn't feel, he decided it was only the storm, casting dancing shadows over the building. Still he went to the door but found the bay area empty. Back inside his office, he gave the room a hard search. There was nothing but emptiness. The chief accountant swiped at a bead of sweat on his lip.

He indulged a bitter nostalgia, watching the thunderstorm pelt the city. The Osaka Building had been erected only in the past two years, right in the heart of commuter Tokyo, where two million people scurried to and from work every day, making the Shinjuku District one of the most suffocating clusters of humanity in the world. Only twenty stories high, the Osaka Building was dwarfed by the fifty-story skyscrapers that now seemed to rise so tall they threatened to punch holes in the sky.

The Osaka Building might have been short in stature, but its power and scope encompassed the globe.

As lightning burst over the skyscrapers, Ashiba moved to the window, his heart heavy. This city had been his home for nearly thirty years, full of memories, of achievement—of shame. He felt as if a dagger had been plunged into his heart, knowing he could never return. He would miss his beloved Tokyo like a father might grieve the loss of a dead son. Tokyo was a city that had been destroyed by nature, by fire and war, but had arisen from its own smoldering ashes to loom bigger and brighter and more bejeweled than ever. The city marked the new Japan, torn between the traditional and the modern. By day the bustling crowds were like a billion sardines swimming in furious waters, filling gleaming skyscrapers with a tightly controlled hysteria for achievement and advancement for the new emperor called yen. By night she was a dazzling neon jungle, a manic glitterdome that lit up the city even in the heart of darkness, where the same hordes choked thousands of bars and restaurants in search of every pleasure, every vice known to man. Yes, Ashiba thought, here was the collision of traditional values and the emergence of the new samurai who moved paper to make millions instead of wielding swords to slay their enemies.

In a final moment of morbid farewell, Ashiba lingered on his fatal obsession, the road that had led to his betrayal.

The chief accountant shuddered at the images of what he had done in the sex shops, how he had unwittingly laid his own trap. But in Japan, he reasoned, you worked hard and you played just as hard. Whatever, he was the new breed of Japanese, he bitterly reflected—he was owed his pleasure, no matter what his dark predilection, after grueling twelve- to eighteen-hour days in a workforce that had made Japan the supereconomy of the world. Even still...

Here nothing less than excellence was expected.

Here nothing more than honor was demanded.

Tormented, his young face pinched tight and his dark, brooding eyes reflecting the storm beyond the windows, he thought of the man who had given him everything, who had made him rich, a man he had betrayed.

Harikami "Harry" Osaka was the new shogun of modern Japan. Or that was the way the old man saw himself, Ashiba thought, and felt his shame and anguish edge toward contempt. Only two weeks earlier he had seen the old man stand near the window of his office at the very spot he was now rooted to. The old man had stared at the skyline of Tokyo, which he still called Edo, and told his chief accountant, "The new dictators of feudal Japan who had warred for centuries, killing each other for land and power and prestige, they are out there, they are everywhere. They no longer wear mail or carry swords, nor even come in the black of night like the ninja to strangle you or cut your throat while you sleep. Instead, they come at us with briefcases and paper and the poisonous mouths of serpents that will strike you from the bush if you even by accident step on them. Beware, Takio. They wear many faces.''

Enough. Ashiba couldn't bear to think of the old man. After all, it wasn't his fault, nor was Osaka to blame. It just was.

Yes, Harry Osaka had made himself the new shogun of financial Japan. That alone made the man worthy of respect.

Ashiba hated himself for what he had done.

Still, the more he thought about the old man and the more he dwelled on the whispered rumors he had caught among his associates, the more he believed the path before him was the only way. For one thing the old man was so serious in his grim and stoic way when he often alluded to the glorious samurai days of feudal Japan that it often frightened Ashiba to the point where he believed failure in Osaka Worldwide would end in mass suicide. Even the Osaka logo featured a helmeted samurai with drawn sword. Weird. And frightening. But beyond the old man's bizarre eccentricity and love of the old ways, there were other signs warning Ashiba it was time to move on. He had no concrete proof, of course; it was just a gut feeling of some deceit or clandestine endeavor on the part of the old man. Whatever it was, it was there, and Ashiba could feel an evil spirit in the wind around Osaka Worldwide.

Proof? Well, there was that mysterious file he had stumbled across on his computer just three days ago. Logged as "Bushino Ichigon," or "the word of a samurai," it showed transactions in the tens of millions of yen, going through what he believed were dummy corporations set up in India, Pakistan and South Africa. With just a quick run through the file, he had believed he was onto something at least sinister, if not covert or illegal. No invoices, no precise points of shipment, no receiver of goods, just initials and words he was sure were code. At first he believed he was being overly paranoid, given the stress and the shame of his dark path. Then yesterday the file, which he had copied to diskette and locked in the drawer of his desk, had been left in the middle of the conference table.

Paranoia became terror when he discovered the file had been erased. Another shudder went down his spine like walking fingers of ice as he thought about the blank diskette. Someone was aware he'd seen the file, someone who had something to hide. Or was someone setting him up? But who? And what was that person hiding? And why?

Lone symbols, words and half words were found on the file, with the words *roulette, chance, rising sword* and *goldwater* attached to money figures. Whatever was being bought and moved had been listed only as miscellaneous material. What material?

Of course, Osaka Worldwide had gargantuan investments in just about everything in every corner of the world. The material could be anything—gold, diamonds, perhaps new oil sites in the Middle East. There had been an Osaka-based petroleum company in Iraq, shipping oil to a Japan in desperate need of fuel from foreign markets, but that company had been abandoned after the Gulf War. What material? *Roulette? Chance?* Perhaps the file contained proposed casino sites. After all, Harry Osaka, with his fondness for gambling, was now looking to open up casinos and luxury resorts in Tokyo and Hokkaido, maybe even Vietnam and Thailand, thus encroaching upon territory owned and controlled by...

By the source of Ashiba's betrayal and shame.

Then his thoughts turned ever darker as the rumors about a secret cult of assassins working for Osaka wanted to take shape in his mind like winged demons. And what about the brutal murders of Osaka business associates in Southeast Asia? Men who had come to Harry Osaka with dreams of expansion into all areas of business but who clearly had their own agendas of attaining wealth. Names turned up in the news—dead men murdered during the night, many of them while they slept the deep and fat sleep of the rich and the hopeful.

Warning signs.

After tonight it wouldn't matter, Ashiba told himself. Whatever was happening in the house of Osaka wouldn't be his concern. All that mattered was getting out of Japan. Later he would deal with the specter of shame.

But how far could he run, how long could he hide with only a million dollars and another million tucked away in a secret account in Honolulu? Sure, it hadn't been too hard skimming from the enormous profit margin. Not when he was in charge of all the books, funneling funds for the major business transactions, his hand in the wheeling and dealing of the contracts with lawyers, nose pressed to the grindstone of the never-ending paper trail of taxes and write-offs. No, with all his billions reaped from an empire that spanned the globe, the old man would never miss the mere pittance of a million dollars. In a last, fleeting moment of regret, Ashiba decided he should have fudged a few more numbers through another bogus company and pilfered another piece of Osaka's fortune. Oh, well, it was too late for such regret.

Heart racing, Ashiba moved quickly for his desk. One last thing remained to be picked up. He didn't know if he could use the Detonics 9, but he would feel a little safer when he met with *them*.

Then, like the sound of a sudden thunderclap, the past, present and future collided in just a few sharp words.

''Takio, have you no sense of shame?''

Ashiba froze behind his desk, just as his hand was poised to open the top drawer. Out of nowhere the voice knifed the air, louder and angrier it seemed than the storm lashing the city. For long and horrifying moments, as he felt like a man who was trapped in a nightmare and couldn't wake up, the question seemed to echo with utter and cold contempt in his ears. If he had been tasting fear before, he now felt pure terror.

Slowly the middle chair swiveled around toward Ashiba.

"My father often says the ways of wealth are not the ways of honor. Surely you have proved him right. And you who have dared to call him teacher!" The woman paused, then snarled, "Traitor!"

Ashiba flinched at the acid she put in her voice. His heart pounding so hard it felt as if it might explode, he found himself unable to pry his stare off the stunningly beautiful heiress to the Osaka megafortune.

"Miji?" Ashiba finally breathed, his voice drowned by a barrage of thunder that felt as if it shook the entire foundation of the building. Swallowing hard, he glanced around the room, wondering how she had slipped in there, like some silent wraith, without his seeing or hearing her. Then the rumors about the woman wormed into his mind, locked him up with an icy dread. He had even seen the closest business associates of Harry Osaka bow to this woman, breaking tradition, addressing her as "Shih," the force of energy and authority.

The petite, slender form in the long black leather coat crossed one leg over the other. Fractured blazes of white light flashed over a small and oval face with high, sculpted cheekbones that Ashiba had seen hypnotize men with their own lust.

The woman gave her long mane of silky black hair a quick toss, then a cold smile flitted over her full, ripe lips. The sudden movement caused her coat to open, and Ashiba glimpsed the hilt of the sword, stuck in a sash around the middle of her silk black jumpsuit.

Miji Osaka chuckled, glancing at the briefcases. "I take it in one of those is the money you have stolen from my father. In the other...well, did you think that a few tapes of my father with prostitutes would bring him to his knees? Oh, Takio, how little you really know about the house of Osaka. But now, of course, there are other things I understand. I often wondered why a young, handsome, charming man such as yourself never looked at me with even a hint of desire. Most men would die to know me, but you always viewed me much as one would look at a piece of stone."

She laughed, a cold, mocking sound, then her voice went hard. "Where my father trusted you, I never did. You think you are so smart, so clever. You never stopped to think that maybe there are spies among spies in the house of Osaka." She narrowed her gaze, and the contempt came back to her voice. "Tell me, did you think the gangsters of the Yakuza could bring my father to his knees when they planted you among us? Did you even dare to think they would allow you to live when you delivered their blackmail to them? I'm sure you already know this, but in just a short while, your masters will be offering my father a final offer they believe he can't refuse. Only those tapes will find another way into their hands.''

She lapsed into stony quiet.

Suddenly Ashiba felt compelled to explain himself, to make her understand. If she only knew how deep his shame cut, if she only knew how broken his heart was.

''Miji,'' Ashiba implored, ''understand, the Yakuza, they had me...''

''Silence! What has happened, you let happen to yourself. I understand that in everyone there is a dark corner of their heart. The secret of conquering the darkness lies in not letting the darkness conquer you. But I would never expect you to understand the way of the warrior.'' Miji let her penetrating stare drill into Ashiba for another moment, then said, ''Do you know what this is, Takio? This is what is called a moment of truth.''

It was then, staring deep into her pitiless eyes, that Takio Ashiba knew he was going to die. So be it. Somehow he steeled himself, clenched his jaw and looked Miji dead in the eye. He might have lived like a dog and brought shame upon himself and the house of Osaka, but he wouldn't die begging for his life. No, it was over. And in some strange way he felt relieved.

"Yes, it was I who left the file for you," Miji Osaka said, "to draw you out and expose you for the dog and the traitor you are. Given time, you might have figured out what it is that my father has planned for the coming return of samurai glory to our nation...given time."

Return of samurai glory? She was insane, Ashiba thought. Feeling the sweat bead on his forehead, he tried to will himself to make a sudden move for the drawer. Frozen.

Slowly, her burning stare never wavering from Ashiba, Miji Osaka reached into her coat. With her small and delicate hand gliding over the hilt of her sword, Ashiba was a heartbeat away from going to his gun. Before he could react, Miji tossed a black silk pouch on his desktop. A fresh wave of terror burst through Ashiba when he saw the white embroidery of the Osaka logo on the pouch. Instinctively he now knew beyond any doubt that the whispered rumours of a secret assassin cult within Osaka Worldwide were true.

"You have two choices. You can commit before my eyes the ritual self-sacrifice, or..."

She started to draw her sword. Thunder pounded the office with even more fury, lightning bursting in a sudden glowing radiance over Miji Osaka's face.

Ashiba hesitated, finally taking his gaze off the pouch, squaring his shoulders. When he balked she smiled.

"So," she said, "I see you believe that even life to a dog on the run is precious."

It was as if she could read his thoughts, smell out the very darkness rotting in his soul.

Somewhere in the back of his mind, Ashiba believed he could survive, could shoot her and walk out of there and catch his flight to freedom. But even as Takio Ashiba bared his teeth and made his move with his eyes locked on the top drawer, some stronger and darker instinct told him he was clinging to a fool's dream, that he would die a fool's death.

Glancing back through the fractured waves of lightning flashes, Ashiba saw the chair had swung away. With terror clawing his throat and shadows dancing in the corners of his eye, he snatched open the top drawer, his eyes searching for the Detonics 9. It took an agonizing, eternal second for him to find the weapon behind a litter of paperwork, but he pulled out the double-action pistol and began drilling half a dozen rounds into the middle chair. Stuffing flew through the air, and the chair rocked against the lead assault, the sound of the thunderstorm raging in Ashiba's ears but sounding as if it came from a distant land. And even as the Detonics cracked over and over in his hand, punching the middle chair back, he already knew she was no longer there even before he found the space empty.

It was what he expected.

It was what he wanted.

Sudden movement boiled up in the corner of Ashiba's eye. He whirled just as lightning sparked off the razor-sharp steel of the sword. The blade swept on for his neck.

Takio Ashiba held his ground and took his death.

IF IT WAS MEANT TO BE, then Harikami Osaka was prepared to die.

Very soon his enemies would invade the shrine, bring to him their dishonor in a vain attempt to shame the house of Osaka. Bring their serpent tongues, their guns and their false image of themselves as men of honor and respect, desecrating everything a true warrior stood for.

Wearing a *kataginu* and *hakama,* the court dress of the samurai, handed down from his ancestors of the Edo Period, Osaka rested a hand on the hilt of his sword, on the soul of the samurai. Since the night would bring death and dishonor, he had chosen to robe himself in black *gi.* Thus he was able to melt into the shadows, even the dark if necessary, far from the fingers of soft light glowing from the rice-paper lanterns. No amount of skill attained from decades of training and practicing in the dojo could ever prepare a man for that moment when he was faced with an enemy intent on his total destruction. One didn't learn how to kill or be killed by sparring with the *jo* or *bokken.* One *did.*

Alone in the main sanctuary of the Shinto shrine, built by his ancestors more than five centuries earlier, Osaka stared at his reflection in the mirror. He knew beyond any doubt he was pure of heart and honorable in purpose. Unmoving, his spirit was aware of all sound, all movement, from the outer shrine to the perimeter and beyond. Indeed, beyond the sanctuary he could hear the light drizzle kissing the gabled roof or dancing off the azaleas that sloped away to the dense woods surrounding the shrine. The storm god, Susa-no-o, had gone quiet, but thunder still rumbled and lightning flashed over the shrine, hurling glowing rays through the open doors or burning white sheets of brilliant light against the screens. The forces of countless spirits filled the shrine: wind, thunder and lightning, honor, shame and death.

For long moments lightning waves shrouded a ghostly radiance around the chiseled visage staring back at Osaka. The warrior narrowed his gaze, peering into his own soul. It had been many years since he had killed a man by his own hand. He was far older now, a little heavier and perhaps a little slower, but he would slay his enemies or die trying. After all, both he and his daughter were eighth *dan* in kendo, the way of the sword.

And Harikami Osaka knew he wasn't completely alone with his fearsome skill, with his purity of mind and honorable single-mindedness of purpose.

At that moment his ninja assassins were out there, crouched in the woods or among the azaleas or standing near in the treasure house, waiting to strike when the time was right.

Feeling the spirits of ancestors in the shrine, he

offered a silent prayer to Yokitomo Osaka, the Great One, to guide and watch over him and his warriors. Then, with the haunting weight of the past and aware of all that had led to the present on his shoulders, he recalled the legends surrounding Yokitomo the Great.

Passed down by word of mouth and by poem, it was said and written that Yokitomo the Great had slain hundreds of samurai during the Edo Shogunate when Tokugawa was turning mosquito-infested marshland into what was now modern Tokyo. One of the shogun's samurai had raped Yokitomo's sister, then the criminal samurai had murdered her to keep his shame hidden. A rampage followed when Yokitomo discovered the truth. Though Yokitomo killed countless samurai of the shogun, the Great One and much of the Osaka clan were chased across the Japanese archipelago to Nagasaki in a bloodbath of vengeance that had seen entire villages wiped out forever, whole bloodlines eradicated for all eternity.

But as great and fearsome a warrior as he had been, Yokitomo had been far more than an avenging samurai, Osaka knew. Beyond the fields of battle, Yokitomo had been priest and healer, philosopher and poet. A Zen master, Yokitomo had been blessed with powers able to return sight to the blind, return movement to the paralyzed with a mere touch of his hand. Thus it was said and written Yokitomo the Great had been a pure, living force of light and fire who could give life or take it. Yes, the legends were many surrounding the Great One and his avenging sword, and they lived on, centuries after his death from ambush by the shogun's samurai.

In his soul, where there was no room for the mingling of fact and fiction, Harikami Osaka knew the legend of Yokitomo the Great was all too real, felt in his heart the spirit of the Great One living on through him. Would he prove himself worthy of Yokitomo's memory?

He had to.

As he wore now the Great One's *gi* and prepared to wield his sword, an enormous pride welled in Osaka.

And those legends were as real to Harikami Osaka as the visions he could still see before his very eyes whenever he recalled that day of infamy, more than half a century ago when he was fourteen years old. Like now.

There was another burst of lightning, this time the fresh waves of light illuminating his stark expression of deadly calm. And the mushroom cloud seemed to rise before his very eyes, as if the memory itself lived in the shrine in the spirit of the storm, as if it were only yesterday, two minutes after eleven o'clock on that morning.

For a long and threatening moment, a bitter hatred knifed through Osaka as he remembered that day. Then the visions leaped like fire from a dragon's maw before his eyes. One moment he was in the courtyard, playing with his younger brothers and sisters. Then, out of nowhere, it was as if the forces of heaven and hell were unleashed in a silent blinding flash followed by a fire in a wind a thousand times stronger than any tsunami. In the time it took a man to blink, he recalled, everything was gone. Destroyed. So sudden and so fast was the fierce annihilation of Nagasaki, he remembered how he hadn't even heard the faintest trace of a scream. Later, after he discovered his entire family had perished in the cloud of fire, it was called a miracle by the Western barbarians that he had survived.

It was no miracle in Harikami Osaka's mind.

It was destiny.

Osaka shut his eyes, fought off the vision, tried to free himself through sheer iron will from the hatred that never failed to fill his soul when he remembered. There was too much to be done to dwell on the hell of the distant past. Tonight, he knew, was either the beginning or the end of his dream for a new imperial Japan. It was his duty to succeed. Death would mean failure, and he didn't intend to dishonor the proud Osaka bloodline, or worst of all, shame the memory of Yokitomo the Great. Nor would the lives of those who had perished at Nagasaki and Hiroshima, both within and beyond his family, go unavenged.

Opening his eyes again, the old warrior stared for another moment into the mirror, reading the fire in his eyes, seeing then the sudden and strange glow that radiated from his face. It was the same ghostly but faint shroud of white light the soldiers had seen when they had pulled him from the rubble. It was the same radiance that doctors couldn't explain but had linked to a series of high fevers he suffered as a teenager and well into his twenties, the same mysterious fevers he had passed on, he believed, and had claimed the lives of his two sons.

Osaka willed his soul to be quiet, knowing the glow came often at night, and always when he was on the verge of uncontrollable rage.

It was as if his soul had absorbed the fire from that storm, as if the radiation from the atomic blast lived on inside of him like a second soul. Whatever it was, it had given him powers very few men knew he possessed. Memories could become living entities before his eyes. Ears could tune into a solitary sneeze from blocks away in the rush-hour madness of Tokyo. Often he would peer into the souls of men, almost hearing their thoughts. Rare nights, while shaking and burning up from the fever in his sleep, he even dreamed the future as if he were right there, then have it pass before his eyes the very next day. The other powers were too frightening even for him to think about, powers of death, where his hand could spear into a man's chest, rip out his heart as if his hand were a steel talon plunging into water.

Osaka drew a long breath deep, then let it out. Concentrating but not concentrating on his breathing as he was taught by his Zen master so long ago, he freed his mind of all thought. Finally, in a state of divine emptiness, the hate and the rage fled him, evaporated as wisps of smoke. Slowly the glow faded. Self-control, he told himself, was the soul's armor of the samurai.

Once again he felt strong, pure, ready. And the mirror told him everything he needed to understand at that moment.

*Know thyself.*

He padded to the middle of the sanctuary, waiting. They were late, but he knew why it was taking them longer than they had arranged to make the trip from Tokyo to the Kanagawa prefecture of the Kanto Plain.

Minutes later he heard the crunch of tires over the pebbled driveway that announced their arrival. Car doors thudded shut, and heavy footsteps sounded in the outer hall. The moaning wind carried the odor of sake and sardines, of spices, cologne and cigars to Osaka's nose. They were coming to him, full of the world, full of themselves. They were a disgrace to all that was Japanese, but he couldn't expect these men—who loved only money, violence and power—to understand that in gaining the riches and the glory of the world they had lost the spiritual. They would prove to be their own worst enemies.

Slowly turning toward the open doors, Osaka watched as the dozen dark shadows of the Yakuza entered the domain of the shrine. As they spread out in a line before him, he let his gaze wander over the bulges beneath the shiny silk of their expensive jackets or the more-discernible shapes of machine guns and machine pistols beneath long black leather raincoats. Several of the gangsters returned his stare with the arrogance of men who believed they were completely in control of the moment. In a show of blatant disrespect, two of the gangsters even grunted among themselves at the sight of a lone old man armed only with a sword.

Finally Osaka looked at his chief enemy. Saki Mitisuma bowed, and the old man allowed the courtesy of a curt nod. Politeness, Osaka knew, was a necessary virtue for the samurai, for courtesy kept the force of the warrior's essence in reserve, to be used at its utmost strength only when necessary.

To know your enemy you had to first become his friend, so Osaka would display the outward appearance of courtesy and respect. The time to strike would come soon enough. Even then, he knew his assassins were moving in, indeed, could feel them, silent shadows delivering death to whatever gangsters were left outside with the vehicles.

Long moments of tight silence were cut by the sound of distant thunder. Mitisuma worked his jaw muscles, his dark eyes piercing with an unwavering stare through the gloom at Osaka.

"Osaka, I come to you with honor and good intentions, but something is telling me your motive is less than what I would like. Be that as it may, I am hoping that, after our last meeting, you have come to see the generosity and the respect I am extending to you by my offer to do business together. After all, that is what we are—businessmen. Both of us, I believe, have the best interests of Japan at heart. Should we pool our limitless resources together, I know we can make Japan the supreme power of the entire world."

Osaka said nothing. They were the ones who felt threatened; they were the ones who needed him. Or rather, they needed his money, his respectability.

Mitisuma glanced at his men, cleared his throat, looking uncertain as to how to proceed. "I am not here to dishonor the house of Osaka nor threaten you. I—"

"If that was true, you would have come alone," Osaka cut in. "Or at the very least these men would have entered this holy shrine unarmed."

"Unless you force me to do something I do not wish to do! Allow me the courtesy to finish."

Osaka stiffened but kept his expression stoic. Mitisuma had already proved himself a thug and a barbarian, but the manner in which he now spoke was insulting.

Mitisuma forced calm into his voice as he went on. "The world has changed, and with the changes in the world we must change or perish, or at best be cast aside like so much ash in the wind. We no longer exist in the military Japan of the shogun. The world seeks money, pleasure and power. Fate dictates a certain course. Fate has brought our paths together. Our paths can join or they can collide. A man of power and honor such as yourself, could be of great benefit to my organization, could help lead our nation to greater heights of glory in this new world.''

"Enough!'' Osaka growled, and saw the anger flare in Mitisuma's eyes. "Say what it is you came here to say, or do what it is you came here to do.''

Mitisuma bristled. "Very well. I want you to do one of two things. You either cease the building of casino-resorts in Japan or you go ahead and build them but turn complete control over to us. I know about your fondness for games of chance. We can find a suitable place for you in the future of any casinos you choose to build. Your percentage could be enormous, and we would not deny you what would rightfully be yours. But we must control them. This is an area of business you are not familiar with. This is an area of endeavor traditionally left to a knowledgeable and privileged few.''

"You want my money but not my direct involvement.''

"Precisely. You join us, you help us build on any site you wish and we will honor our commitment to you. I am willing to go so far as to even allow the Osaka name to be the one that honors any casino. Think of it. Together we could build the gambling supercity of the world, far greater, more powerful and wealthier than Las Vegas and Monte Carlo or anything Hong Kong has to offer combined.''

Osaka peered into Mitisuma's eyes, let the silence drag, made the man feel his fraying nerves. The old warrior could find no soul in him. Behind his gangsters, Osaka then caught the flicker of the first shadow beyond the doors.

"Well?" Mitisuma prodded. "What is your answer?"

Somehow Osaka controlled his outrage. This gangster who would come to him, a warrior who could trace his proud samurai lineage all the way back to the first shogunate of the Kamakura Period, and dare speak to him in the name of honor. This snake in human skin sold the sons and daughters of Japanese into prostitution and brought white poison into the country, which ruined countless lives and was eroding the already shaky foundations of time-honored Japanese tradition. This same creature had used his own sin against him and was on the verge of attempting to publicly shame him unless he bowed and crawled into the same viper's nest. Never. Blood was about to atone for his own sin against the house of Osaka.

Slowly the old warrior drew his sword. Mitisuma stiffened, fear dancing through his eyes, his men reaching into their coats. The Yakuza leader waved his hand at his subordinates and barked, "Wait."

"I have something for you," Osaka said. "It is both a gift and my answer."

He tapped the polished cedar floor with the tip of his sword, then turned his head slightly as the doors slid open behind him. A slender shadow appeared in the doorway a moment later. Lightning flashed through the room, and in the light Osaka caught the outrage in the eyes of Mitisuma at the sight of the woman.

Osaka waited as his daughter slid the first, then the second briefcase across the floor, and they stopped at Mitisuma's feet. Nodding, the Yakuza leader let his stare linger on the briefcases, then Osaka before he ordered one of his men to open the briefcases. Opening them, the gangster displayed the money and the videotapes for his boss.

"Now you understand why you were late," Osaka said as the shadows multiplied beyond the screen. "Your student never showed for his delivery."

As silent as a summer breeze, Miji Osaka moved up beside her father. Then the black pouch leaped up in her hand, hurling the head of Ashiba out and across the room. Alarmed, Mitisuma caught the head as it slammed into his stomach.

"I see now your idea of honor, respect and generosity," Osaka said, "is blackmail and extortion."

Mitisuma bared his teeth, still holding the head, and looked Osaka straight in the eye. "No, what I see is a foolish old man who would rather hold hands and do business with those who are not our own!"

Calm, Osaka ran a stare over the Yakuza hardmen, then said, "You are not my own."

Mitisuma let the head fall. "Kill them!"

The gangsters were reaching inside their coats, breathing in, giving father and daughter the opportunity to strike first. Breathing out, they split up, moving as fast as the winks of lightning before the gangsters cleared leather. Body and mind fused by tremendous unleashing of their fighting spirit, the Osaka team of death exploded into the ranks of their enemies.

In the next lightning flash, more sudden death swept through the Yakuza from behind, beside and below just as father and daughter drew first blood. In the corner of his eye, Osaka, his blade sweeping and slicing through necks and hands holding blazing weapons, saw the black-garbed ninja burst through the open doors on the flanks of the enemy. Altogether eleven silent wraiths in hoods and masks plunged into the midst of the suddenly panic-stricken gangsters, the tempered razor-sharp steel of their *katana*s flashing as swiftly as the lightning beyond the shrine. There was an initial moment of hesitation and shock by the Yakuza hardmen as they realized, too late, a trap had been sprung.

Heads flew through the dark. Gangsters screamed as their arms thudded to the floor, fingers still triggering pistols from the final electric pulses of severed nerves. A ninja burst through the trapdoor between a hardman's legs. Just as the man began to spray the room with an Uzi submachine gun, the ninja drove his sword through the gangster's groin. So deep and so tremendous was the killing thrust, so fueled by his own adrenaline, the ninja came out of the hole, his human trophy impaled on his sword. With superhuman strength the ninja lifted the wailing gangster in the air, then hurled his victim through a paper screen.

The slaughter lasted only a few more brief moments. Light as a feather, swirling through the enemy ranks with the breath of hot lead whizzing past his ears, Osaka claimed another head. The polished cedar underfoot became shiny and slippery with running blood as headless, dismembered or disemboweled Yakuza dropped where they stood. Still a few of the luckier or more-determined gangsters fired their weapons even as they took driving steel through the heart. Three ninja caught bursts of machine-gun fire in the stomach at point-blank range, and, drenched in crimson, were kicked through the paper screens.

Miji Osaka delivered more instant death with skewering thrusts, silencing the final barking weapons.

While the dead hammered the floor all around him, Osaka saw Mitisuma dive for a discarded pistol. Spurred on by righteous fury, he drove his sword through the Yakuza leader's arm. Horror bulged Mitisuma's eyes at the sight of his limb hitting the floor behind a gush of blood. Before he could scream, Osaka pounced on his back. With a knee in his enemy's back, pinning him to the floor, Osaka fisted a handful of hair and wrenched Mitisuma's face up to his own. The old man pressed the blade to his enemy's throat.

"This is what is called a moment of truth, Saki.

If you wish to live, you will ask me to spare your life."

The agony in Mitisuma's eyes vanished behind a stare of unwavering defiance. "I will not."

"I understand," Osaka said, and wrenched back on the blade.

Releasing his enemy, the old man stood. Feeling the presence of his daughter as she slipped up behind him, Osaka stared at his image in the unbroken mirror. It was sacrilege, he knew, to stain the shrine with blood, but he had cleansed himself in the slaughter.

Sin for sin, he had won back honor for the house of Osaka.

## CHAPTER FIVE

*Washington, D.C.*

A full day after touching down at Andrews Air Force Base, where the terrorists had been handed over to the FBI, Bolan's self-imposed solitude had come to an end. Standing at the window of his suite at the Key Bridge Marriott, Bolan sipped his coffee. Behind the Executioner, Hal Brognola took a seat near the table by the dresser. The soldier could feel the big Fed's grim stare boring into the back of his head as Brognola opened the file.

The Sphinx File, Brognola had called it, full of questions and riddles with no clear answers in sight. There was nothing but the specters of savages waiting in future shadows for the warrior.

As soon as he had hit the tarmac at Andrews, Bolan had been met by Brognola and whisked away in an unmarked car before the FBI had time to converge on the C-130.

"This thing isn't over," Brognola had said.

Those four words still haunted Bolan as he stared

down through the window at the midmorning traffic
jostling to get across Key Bridge for M Street in
Georgetown. He felt the specters of the dead commandos on his shoulders, the weight like a hundred
pounds of steel. Life had ended on the battlefield for
too many fine young soldiers. No amount of debrief-
ings, rife with solemn congratulations and promises
to the families of those soldiers who had given their
lives in Lebanon, would ever do them righteous
homage. Whatever honors were bestowed upon those
soldiers, Bolan knew the Pentagon, the CIA and the
Justice Department were staying tight-lipped and
evasive, trying hard to keep the lid on the identities
of all parties involved in the Beirut raid. In time there
would be leaks about the identities of the dead commandos, whether it came from hungry newshounds
or family members. But the man from Justice would
keep the cover of one Colonel Pollock in the dark,
even if he had to end up issuing a litany of denials
before a thousand cameras. No doubt, it helped that
the President had privately pledged to back Brognola
all the way.

One thing Bolan knew for sure was that a dark
light was moving his way. It wasn't so much what
Brognola had said; it was what he hadn't said. Whatever was ahead for Bolan, Brognola had looked and
sounded ominous during the Beltway drive. But the
big Fed had given the soldier his privacy, sensing
that everything that had happened in Lebanon could
have gone either way and that only Bolan's battle-

tested skill, a little bit of luck and a whole lot of daring had pulled off the impossible. So the man from Justice had simply informed Bolan that he needed another day to put some more pieces of Intel together, then he'd get back to him ASAP.

Now it was time.

Bolan turned and saw his old friend spreading the photos of the players across the table.

"So this thing isn't over."

"Far from it. In fact it's only just begun if my hunch is right. But we all knew the deal before you and the others went into Beirut."

"Now we brace ourselves for the fallout, the backlash from the extreme factions of the Islamic world. No American citizen is safe right now, especially in the Windy City."

Brognola put steel into his eyes and voice, but his agitation wasn't directed at Bolan as he said, "What happened in Chicago can't happen ever again on any piece of American soil. I think this country made that statement to the world, loud and crystal clear. That's why I need you to follow up on what I've got."

Bolan nodded, both men well aware their duty to their country would never end. Not until they were six feet under.

Suddenly the attorney general was on the news, giving a statement to the press that the terrorists responsible for the atrocities in Chicago had all been caught. No details were divulged about where the terrorists were being held or what was being done with them, but the AG went on to echo an earlier statement by the President, saying justice would be swift and uncompromising. Bolan clicked off the television; he'd heard more than enough.

The big Fed worked his jawline. "It makes me sick to my stomach when I think about what those bastards did. Five attacks in the early-morning hours on unsuspecting civilians. They were well-planned hits, designed to follow one right after the other. There were 221 dead and now you've got the Lebanese authorities, who we know gave these bastards refuge, shouting to the world that America has effectively declared war on their country with its 'criminal attack' in Beirut. Unbelievable. I'd like some of those outraged officials to look right down into the open caskets of our dead who were incinerated by a thermite explosion in the lobby arcade of the Sears Tower."

Bolan became filled with his own hot but tightly controlled anger, all too familiar with the atrocity. Starting at Chicago's O'Hare International Airport, two members of the Death Brigade had walked into the busy terminal and cut loose with automatic weapons, killing twenty and wounding another thirty before security and police had fulfilled the perverse martyr wish of the Iraqi fanatics. A series of four devastating explosions had then ripped through the city. Damage inflicted on the buildings and in the streets of Chicago was estimated in the tens of millions. But a price tag could never be put on the human life sucked into oblivion during a few seconds of the venting of the hate and rage of twisted minds.

Brognola stared at Bolan, frowning. "I can tell something happened over in Lebanon besides what I already know. You want to talk about it?"

"It's ancient history, Hal. Let's just say the blood of too many good soldiers was shed to not see this thing through to its conclusion. From here on I'd just as soon the law handle the terrorists I brought back. That was the mission."

"That's the problem, Mack. I wish it were only that easy." Brognola paused, then pushed on, putting a sympathetic touch to his voice. "Those soldiers will be buried with full military honors—you know that. As for Watkins, something tells me he had it coming to him. If I hadn't gotten you put in charge, the whole thing would have turned out different—a total disaster. From what I could glean from my own sources in the intelligence community, the late colonel had a bad track record but he had friends in the CIA. Watkins was a paramilitary operative for the Company, what is referred to in the martini talk of the intelligence community during happy hour as 'an animal,' a borderline criminal who wrapped himself in the Stars and Stripes but who was out there for himself. No telling how many innocent people have gone down for good in his line of fire or executed outright so he could achieve what he thought was his duty."

Grabbing a chair, Bolan sat next to Brognola.

Watkins was dead. Lebanon was behind him now. Shadows of a future battlefront were amassing on the distant horizon.

"What have you got, Hal?"

Meticulously Brognola laid out the black-and-white pictures.

"What I've got is some bad gut feeling, the worst I've had in years. I've managed to put some pieces together, but there are too many loose ends. Our wizards at Stony Man have been working around the clock on this—and on what I might have in store for you beyond Chicago."

A tight smile appeared on Bolan's lips as he thought about Aaron Kurtzman and Akira Tokaido. Before deciding to take his brief downtime, the Executioner had spent a few hours at Stony Man Farm. Brognola had sat with the computer sorcerers for some time, putting together the Sphinx File.

Brognola tapped the photo of a swarthy, bearded face with the fiery gaze of the extremist Bolan had seen thousands of times. "Abdullah Muftazi," he said. "He was caught when the police converged on the bomb site that ripped through the lobby of the John Hancock Center while another van loaded with C-4 killed forty-five people right out front on Michigan Avenue. His comrades went down in a hail of gunfire on Michigan, but Muftazi threw his hands up. Apparently he decided he didn't have the stomach for martyrdom. The FBI has been sitting on him since."

Bolan listened intently. Brognola informed the soldier it was Muftazi who had helped turn the tide, giving the FBI the hideouts of his comrades on Chicago's outskirts, who were then caught, details of weapons smuggled and stored, as well as forged passports and IDs to get them into the country—the whole nine yards on the workings of the savage strike on innocents. He'd also supplied leads to the possible overseas whereabouts of those who escaped.

"Then he stopped talking," Brognola said, "and started railing about a conspiracy on the part of Americans, hinting that his fanatic brothers had help getting into Chicago and getting out. Now he's demanding full immunity for his crimes before he says another word. I had agents interrogate him, but he's not talking to them, either, saying he's afraid for his life, babbling about the forces of the East and the West coming together to destroy America. He's yours. I've got a Learjet on standby at Dulles and can have you in Chicago this evening. You're going in as Special Agent Michael Belasko. I've called in some markers, pulled all the right strings, but now I owe some favors. You've got carte blanche. You're to pick up this bastard and sit on him. Then you'll be working with the FBI and a contingent of marshals to make sure the guilty get their day in court."

"What am I supposed to do with Muftazi?"

"If his story is bullshit, you're the one to find out. If not, if there's a dirty wind somewhere among the ranks of our own, it will blow your way."

Bolan had known Brognola for years, trusted beyond question the big Fed's instincts, however shadowy with little or no concrete basis. Just as he trusted his own bad gut instincts, honed by grim and savage experience. More often than not, Bolan knew, a warrior had to go with instinct when there was nothing tangible before him. And more often than not, acting on a hunch proved the difference between seeing the next sunrise or taking a bullet. Bolan let Brognola keep the floor, uninterrupted.

The big Fed spaced out a series of pictures of six men on a city street. Four of them, dressed in either windbreakers or dark suit coats and wearing sunglasses, were Occidental. The two other subjects in the photo were Oriental, sporting expensive tailored jackets and slacks.

"This is Special Agent Mark Withers," Brognola said, pointing at a lean figure with white hair and who struck Bolan as wearing a tight if not slightly paranoid expression. "He's in charge of the joint FBI-marshal task force sitting on the terrorists. This photo was taken by one of my men I had tail Withers, right in front of the Ritz-Carlton in what is known in Chicago as the Magnificent Mile. It's where a lot of big money, domestic and foreign, gather to do business. You don't even show your face in this stretch of Chicago unless you're clearing six figures a year.

"So, what are some FBI agents doing in that part of town, with what sure looks like some Japanese associates, our Feds looking around like they're waiting for a trap to be sprung on them from the shadows? At first I thought Muftazi was blowing smoke about this East-West conspiracy. But about the only thing he told my agents was that 'traitors walk among you.'

"So I did some digging on the head Fed honchos. Turns out Withers and five other agents in his unit have a distinguished track record as lead investigators working the Chicago field office on organized crime. They've brought down a few button men during their careers, but more importantly they've nailed a couple of capos. More importantly still, they broke up a connection between the Chicago Mob and the Yakuza during a brief but unsuccessful stint when the Japanese gangsters were looking to link arms with the Chicago bosses and set up shop. Right. East meets West."

Bolan met Brognola's dark stare.

"The picture gets more ominous," the big Fed went on. "Here it is. Six weeks to six months after Withers and elite company put their catches into the Witness Protection Program, their prized songbirds turned up dead. The Chicago boys went out with a bullet through the head. The Yakuza informant and his two samurai were found with their heads lopped off. Only a few people in the FBI, beyond Withers and his men, knew where these witnesses were relocated. A follow-up investigation into the executions hit a stone wall.

"Withers is calling the shots in Chicago," Brognola went on. "Let's just say, for starters, the man has a real bad attitude. But he has clout and is considered reliable and is respected by his superiors. He obviously jerked some strings to get what he wanted. Withers declined to use a site other than the one of his own choosing to hold the prisoners. The task force has erected a makeshift military installation, a good fifty miles south of Chicago on government-appropriated farmland. Crazy, I know. But is there some method to Withers's madness? You have the obvious problem of logistics of transporting the prisoners to Chicago. It will be done by Huey, then by van once the choppers set down at some site preselected by Withers. Anything can happen along the way, which is what worries the hell out of me. The trial starts tomorrow, at night."

That news caught Bolan by surprise. "Justice is swift on this one."

"Maybe too swift, but the AG got all the paperwork moved to get this thing under way. Indictments were filed, and the date for the beginning of the trial was set to go tomorrow night, whether or not you made it back with the terrorists you were sent to Lebanon to retrieve.

"Now, there will be a ring of security around the Richard J. Daley Center, where the courthouse is located, enough snipers on the rooftops of every building along Randolph, Dearborn, Clark and Washington Streets that not even the Four Horsemen of the

Apocalypse could breach it if their intent was to free those fanatics in some suicidal assault. But I'm worried just the same. Withers somehow got it all done his way, and I have a hunch that something is going to go wrong. I'm bracing myself, and sending you, to confront one of two possible nightmare scenarios. One, there will be an attempt to free the terrorists. Or two, they are being delivered for execution before we all hear the words, 'Court is now in session. All rise.'" Brognola paused, then said, "I want you on Withers the whole time."

Bolan broke the big Fed's piercing stare and studied the photo of Withers and the Japanese. He saw something on the right hands of both Japanese, some sort of marking. Brognola laid another photo in front of Bolan. As if guessing what the Executioner's next question would be, Brognola showed him a close-up photo of those hands, obviously taken by the lens of long-range cameras. Bolan couldn't quite make out the markings on the hands, but they looked like tattoos.

"Are these men Yakuza?" Bolan asked.

"No. Does the name Harry Osaka ring a bell?"

"Vaguely. I don't read *Forbes,* but I know the Osaka financial empire reaches around the globe. You turn on the six-o'clock news, you're liable to hear about some American company he's bought and built back up from near ruin."

"Right. Harry Osaka is one of the richest men in Japan, maybe the entire world. The man has major stock, is a shareholder or outright owner of just about any area of business you can name, both here and abroad. He even had an oil company for a while, based in Iraq. The Gulf War ended any oil ambitions the man had. Another thing—he's personally shaken the hand of Saddam Hussein.''

Bolan looked up, right into Brognola's stare. Bad gut feeling washed like a hot wave over the Executioner.

''Osaka is the economic shogun of Japan. Right now he's having problems, rumor has it, with the Yakuza. Seems Harry-*san* has a love for gambling and is encroaching on turf traditionally left to the Yakuza.'' Brognola tapped the close-ups of the Japanese. ''Those markings on their hands? It's a samurai in helmet with his sword drawn. That's the logo of Osaka Enterprises Worldwide. I haven't been able to identify these men and, of course, I'm not going to ask Withers who they are. My feeling is they're more than just associates of Osaka setting up a new business venture here in America.''

''Security?''

''Maybe more.'' Brognola cleared his throat. ''If this thing reaches beyond Chicago across the Pacific, then…well, how do you feel about going to Japan with a proposal to open casinos in league with Harry Osaka?''

A grim smile touched Bolan's lips, but he knew the big Fed was deadly serious. An ill wind was sweeping America, and Bolan was marching right into it.

"Let's deal with Chicago first," Bolan said. "If the winds blow in the direction of Japan, well, I'll pack a sword later."

## CHAPTER SIX

*Chicago, Illinois*

FBI Special Agent Mark Withers was at the threshold of life or death. Everything he had planned, schemed, hoped and, yes, killed for during the past ten years, would either have him coasting toward the future of a new life in a distant foreign land or blow up full in his face like the flying shrapnel of a live grenade. If something, anything, went wrong now, justice, the real justice of the law of the land, would bring down on his head a life sentence in the state penitentiary at Menard. If that happened, eating a Magnum sandwich would be far easier than being marched down a cell block full of howling cons hungry for his blood.

Driving the unmarked black four-door sedan south on Wacker, Withers felt as if he had a bundle of dynamite in his belly, the fuse lit and burning. Then he drove past the monolithic landmark that was the Sears Tower. There the mental image connecting his frayed nerves and mounting paranoia and anything that smacked of explosions sent invisible fingers of ice walking down his spine. Even now, more than two months later, the scuttling lunch crowd wore the expressions, he thought, of civilians hunkered in a bomb shelter and braced for a ferocious enemy bombardment. It didn't matter if it was on Michigan or Wacker, in office buildings, bars or restaurants, in Chinatown or uptown or in the huddled masses aboard the elevated trains or in cars fighting the Loop.

The smell of fear was all over the city.

But Withers could understand the sense of morbid dread, terror and outrage that gripped the masses whenever they ventured into the streets of Chicago these days. Whether they lived fat and safe in their mansions in the Gold Coast or clawed out a wretched existence in the South Side, the fear was pervasive. Around-the-clock fear was sucking up the energy of this town in a vacuum of terror sparing neither cop, crook nor civilian. No doubt, to everyone in the city it seemed like only yesterday when human torches had hit Wacker Drive or Franklin Street. Flailing limbs going everywhere, bansheelike screams knifing the air so shrill and loud they could be heard clear to Lake Shore Drive. They were human torches he had helped to ignite, civilians he had helped to mow down in the terminal at O'Hare or blow up into countless shredded remains at selected strategic points across the city. Not directly, mind you, but there had been a conspiracy within the conspiracy, a plot of doom and destruction that now shoved more problems at Withers than he cared to think about. Unfortunately, though, today still carried the ghosts of yesterday, still swept the stench of the dead right up his nose. Withers was all too grimly aware it was coming full cycle again in collision with tomorrow.

Conspiracies, shadows of doom and loose tongues that knew too much were all around Withers. One of his greatest threats was that Iraqi bastard being sat on by a couple of his agents and marshals in a renovated River North condo. But if Muftazi was thinking about singing to anybody who might listen or anybody who might hand him the keys to his freedom, then the Iraqi was going to be proved wrong. Dead wrong.

A low bank of gray clouds scudded over the imposing skyline of the Windy City, but Withers always kept his dark aviator shades in place on his handsome visage, sun or no sun. And these days he never went anywhere without his 9 mm Beretta in shoulder holster, with the backup .357 Magnum Colt Python on his hip. His enemies, he knew, were everywhere. Like the Japanese bastards and the Iraqi connection he was holding hands with in the shadows of the night.

Thinking about his Japanese contacts now, he decided they might be the reason he was ready to take big money from the East to free the Death Brigade captives, but he and his team were the driving force.

Without him the Japanese were dead in the water, he thought, and they might as well commit hara-kiri before this thing even got off the ground. And with that vision of disembowelment fleeting through his mind, it was suddenly too unnerving to dwell on the full ramifications. But he and his men had thrown it all on the line, which meant there was no turning back now. Whatever the connection between the Japanese and the Iraqis, Withers didn't care.

Still, he knew enough, had caught the implications and hints during those midnight sessions to know this was deadly serious business, to be aware that this thing was going to reach around the globe and he had damn well better fulfill his end of the bargain—or else. As sure as there would be snow on the city and icy wind slicing with Siberian strength off Lake Michigan in the next couple of months, a nightmare plan was about to unfold.

The following night, in fact.

Either way, Withers didn't give a damn about the pact between the Iraqis and the Japanese. He was in it for the money, plain and simple.

He checked his partner, knowing his eyes were hidden but hoping his expression didn't betray the bad case of nerves shooting fire through every nerve ending in his body. Gratefully he found his long-time ally, Special Agent John Turnbull, giving the crowds a look that was something between contempt and tolerance. Withers allowed a tight smile as he turned on Jackson, then swung south on Canal, keeping the long circuitous route in case there was a tail. A man never knew these days who he could trust.

But Withers had known Turnbull for years, the bond going all the way back, a century ago, it seemed, to their training at Quantico. Both of them were indeed linked by the dark secrets of the past. Theirs was a mutual joined path, carved by a knife of treachery and deceit, and they had followed it straight to this crossroads in Chicago. Hell, he thought, Turnbull was his mirror image, the two of them sharing common beliefs and attitudes about everything from handling capos to affirmative action. They were the links in a strong and unbreakable human chain of righteous rebellion, he believed. Being FBI agents, they would never come right out and rail at the system or condemn the country for its downward liberal slide like their associates in the right-wing paramilitary organizations—shadows they had kept over the years at a good arm's length but guys with the connections to land him the necessary hardware whenever he needed it.

Unlike the racist, antigovernment, would-be Hitlers out there in the heartland, Withers and his men maintained a quiet and controlled and secretive indifference toward America and what America had become in their view. In their hearts they kept it all hidden from public scrutiny, but shared a belief that they lived in a country out of control. No question in his mind—it was dog-eat-dog out there, where money ruled, where kill-crazed punks ran amok in the streets, armed to the teeth, could even kill a cop and get a slap on the wrist because maybe their constitutional rights had been violated. As law-enforcement agents they constantly endured the insane wrath and simmering hostility from too many out there who had no respect for the law. Worse still, they shouldered too often the apathy, even the outright contempt, of civilians who wanted nothing more than to maintain the crumbling walls of their own little enclaves as long as they didn't get hurt.

Life had turned ugly all over the land. Nothing but fear and rage came at a man, from both sides of the tracks. It was beyond mind-boggling. Withers was forced to live in—no, protect—a sick or silly society that had become one large bed of special-interest quicksand and moral decay, but a quagmire he wasn't going to drown in.

Turn one way, and he saw ass-grabbing officials and politicians out for themselves. Look the other way, and special-interest groups were right in your face, showing any man with a real pair that they were interested in only their plight, imagined or not, whining all over the place every time you turned on a morning talk show. These days right was wrong and wrong was right. It was all beyond hope, beyond redemption, Withers believed. Sure, they might have wrapped themselves in the Stars and Stripes, staunchly believed in their duty to law and to country. But things change, and life has its own way of waking up a man.

Quiet ways, right, but you got the message. For instance, since the terrorist attack on Chicago, the city observed a moment of silence every morning at 0900 sharp, but Turnbull privately called it a moment of triumph, when the winds of change were sweeping America. Well, Withers understood the man's sentiments. Turnbull was simply echoing that wake-up call to America.

But like the system he privately cursed and loathed, Withers had long since lost control of his own life, both personally and professionally. Like Turnbull and the others in his inner circle of conspirators, Withers was divorced, either faced with huge alimony and mounting debt or scurrying to keep in the dark a fast but clandestine life-style of good food, hard drink and warm women. Then there were those shadows of past sins haunting them all to keep up the good life while clinging now to the last shred of hope of putting it all behind in some remote corner of the earth.

First there was the extortion of midlevel drug dealers or the strong-arming of lower-level mafiosi, another hundred lifetimes ago.

Second they themselves had done a contract killing of a federal witness or two under their protection along the way. Even if a couple of them hadn't outright pulled the trigger, they all shared the knowledge, as well as the guilt. So, he thought, fate had somehow sealed the now and the future for all of them. And all they had ever wanted was a little more rightful piece of the pie.

You bet, Mark Withers had his own ideas about balanced budgets and affirmative action. That was why he'd taken the offer from the Japanese envoy he'd been introduced to after his takedown of the Mob-Yakuza connection several years back.

Withers glimpsed his big crew-cut partner giving his watch a long hard look. A scowl touched the corners of Turnbull's big, granite-hard face before he pushed his dark shades a little higher up his hawkish nose. Stop thinking, stop worrying, Withers told himself, putting his concentration on the drive between the canyons of office buildings along the riverfront. A couple of turns, east on Harrison, then south on Wells and he was heading for the South Side.

"All this dodging and weaving, looking over our shoulders, we're going to be late," Turnbull said.

Withers gave his partner a look, not sure whether he cared for Turnbull's tone. "Better late than not getting there at all. Caution, my friend, and patience. We've covered our tracks this far, so let's not get careless now. The Japanese will keep."

"They have our million."

"And we've got what they need. Relax."

"I'm relaxed. I'll be even more relaxed after tomorrow night when this thing is behind us."

Withers worked his jaw, the tension knifing up

from deep in his belly, driving some bile into his throat. There were details to iron out with the Japanese, logistics to go over, arrangements to nail down. And there was money to take.

"Look at this human shit," Turnbull said, nodding at a few winos shuffling in front of a liquor store. "You know, we spent a lifetime trying to make things better, either fighting for or protecting a bunch of ungrateful civs. These days there's so much human feces around it would take a hundred lifetimes to flush it and a lake ten times the size of Michigan to take it. Duty, honor, fidelity, all that crap. You work hard, do what's expected of you, pay the bills, provide for the family, then one day you come home and your wife tells you she's leaving you for another guy. Takes the kids, the house, everything but your balls. One day, just like that, it all goes up in smoke. Wake-up call, that's what it is. Just like the bombs and the bullets that ripped through this city. Wake up, people, smell the shit you smeared yourself in." Bitterness edged toward hate in Turnbull's voice as he added, "The world can kiss my ass."

Withers showed Turnbull a mean smile. "Good to hear you're not about to get a conscience on me."

Turnbull patted the bulge of the pistol beneath his jacket. "I got all the conscience I need right here."

They fell into grim silence as Withers worked his way through the streets, killing more time but wanting to be sure they weren't followed. Tuning out the clamor of elevated trains and the blare of distant horns, he guided the sedan to the storehouse that was nestled on some river frontage. Finally Withers swung into the long, narrow alley, then gave the area a hard look. He cursed. There was no sign of their Japanese contingent. Parking the sedan beside the back door of the redbrick storehouse, he killed the engine.

"They'll be here," Withers said to Turnbull, who was scowling around the alley, showing the first hint of nerves on his big-boned face.

It obviously gave Turnbull too much time to ponder some problems, since he said, "What's the story on this Justice agent, this Belasko guy Washington is flying out here?"

Withers felt his heart skip a beat. "It's news to me, but we'll deal with him when he gets here."

"Well, he'll be landing in a few hours. We're supposed to greet the guy with open arms at the base, then march him right to Muftazi. That's straight from Washington."

"Fuck Washington. Fuck Muftazi. I'm in charge, and that's straight from Washington."

"Yeah, well, it makes me a little nervous just the same. Tells me somebody in Washington thinks they know something. And Muftazi is so nervous he could shit himself you look wrong at him."

"That's another thing I need to talk to our Japanese buddies about. Before this Belasko gets a chance to lay eyes on him, Muftazi is going to be a bad memory."

Turnbull chuckled. "A little ninja action maybe to get this thing kicked off?"

"Something like that."

Turnbull turned somber. "I have to tell you, I don't trust our Japanese allies out of my sight. Whatever it is they want with the Iraqis, it's important enough for them to risk their lives with this kamikaze action. Not only that, it's as if they've known all along one day they would call in our marker. I mean, they're not even connected to the Yakuza, but these same guys did the hit on the informant. Like it was a message to us. Christ, it's almost spooky, the way they look right through you, like they know some secret."

"The only secret they'll know is what's in here," Withers said, patting the manila envelope on the seat beside him. His partner frowned, and Withers could tell some of Turnbull's cold calm was melting around the edges. "Listen, I'll handle this Belasko guy, if that's what's eating you. I mean, how bad can it be? I've dealt with and beaten Justice guys before without them even knowing it. This guy will turn out to be just another clown in a suit with a badge. Probably the first stretch he's ever seen away from behind his desk."

Turnbull grunted. "You're probably right."

"I am right. That's all you need to know."

Suddenly Withers saw the vehicle loom in his

rearview mirror. First one, then a second black limousine pulled up and parked on the sedan's rear.

"Well, well, payday just rode in. Our fearless
samurai from the East. About time," Withers said,
grabbing up the manila envelope. As soon as the two
men started to bail out of the sedan, the Japanese
disgorged from their limos. Withers counted thirteen
grim-faced Asians. All of them had their eyes hidden
behind dark sunglasses, and stood their ground with
that stony expression Withers had come to know and
distrust. Worse, it never failed to strike a nervous
chord in him the way they wore that stoic demeanor
like a porcelain mask. Nor did it ever fail to flare up
his indignation the way they looked at him as if he
were something they'd just stepped in.

The short lean one with the scar on his left cheek
was their contact, and Withers made a beeline
straight for Misimoto Harisomo. The six times he'd
met with Harisomo over the past four years, three
times in the past six weeks alone, Withers had always walked away with the feeling the scar-faced
man thought himself superior, meaning any Western
type was supposed to kiss the ground he walked
on—samurai honor and all that. Even still, their contact knew far too much about them to not keep up
some appearance of respect and continued cooperation. For starters, there was never any hint of threats
or blackmail or extortion by the Japanese. No, they
simply handled the sordid past of Withers and his
men as if it were just another aspect of doing busi-

ness. Withers knew better, the clincher his fearful belief their swords would turn on him if it came down to us or them.

Beyond his apprehension of them and ignorance of their ways, there was still a part of him that respected the Japanese. Unlike his country and its people, he thought, the Japanese were one blood, one culture, one history; they honored and respected their own above and beyond all and anyone else. Little wonder they looked down upon the West, with its families shattered and scattered all over the map, misplaced and mismatched fragments of the so-called melting pot, most Americans displaced of character and commitment, detached from any sense of honor or loyalty. It was truly a sick and sorry world, he decided. High time to bail out of the sinking ship before the whole country erupted and he was left with nothing but more regret, more anger, more bewilderment.

Locked onto Harisomo, Withers sensed right away he was getting the same smug once-over from the Japanese. Then his gaze flickered over the hilt of the sword poking out of the black leather trench coat swathing Harisomo like a second skin. Withers almost stopped cold in his tracks; he could tell the Japanese were packing some serious heat beneath their silk jackets or leather coats. It was unbelievable that they were riding around Chicago as if they didn't have a care in the world, as if they weren't about to set the town ablaze with a hellstorm that would make the Great Fire of 1871 look like a weenie roast for Boy Scouts.

"You're late," Withers said.

The trace of a cold smile flickered over Harisomo's lips. "Traffic was...how do you say—a bitch?"

Great, Withers thought, now some samurai comedy.

"You people have your own private air fleet, and you can jet back and forth across the Pacific in about the time it takes to watch a three-hour movie, but you can't show up for the most important meeting of our lives on time."

"We are here now."

Disgusted, Withers turned his attention on the briefcase Harisomo held. Right away hot anger flared in him when he saw the samurai on the briefcase—the frigging Osaka logo.

"The money in there?"

Harisomo stared at the FBI man, letting the silence drag. "It is what you wanted, am I right?"

Withers shook his head. "You might as well tell the whole city of Chicago what we're doing."

Harisomo's face turned to stone. "You worry too much, Withers-*san*. Consider the briefcase a humble gift. If it bothers you that much, change the briefcase."

"Let's get inside," Withers growled. "We've got a lot of ground to go over."

But Withers found the Japanese holding back, giving him a strange look. He keyed open the door, then said, "Well?"

"We do have a lot to talk about, you are right, Withers-*san*."

What the hell was that supposed to mean? Withers wondered, watching the Japanese then move with a calm swiftness, a tranquillity of motion almost that he found eerie. The agent tasted fear on his lips, the weight of all his past sins bearing down on him with a sudden invisible force. It was hardball time, or else. They knew everything, and he was going to play. To cut that fear a trifle deeper, Withers knew what these guys were all about, knew their work firsthand—swords, throwing stars and all, plus a few hand cannons and some machine guns for good measure.

Whatever they were, they were ready for that kamikaze action. And they were exactly what he needed to pull off the second great fire poised to sweep the Windy City.

But Mark Withers wasn't about to bow to any man, no matter what he was or what he thought he knew.

The next day was going to settle all business, wrap up the past, present and future in one nice little send-off party from Chicago. Right then, Withers heard Turnbull's bitter words echo through his mind.

The world could kiss his ass. You bet.

*Japan*

HARIKAMI OSAKA AWOKE suddenly from the nightmare. Snapping upright in his raised bed, he shivered violently as he felt the sweat running down his back, soaking his kimono. Then he felt the fire in his brain, the fever, one of the worst he'd had in some time. Somehow he stifled the cry of agony with an iron will, but a sharp grunt knifed its way out of his throat.

Alarmed, he jumped off the bed and dipped his hands into the cool waters of the basin. With controlled fury he doused his face and neck. Then he concentrated on his breathing, driving the fire from the center of his brain, remembering what Zen Master Tokishoma had once said. *Disease can be mastered by the will. Everything is in the mind, and all comes from the breathing. Inspiration takes in the life forces of the cosmos, breathing out correctly releases the energy of the universe through the body.* Control the fire, he told himself, breathe correctly.

But this was a new fire, stronger, more powerful than all the other fevers combined. It had brought on all the jumbled, horrific images of the past, a floating but fleeting maze of living entities in and beyond his mind, it seemed. For the most part the visions lived before him as they always did, but this time the fire was accompanied by an unshakable fear. Some voice in the fire had warned him to be wary of the future but to embrace the coming calamity with all the calm of the true samurai. But the images of that day so long ago overpowered any shadowy vision of tomorrow right then, displacing for the moment the face of a future enemy he had seen in the depths of the nightmare. Still the face fleeted before him in the darkness. Was it imagined? Real? Brought on by the fever?

With sheer willpower Osaka shook the images of the countless charred bodies from his mind after what felt like an eternity. The fire then receded from his head moments later, only to boil down deep into his belly. And as his head cooled, the fear grew stronger, wanted to seize control of him with its unknown demons. But what was he suddenly so afraid of?

Osaka took up his sword. Before he knew it, he had lit the lanterns in the quarters. Before he was aware of it, his wide-eyed stare was wandering over the myriad prints from the Edo Period, a collage of swirling, meshing color of samurai in battle covering the length of all the screens. From out of nowhere he believed he heard the roar of battles past come to life in the Osaka castle, heard everywhere the clang of swords, the screams of men falling horribly wounded or slain in battle. And for just a moment, in his delirious state, he believed the prints actually moved.

Calm slowly fell over Osaka. The visions faded, the sounds of battle left like a receding wave from the room and the world stopped spinning. It helped to focus on the scroll, the flower arrangement near the hearth. They were real.

He moved back for his bed, sword in hand, still braced for any shadows to come rushing at him. He sensed the room was alive with countless spirits.

Then his stare fixed on the bed, the spot that had been vacant for years. He felt the ghost of his wife in the room, wondered if she knew his shame over what he had done to her memory. Men were allowed their pleasures outside of marriage in his country, he knew, but to be caught—no, filmed with prostitutes as a weapon of blackmail—was unspeakable shame. Even though his immediate enemies were dead, buried in the countryside, they would be missed, and more enemies would come for his blood. The future, though, whatever it held, had to be faced down with all the strength and determination of his ancestors combined. If dishonor befell the house of Osaka again, he would have no choice but to commit seppuku.

Choking down his grief, unable to remove his eyes from the bed, he recalled how his wife had passed on after long and agonizing suffering from cancer. Radiation sickness had claimed her life; he was sure of it. No amount of money could have saved her, nor the lives of his sons. In that one grievous respect alone, money was useless.

But there was power, Osaka decided, in their deaths, more fuel still to feed the fires of vengeance.

More and more he felt drawn to his destiny. Perhaps, he thought, even after all those years since the bomb, he was now dying from radiation sickness himself. If that was the case, then he would have to act more quickly than he had originally planned.

Osaka walked toward the east window. There he gazed out at the blackness shrouding the sprawling reaches of his immaculate flower gardens, toward the horizon. He recalled the face in his dream, tried to get a clear picture, but it was only a veiled visage. Beyond the shimmering pall of recollection, he knew the face was that of a future enemy. It was a dark-haired man with the steely, determined stare of a warrior who had known much death and violence in his lifetime. Perhaps. All he knew was that the man in his nightmare vision was Occidental.

Some future battle awaited the house of Osaka—he was sure of it, and the enemy would come from the West.

Osaka stared for a long time past the distant hills. Right then most of his warriors were across the ocean. They would succeed or they would die in America, beginning a battle for the future of the world, for the triumph of the house of Osaka. When the dust settled and the flames died, he knew he would be faced with new challenges, new duty.

But the Occidental face in his dream flashed back to him. He wasn't sure why, but he knew he had to face this unknown, undetermined enemy soon. Osaka would be ready. He intended to greet any potential enemies from the West as honored guests. Know your enemy first as friend.

"Foreigner," Osaka breathed. "I am ready for you, whoever you are."

# CHAPTER SEVEN

*Chicago, Illinois*

Misimoto Harisomo kept his hand on the hilt of his sword. He could neither trust nor respect any man who would abandon his duty to lord and country. It was dishonor. But sometimes, he believed, a man had to walk with the devil to reach the lofty heights of perfection, to catch even a fleeting moment of paradise on earth. To Harisomo, whose only lord and master was Harikami Osaka, Mark Withers and his men were devils, but they were necessary tools. What he had been sent to do for his lord was far more important for the future of Japan than the momentary shame of allying himself with creatures who worshiped only money and their own desires. Indeed, his duty was even more important than his own life. Yes, if he didn't succeed, if capture looked unavoidable, he would commit seppuku, right on American soil if he had to.

Patiently Harisomo waited while the FBI men checked the money in the briefcase before turning their attention to the more important business of weapons and the battle plan. While Withers prattled on about details of the strike, matters that they had already gone over two weeks earlier, Harisomo made a show of perusing the map of the city. Withers indicated places near the courthouse marked in red ink, places that he claimed had holes in security, potential breaches he had purposely created. The man proud in his conspiratorial way.

"Are you listening to me?"

Harisomo glimpsed the agitation on the FBI man's face and nodded. "Go on."

And on and on Withers went, jabbing the map on the desk many times. Assuring him everything would go off without a hitch if everyone worked as a team, in sync, struck at the same time, and that included the Iraqis. Then reassuring. Then wanting reassurance.

Harisomo was tiring quickly of Withers and the man who looked like a bulldog, the giant called Turnbull. He knew all about these men, how they had betrayed their country, abandoned their duty to work for themselves, knew about these agents of the law long before they armed the Iraqis with weapons they'd purchased from the various hate groups in America. No, the FBI men hadn't outright delivered the weapons of mass destruction used to kill, terrorize and inflict horrific damage on the city. Instead, they had used conduits of the paramilitary groups to nail down the deal, take the money from the Iraqis.

Indeed, Harisomo knew too much about the FBI men. Sometimes knowledge in itself could be revolting.

What these FBI men could have never guessed, though, was that Osaka Worldwide had spies and informants all over America, entrenched in the corporate and legal and illegal world. That one Yakuza turncoat had meant nothing to anybody, Harisomo reflected. But the execution had been a way in for Osaka when Harisomo had contacted Withers and employed persuasion to be able to assassinate the informant on American soil. What Withers had certainly figured out by now was that the execution had merely been a method by which to snare him, use FBI status as a favor owed in the future.

That was something else Harisomo had always admired about his lord, aside from his unwavering, unflinching sense of duty and honor. Lord Osaka was always thinking and planning ahead, as if he knew the way before the path even presented itself.

Well, the way had showed itself and the time had come. Bets had been placed, Withers had lost and markers had been called in. Lord Osaka wanted the Iraqis freed, or killed, at worst. No, they would be freed, Harisomo corrected; plans had been laid to see this present course of action through, and soon the Iraqis would be whisked straight to Japan. Osaka Worldwide had plans, a megascheme that could have Osaka conquer the Western world, or at least put

Japan at the unchallenged forefront of all global enterprises. First, though, they needed the Iraqis.

For a long moment, hearing Withers from some great distance as he indicated what would be the safest places near the Daley Plaza to hole up the strike force until they could be unleashed at the appointed hour, Harisomo silently cursed the misfortune that had led him to this incredibly risky endeavor. He had never liked doing business with Islamic extremists in the first place, seeing them as too foolish in their zeal to die over religious ideology or a piece of land. It was insanity. What honor was there in dying when the cause wasn't clearly defined? Maybe he simply didn't quite understand how the Arab mind worked, but he had certainly seen enough evidence of their madness in the past couple of months to make him think twice. This whole vendetta of their Iraqi allies, their going off to vent their hate and rage on America at a time when Lord Osaka needed them, was utter madness. Then they'd been caught and had to be rescued. Oh, they had better show due gratitude and respect when Harisomo got them safely out of America and on Japanese soil, or he would cut off their heads personally.

"Now, let's take a look at what we paid for," Withers said.

Harisomo followed the FBI man across the room to where large crates were stacked in the corner, receiving yet more reassurance that this storehouse was safe. There was nothing to worry about. Incredible.

The more he read the doubt, worry and fear on the face of the FBI man, the more Harisomo began to think there was plenty to worry about.

Withers began to open the lids on the crates, displaying a variety of weapons, then named them: M-16 assault rifles with attached M-203 grenade launchers; Uzi submachine guns; Ingrams with attached silencers; grenades, both fragmentation and incendiary; a half-dozen LAWs, RPGs and six MM-1 Multiround Projectile Launchers, which looked to Harisomo like some squat, futuristic weapon more fitting for a woman than a warrior.

Harisomo continued to give Withers half an ear. The agent rambled on about how the twenty thousand pounds of plastic explosive and dynamite were safely stored, dispersed in warehouses across the city, how the explosives would have to be planted at preselected sites near the plaza and across Chicago, details about how to do that. He'd have the radio remote control, and he would signal the start of the battle. Other boxes would be given to the Iraqis and to Harisomo, his people.

"When this goes down," Withers said, "I trust you understand you're going to need more than a few swords and some ninja techniques."

"I understand perfectly," Harisomo said. "The other half of our force, the Iraqis, they are already here in the city. They are ready and know what must be done."

"Right, so you told me. Flown in two and three

at a time. I know all about the forged-passport routine, falsified documents, the paper trail that gets laid out. That's all real swell, but when it hits the fan, a whole lot of people are going to die. Let's see we don't add ourselves to the body count.''

Still enduring, Harisomo listened to more false pride, about how shadows work within shadows, about speed, daring and seizing the moment from the initial strike on. If some civilians got caught in the cross fire, well, that was their tough luck. The night and the confusion of battle would provide them with the necessary edge. Darkness. Use the shadows. This gaijin, bloated with ego, couldn't even begin to fathom the cunning and the guile of the ninja world.

''So far it's been enough to get here, but we all know getting in is just the start. Now, we've gone over the escape plan, but once again, getting there and then getting out of here isn't even half the battle. The right people have been paid off to help us get out. That includes a fat chunk of cash I had a man deliver to the right people in the FAA, reel in key people at O'Hare military and Fort McCoy. But just because airspace is protected doesn't mean we're home free by any stretch. When it goes down, I suggest you keep some of this firepower for yourselves and give the Iraqis only what they need. But before we go over the escape route one last time, there's a problem we need to discuss. An Iraqi problem.''

''Something has happened I do not know about?''

''You could say that.''

Harisomo peered hard at Withers. "There are only two of the Iraqis I am primarily concerned with. Zabir and Abriz, the one who was just captured in Beirut. Their lives are to be guarded like the most rare of gemstones."

"Gems or whatever you want to call them, they're not the ones causing me a problem. It's one of them I'm sitting on in town. Muftazi. In just a short while a Justice Department agent will be here to pick up and question Muftazi. The Iraqi thinks he knows something, which he doesn't. Well, not really. What I mean, he has some idea of how this town went up in flames two months ago. Bottom line, if he becomes my problem, then he becomes your problem. I can't very well walk into the room and just put one through his head. If you follow me."

Harisomo became suspicious. It could be a trap. After all, the FBI men had their money, or most of it. Harisomo had kept some leverage in reserve.

The Japanese decided to turn up the heat, search for any hidden motives. "Give me the location of where he is, the room and the layout of the building. I will handle it personally."

"It will have to be soon. As in the next few hours. Of course, I'll have to work out some details of getting you in, but I've got two men I can trust guarding the guy."

"I said I would handle it. I hope, Withers-*san*, for your sake, you are being frank with me. If you are not..."

Harisomo let it trail, waiting as Withers looked prepared to vent anger over the insult of not being trusted. The FBI man scowled but gave Harisomo's short sword a long look and reined in his emotions.

"As honest as you've been with me."

"Good," Harisomo said. "Then you will get the rest of your money when this comes to a successful conclusion."

Harisomo got the expected outraged response.

"What the hell are you saying?" Withers snarled. "We had a deal."

"We still do."

Turnbull was opening the briefcase, riffling through the packs of hundred-dollar bills. "I thought it looked a little light."

"How much?" Withers growled at Harisomo.

"I owe you another quarter."

"When do we get it?"

"When this is over and we are safely out of the country."

"This wasn't the way business was supposed to be handled, my samurai friend," Withers said, fighting hard to control his fury. "Not only that, but a lot of this hardware I paid for out of my own pocket. Not to mention bribe money."

"This is not about money, Withers-*san*. This is about honor and duty."

"No, this is about something you've got going down with the madman of Iraq. I've caught enough to know you've got your own ideas about a New World Order.''

"Enough. Your problems are your problems. My duty is my affair.''

"That's where you're wrong, pal. If I go down, we all go down. What's more, my men and I will be flying out of the country with you. That was part of the package. You give me your word now that we are guaranteed safe flight to Japan and that we will get the rest of our money.''

Harisomo balked. A samurai never had need or reason to ever give his word of honor, either verbally or on paper. Honor was unspoken. But he couldn't expect these men to understand the way of the warrior.

"Your word?''

Harisomo gave the FBI man a curt nod. "Very well. You have my word.''

"We've come too far to screw up now,'' Withers went on. "I want out of this country safely, and we all want this to succeed. The future, my Japanese friend, that's what I'm looking forward to. A new life. A new identity.''

"Then we shall see how it all goes.''

"What the hell's that mean?''

A thin smile cut Harisomo's lips. "Allow me to tell you this about the future. It is something no man should look to, anticipate, promise or even fear. We are all dead or dying actors playing out a live drama with an unwritten ending. You should neither rush to nor avoid the end. Acceptance of death, if it is meant to be, is the greatest glory one can give to his lord and master. Even give to the Creator.''

Harisomo gauged Withers closely for a reaction. No, the FBI man didn't understand at all, instead showed even more doubt and fear. Harisomo might as well have been talking to himself. He couldn't wait to be finished with these barbarians.

MACK BOLAN WAS the only passenger in the six-seater cabin of the Gates Learjet 24F. Alone with mounting and disturbing thoughts and a slew of unanswered questions, he'd had plenty of time to mull over Brognola's Intel, sort through the rumors and establish a game plan during the flight to Chicago.

He was going in, low-key, with no hardball questions, no flare-ups, no muscle flexing. If Withers and some others who might or might not have chosen to tarnish their badge and duty with dishonor...well, a quiet, unassuming approach could prove more effective in rattling some cages than going in with shoulders squared and steely eyes drilling through everybody.

But something was feeling wrong to the Executioner. With grim resolve he intended to flush out any traitors, step on and crush the heads of any vipers on either side of the law. That was his mission. Justice was going to be served to the guilty. Whether it came from the end of a gavel or from his own weapons, the choice was up to any guilty players involved in the business.

Make no mistake, he had come prepared to serve justice the hard way if that was what it took. Beneath his black leather jacket, the 9 mm Beretta 93-R was tucked in shoulder holster, with the .44 Magnum Desert Eagle riding quick-draw leather on his hip. In his duffel bag was a change of clothes, including combat blacksuit, webbing and military harness, as well as an Uzi submachine gun and plenty of spare clips for all three pieces of hardware. Beyond that, dressed in gray slacks and wing tips, sporting dark aviator sunglasses, Bolan could have been a regular guy coming to the Windy City for a little R and R.

Dark suspicion began to nag him even more when the pilot angled in for a landing on the hastily constructed runway. Starboard, Bolan stared out the cabin window. The makeshift compound-prison was erected smack in the middle of sprawling farmland acreage. The compound perimeter was ringed by woodland to the east, west and south, with Bolan counting at least a dozen vehicles, vans and unmarked cars surrounding the farmhouse. Maybe ten assault-rifle-toting men in windbreakers were strolling the area around a long, low-lying structure to the south. That would be the holding pen for the terrorists, Bolan knew from Brognola's layout of the compound. Another hard search from above and the warrior took in the woods around the compound perimeter, saw other farmhouses and country roads branching off in all directions in the distance. The site had plenty of open land. Too much. A force of mercenaries or terrorists determined to free the fanatics wouldn't have much problem penetrating the perimeter.

So close now, though. One day away from justice for the savages who killed so many so wantonly, he thought, watching the long shadows crawl across the quiet countryside south of Chicago as the setting sun was swallowed up by a dark bank of clouds to the west.

The land of Lincoln looked peaceful enough, but Bolan came alert to the sudden scrambling of lawmen racing for the incoming aircraft.

Moments before the jet touched down, the Executioner saw even more Feds with assault rifles come charging from a large white farmhouse toward the runway. Running like hell, about twenty men in windbreakers with either FBI or US Marshal on the back converged on the runway. Their weapons were now held steady and poised on the jet.

What the hell were they doing? Bolan thought. They looked as if they were set to cut loose any second, without warning, without reason. Brognola had called the base personally, alerted them to expect the arrival of Special Agent Belasko. Now there was this sudden rush of force, men tensed with prebattle nerves, as if the compound were being hit. From the cockpit the pilot echoed Bolan's alarm, but he ordered the Justice flyboy to stay calm.

The jet bounced, then began its long taxi toward the armed phalanx. Bolan was up and out of his seat as soon as the jet rolled to a stop. He opened the cabin door and found himself staring down at nearly two dozen M-16s, right in his face, locked on.

Unmoving, Bolan filled the doorway. "I'm Agent Belasko. You want to tell me why I'm standing here about to be cut to ribbons by you men and sent back to Washington in a body bag?"

So much for a soft landing and easy approach.

One of the agents lowered his M-16, a flicker of embarrassment tightening the soft flesh of his clean-shaved, almost baby-pink face. The agent looked confused and said, "Belasko? We were told you'd be coming in at Midway."

"Who told you that?"

"Agent Withers. He radioed about an hour ago and said he was going to Midway to pick you up."

Bolan said nothing, but a wave of ice fell over him, warning bells going off in his head. Just like that, actions were speaking louder than words. As he stood there, looking at the bewilderment on their red faces, the Executioner's bad gut feeling edged toward a time bomb in his belly.

And it was ticking down, hard and fast.

# CHAPTER EIGHT

Togged in ninja black, his sword firm against his back shoulder, the slender nylon rope coiled tight around his arm, Misimoto Harisomo leaped from the chopper. A ten-foot drop took him to the roof of the target building with catlike grace. Moving across the sprawling rooftop, melting in with the blanket of night draped over the city, the ninja assassin swiftly and silently padded for the far south corner of the high-rise.

As the helicopter streaked away for the towering canyons of buildings to the east, Harisomo crouched near an air-conditioning unit. From the air he had seen the white sheet on the roof the FBI had laid out, marking the building. So far Withers was proving truthful.

For long moments, as the slipstream of the swift, bullet-shaped chopper washed over him, giving way then to a howling wind lashing over the roof, the assassin took time to gather himself, get his bearings, reflect.

Harisomo was driven by and inspired by his own ghosts, fueled by his own pain.

From there on, it was trial by fire. He couldn't fail. This was both an assassination and a test of truth. Should anything go wrong, if the balcony door wasn't unlocked as Withers had said, if he encountered more than two marshals inside the condo, then Harisomo knew he had been set up, betrayed.

Snugging the rope higher on his shoulder, Harisomo peered with steely eyes from behind his cowl and mask at the partially lit buildings looming east of the high-rise. As an assassin, he always needed to know the layout of the strike area and immediate perimeter. So far the FBI man's intelligence looked accurate enough at a first sweeping glance.

As the wind whistled over the roof, the ninja felt haunted by the memories of two nights earlier, where his sword had drawn blood in the shrine. Where he had fought, side by side, with Lord Osaka. And Miji. For a dangerous moment of weakness, his heart ached for his lord's daughter. How he longed to have her hand in marriage. But she was always distant to him, almost cold, their relationship seeming to be nothing more than the duty of serving her father and Osaka Worldwide. It was painful and confusing to him. Lord Osaka had hinted but never promised him her hand in marriage. Perhaps if he fulfilled this mission successfully, he thought, Miji would come to see him in a new light.

The ninja assassin looked over the edge. Three

over and two down. Quickly he removed the rocks holding down the blanket, furled up the landing flag and shoved it down a vent. When that was done, it would be clear what had happened, but he planned to leave the honorable law with as few clues as possible.

The ninja assassin secured the rope around the air-conditioning unit. He had fifteen minutes before the chopper returned.

It could be a lifetime if he was betrayed.

BOLAN SAT in the back of the sedan in hard silence. Closely he measured Agents Withers and Turnbull but never let his gaze focus on either man for more than a few moments, just long enough to let them know he was there, make them feel their nerves. Silence could prove the tool that would erode what Bolan was sure was a front the agents were displaying.

And during the drive north, the soldier was getting mixed signals from the special agents. When Withers had rolled into the compound, nearly an hour after Bolan had touched down, the man had been full of apologies, offering a litany of excuses. All of it sounded a little too pat, too rehearsed, but Bolan let it ride.

Now they were heading north up the Dan Ryan Expressway. The lit skyline of Chicago loomed in the distance. The Sears Tower and the Hancock Center jutted like twin giants into the black sky of night, but Bolan wasn't interested in the scenery.

He was thinking Brognola was right. Traitors walked among the ranks of the law.

"Do you have any questions, Belasko?" Withers suddenly asked, sounding as if he needed to talk to hear his own voice.

Bolan kept a poker face. "Not that I can think of."

Withers and Turnbull gave each other a look.

"Listen, I know you're not too happy about the mix-up," Withers went on. "All the running around we've had to do, nail down the logistics of moving the prisoners, security arrangements at the court-house—I mean I would've sworn one of my men told me Midway. Maybe I didn't hear him right."

"So you've said." Three times, in fact, Bolan thought. "You're here now."

Bolan got a look from the man in the rearview, caught the trace of a scowl wanting to work the agent's lips.

Withers cleared his throat. "I don't know what this Muftazi thinks he knows, but I have personally questioned this sack of dung. If you want my opinion, he's blowing smoke, trying to cut a deal. Probably figures if he throws enough shit on the wall, some of it will stick."

Bolan said nothing. What he wanted to ask, but didn't, was why Muftazi was being held in Chicago, away from the other Iraqis.

Withers gave the rearview and Bolan another look, had to have guessed the unspoken question—or read Bolan's suspicion.

"I couldn't very well keep Muftazi with the others. Not even on the same compound. You know, his turning informant. Might stir some real anger among the natives. I got enough problems as it is. We're talking about the trial of the century here. I mean, they couldn't even find a defense lawyer who wanted to touch this case. Finally three Arab Americans came forward. Pro bono, I heard. Muslims sticking together, all that."

Bolan was beginning to think the man really did have more than he could handle. Problems, right. The man was trying hard to keep everything at face value, overdoing it, maybe even pushing to get a feel on "Agent Belasko."

Bolan hadn't survived his hellfire trail by taking anything for granted. His instincts were flaring up as he caught shadows in the stares of both agents, a slight quaver in the voice of Withers. The guy was fighting hard to keep it all together, and it didn't have a thing to do with logistics of transport or security.

Withers gave a strange and sudden laugh. "I try to look at the upshot of all this. Uncle Sam got his balls back. I mean we leaned hard on Muftazi after this went down, no good cop–bad cop action, either. We broke him. Without him the others would have never gotten snatched out of Beirut, brought back to the States where they will get exactly what they deserve. I tell you, when I heard about the commando raid that grabbed those bastards, well, it just goes to show that when Uncle Sam puts his mind to something, he can do it like no one else. They ever find out who pulled that off, I would personally like to shake the hand of each and every soldier who put it on the line over there to bring Saddam's butchers back. I mean, those commandos rolled right into Beirut, took no crap, not even from the Lebanese army. Heroes is what those U.S. boys are. I wouldn't only shake their hands, I'd be at the White House, right in the President's face, telling him he should give those heroes the keys to every city in the country."

Bolan allowed a tight smile, meeting Withers's gaze in the rearview. "Is that right?"

"You damn well better believe it. Those guys are heroes, last of a take-no-shit, stand-up breed from the looks of what they did over there. Of course, you've got the frigging press all over the place, foaming at the mouth to find out who they are. I mean, those soldiers were to come forward, there'd be book deals, movie deals thrown at them. They'd be set for life."

The man now showed a decidedly greedy nature to Bolan. More fuel for the fire of the soldier's suspicion. Let him talk.

"What do you think, Belasko?" Withers said with a sudden touch of condescension in his voice. "Those guys heroes or what?"

"The fact that they haven't come forward," Bolan said, "means they weren't in it for the money or the glory."

Again Bolan was treated to an odd look from Withers.

"Guess so," the man said.

The guy was talking way too much, Bolan decided. Turnbull had even given his partner a look that suggested he wanted to smack him right in the mouth.

"So, what's the story, Belasko?"

"Story?"

"What do you plan to do with Muftazi?"

"Ask some questions. See if what he's throwing around will stick to that wall."

"Then what?"

"Then I'll be riding with you tomorrow night."

Withers pinned a hard stare on the rearview. "What's that?"

"That's another reason why I was sent here. Washington seemed to think you might need an extra gun."

Now Bolan sensed the man was really wrestling with some bad feeling, some secret, dark demon.

Withers and Turnbull lapsed into a cold silence.

Finally Withers said, "I'm not sure I follow Washington's thinking on this. We've got it covered but, hey, we're both on the same side, Belasko. I'm here to cooperate."

Bolan met the agent's gaze in the mirror, cocked

a half smile even as he felt a cold, deadly wave drop over him. "That's good to hear."

THE NINJA ASSASSIN dropped like a falling stone down the wall. The balcony was beside him now. Rope in hand, he clung to the dark wall for a long moment, invisible. Far below, the life of the city rushed up at him: car horns, sounds of the elevated trains in the distance, a siren from somewhere far across town, wind howling in his ears.

But something suddenly felt wrong. There was a force near the door. Had Withers betrayed him? Harisomo wondered. Was the FBI waiting? A room full of guns drawn down on him as soon as he landed?

Too late now to go back up the wall, but retreat was the furthest option from his mind. There would be no escape now anyway.

Pushing out from the wall, Harisomo flew the several feet toward the balcony just as a big man he had never seen before rolled through the doorway. Harisomo suspected it was one of the marshals. He checked the door, a funny look on his face.

The man's odd expression turned to shock and fear at the strange and sudden appearance of a dark shadow falling from the sky.

Harisomo unsheathed his sword in an eye blink, turning the marshal's hesitation into his death. A deep and powerful thrust straight into the chest skewered the man's heart, the tip of the blade poking out the marshal's back in a gushing torrent of crimson. Before the lawman dropped and Harisomo slid the blade from his chest, another marshal was leaping from a table across the living room. They had been playing cards, the ninja saw, but now the second marshal was alert to the fact that this was no game. It was life or death. And death had come from him, out of nowhere.

This distance was too great to reach the lawman with the sword as he clawed for a shoulder-holstered pistol. Sweeping through the doorway, Harisomo pulled a *shuriken* from a pouch around his waist. As if it had a life of its own, he hurled the throwing star. A heartbeat later the star thudded into the lawman's throat. Surging on, the ninja drew more blood with his sword, driving cold steel through the marshal's belly. Pure horror stared back at Harisomo, the lawman torn between grabbing the star in his neck or digging out his weapon. With an explosion of ferocious energy from deep inside, the ninja sliced the blade sideways, a wrenching blow he felt rip through vitals like mush, grate bone before tearing out his target's side. The awful gurgling noise died with the marshal.

A startled voice called out from near the kitchen.

"What is going on out there? I am trying to sleep!"

The voice had a thick accent. The speaker was an Arab.

Harisomo crouched by the wall near the kitchen. He heard footsteps, then a swarthy, bearded face came around the corner. Muftazi came to life, but in the next instant he was put to sleep forever.

Harisomo sprung at the prime target, and he saw the Iraqi's eyes go wide with utter terror, two white orbs that looked set to explode from their sockets at the sight of his onrushing death. Muftazi's mouth opened, but the scream never came as Harisomo drove razor-sharp steel clean through the Iraqi's neck. Bulging eyes and vented mouth went with the severed head.

The Japanese caught movement from behind and whirled, the headless corpse standing erect behind him for a frozen second, spurting red fingers in the air before toppling.

Crouched, Harisomo moved for the door as it slowly opened. Poised to deliver death, he held the sword forward and low by his side in a two-handed grip.

After several steps toward the door, Harisomo froze. It was one of the FBI agents, a man he knew as Smith, standing in the doorway. Incredible, Harisomo thought. What was he doing? Checking to make certain the assassination was successful? Prepared to spring a trap?

A dangerous moment of indecision followed as the tall, blond-haired, blue-eyed agent stood paralyzed in the doorway. There was a look of revulsion on the agent's face as his gaze wandered over the carnage.

Harisomo waited. An expression of profound confusion, a look of self-hate, slowly dropped over the agent's face.

Smith looked at Harisomo and said quietly, "Go. Get out of here."

For just a second Harisomo thought it might be better to slay the man. Then again, he decided the agent's nerves or a sense of shame had compelled him to look inside. Whatever, the assassin put him out of mind. He wiped the blood off his sword on the Iraqi, then retrieved his throwing star, intending to give them as little evidence as was necessary.

Pocketing the star, sheathing the sword, Harisomo looked back as the agent gently shut the door. These FBI men were incredible, he thought, torn, guilt ridden. One of them even seemed uncommitted to his own treachery.

Disgusted by what he'd seen on the FBI man's face, Harisomo padded back to the balcony. High above the murky gloom of the street below, he leaped off the balcony edge and grasped the rope, making a successful escape.

BEFORE HE EVEN SAW IT, Bolan knew what had happened, and why.

The condo hallway was a flurry of grim activity. A swarm of FBI agents and U.S. marshals crowded the open doorway to the condo housing Muftazi. Agents were barking into walkie-talkies when Withers rolled right up to them, demanding to know what was going on. The entire floor, Bolan had been informed by Withers, had been taken over by his agents and marshals, sealed and secured. Supposedly. Now this.

"We've got a bloodbath inside, sir," an agent told Withers. "The bastard, or bastards, must have come through the balcony. The door was supposed to have been locked. It could have been picked. But there was no sign of tampering that I can see."

Bolan gauged all of their reactions, a mix of rage, frustration and confusion, and listened as he heard about the executions. Muftazi's head had been sliced off. Two marshals were dead, gutted like fish. One marshal had his heart nearly ripped out of his chest; the other lawman, Bolan heard, looked like some object had been driven into his jugular before he was pierced by some sort of knife.

A great mystery was hitting the FBI men and marshals full in the face. It was no mystery to Bolan.

It was planned.

Withers turned on an agent who looked as white as a sheet. "Goddammit, Smith, you and Markinson were supposed to be inside with them."

Bolan wasn't convinced by the anger in Withers's voice or Smith's lame excuse that he had been inside only minutes before. Everything had seemed fine. Muftazi was asleep. Marshals James and Mullins were playing cards. Smith was about to relieve them, then decided to go back to monitoring the hall, where he thought he heard suspicious noise at the end of the corridor.

There was some huffing on Withers's part, more outrage, then he grabbed a walkie-talkie and ordered his men to get to the roof, give it a thorough sweep. When asked about Chicago PD, Withers snapped he would handle the local cops, then stormed into the condo.

Following the Fed, Bolan surveyed the carnage. Out of the corner of his eye, the Executioner watched Withers sweep around the living room with wild eyes and voicing what sounded like righteous outrage.

The soldier just stood in the middle of the living room. His gaze fell on the headless body that someone told Withers was Muftazi.

Bolan met the special-agent-in-charge's enraged stare from across the room.

"Dammit, Belasko, I don't know what to say."

Neither did Bolan, but he knew what to do.

From there on, the Executioner intended to turn up the heat, little by little, until the vipers came writhing out of their nest to strike.

The doomsday numbers were rolling hard in Bolan's head.

# CHAPTER NINE

Whispered oaths had been pledged in the dark to his brother Iraqis by two of the FBI agents. Rumor had it they were going to be freed. Hang in there, stay strong, ride it out. Soon they would be out of America.

Or so Hannibal Zabir was telling Abriz as they sat in the hot, tight confines of their cell.

"I know all about promises," Abriz said with a bitter edge. "I was sworn safety in Beirut. Now we are faced with death in the very country I despise with every fiber of my being. How can you now trust the word of the same men who imprisoned us?"

"I can tell they are being truthful."

"You can tell."

"There is a hatred in their eyes for their own, a rage in their voices when they talk."

"When is this supposed to happen?"

"He did not say."

They were speaking softly in Arabic, dark gazes never wandering for more than a few moments from the barred window. Breaking Zabir's impassioned stare, Abriz gave the cell a quick look, his eyes flashing with hate and rage. Three other members of the Death Brigade, Zakan, Atawi and Muhammad, were clustered on cots along the wall. All of them were hunched shadows, sweating heavily beneath the soft glow of the naked lightbulb hung by a wire from the low ceiling.

The remaining brothers of the revolution were locked down in groups of four or five in other cells in the concrete building hastily erected by the Americans. They were given two meals a day of bread, some sort of gruel and water. He had been told by Zabir they were rounded up, every few days or so, marched to a primitive shower facility where they washed under the glowering eyes of armed guards.

So far Abriz had yet to see a shower; indeed, he was still ripe with the stench of the Beirut fiasco. Keeping him starved and unclean, was this the American idea of justice? Did he not have what they called constitutional rights in this land? So far he hadn't even met with his lawyers, the three Arab Americans who had chosen to come to their rescue. That alone was a sick joke to Abriz, who was sure those lawyers were seeking notoriety that would have them writing books and signing movie deals when this was over, when a jury of infidels handed them all a death sentence.

Abriz felt like a caged animal. The mere idea of imprisonment was threatening to drive him into a murderous rage. If he could get his hands on one of the guards outside, he would pull him tight to the barred window, crush his throat with his hands, rip his eyes out with his fingers.

It was all too shameful and infuriating to even ponder that it was all going to end where it had started—in a trial in the very city he had attacked, where all that was left were the motions of going through American justice, then hearing a sentence already determined by the infidels.

Looking back briefly, he now thought it was all insane, even unjust. Was he doomed for martyrdom whether he wanted it or not? First there had been the American contacts he had sought out when he'd landed in Chicago six months earlier. They were members of a hate group, who had been eagerly searching out an opportunity to attack their countrymen, show their government how much they hated its laws and system. Where those men had been hungry to make their statement to a government they despised but were seeking to change through violence, Abriz had only been interested in revenge for the Great Satan's attack on his country. Driven by the ghosts of the dead from the bombings that had leveled Baghdad, killed women and children, Abriz had simply come to America to get an eye for an eye.

Yes, success first, then failure, second and last in Beirut.

Worse, there had been business with the Japanese, waiting to be played out when he returned to Baghdad. How disaster had struck its cruel blow by a twisted fate. Now what he had planned with the Japanese looked finished forever. There would never be the ultimate revenge, the final justice served up on his hated enemies. Or was there a way out? A way back? A way to finish business?

As if reading his thoughts, Zabir said, "We have our friends in Tokyo to think about when we are freed. I must say this, and forgive me, Mahmud, but we let them down by coming here in the first place. Surely they know what has happened to us. Perhaps we have lost what they would call face, but we both know too much is at stake for even them to let us rot here, to face a grave future at the hands of the infidels. I do not know for certain, but I have a feeling...I feel perhaps they are somehow behind the fight for our freedom. The man relayed a message— East and West are coming together for a big party."

Abriz peered at Zabir. "You talk as if this is really going to happen."

"It had better—no, it will happen. He told me. I know now who it was who sent our weapons supplier, who made the deal, who took our money. He worked from the darkness the whole time, but it was he who assured me and the others in this cell that our freedom was being worked out. While showering with the others, I spread the word. They are holding strong with patience and faith, I assure you."

Abriz peered hard at Zabir, then looked at his other comrades. They wore the same deadly serious expressions as Zabir. Were they mad? Were they fools? No, it was something else, a new radiance about them. Behind the anger in their eyes, Abriz saw the glow of hope in their penetrating stares. Yes, the Japanese. Traitors among the Americans. Deals within deals. It made sense. Yes, a conspiracy was in the works. He could see it in their determined stares, feel it like an electrical charge in their silence.

Abriz then thought back to the long flight from Beirut to America, recalled the big, dark-haired man who pulled off the daring, the impossible. Still, even when he'd been seized out of Lebanon, something had clung to his mind, telling him there was still hope as long as he was breathing. He knew he had allies out there, noble men in high places, but shadows lurking nonetheless with their own hidden agendas.

Abriz suddenly remembered trying to look right through the big American commando while sitting there, remaining somehow as cold and steely as the chains around his wrists and ankles. It had been no front. Abriz had felt strong even in captivity, believing in the power of God to set him free. But the feeling of hope had been short-lived, vanished like a pin stuck into a balloon as soon as he touched the tarmac when he'd landed in America. Reality took hold, fear and rage seizing him when the FBI and the U.S. marshals whisked him off to Illinois.

Once again, though, Abriz was feeling hope, the power of his faith suddenly surging hot blood through his veins. He showed his brothers a smile and nodded. He was with them.

"Very well. But when the moment comes, when we are set free, hear me when I tell you I intend to leave this country once again with the blood of many infidels on my hands. If our friends from the East are somehow behind what you say, then we owe them much. We owe them what we promised. We owe them the right to their own vengeance on the infidels."

Mahmud Abriz felt the smile spread over his face. He felt strong, in control again. No chains, no walls, no amount of armed infidels would keep him from completing his task.

From delivering to Saddam the nuclear bomb.

More than ever, Mahmud Abriz believed he had a special destiny to fulfill. It was the will of God.

"IT's GOING TO HAPPEN," Bolan told Brognola. "When, where and how are the only questions left unanswered. I read conspiracy all over this."

Slowly pacing the suite of his North Lake Shore Drive hotel, the soldier held the phone in a tight grip. The Executioner laid it out for Brognola, from the landing at the compound to the arrival at the River North condo.

"How are you going to play it?" the big Fed asked. "You'll be right in the middle when it happens."

"So far a low profile has made the vipers nervous.

There's no reason to change tactics, especially now. Staying in the background, they're coming to me, tipping their hand. I get the impression Withers doesn't know if I'm suspicious, or if I'm scared because I might be inexperienced or incompetent. He's trying to get a read on me. The more he tries, the deeper he sinks.''

"The way it's falling tells me it's been in the works for some time. But behind this conspiracy is a driving force we don't yet know about. With these executions you've now got players who could come at you from all directions. You don't know who you can trust.''

"There's no telling how far this thing reaches. Could be those marshals were sacrificed for the cause, whatever that is. How many are involved altogether, I intend to find out.''

"You'll be riding with Withers tomorrow night, I take it?''

"All the way. From compound to courthouse.''

"You think an attack will happen tomorrow, on the way in?''

"That's my hunch. Once they get them inside the Daley building, it would be suicide to try and break out Abriz and the others by force. It has to happen on the way in.''

"What about an assault tonight?''

"I don't think so, but anything is possible from here on. This entire operation has been handled so officially unofficial that Withers has been given carte blanche to whatever the hell it is he wants. I've never felt so right about something so wrong for as long as I can remember."

"Tells me there's going to be some serious house-cleaning high up in the FBI. Especially if someone in the Bureau is covering for Withers. Where is he now?"

"Withers is tied up for a tough stretch with Chicago Homicide. I left him about an hour ago. One of his agents took me to get a rental car, then I told the man I'd be seeing his boss later at the compound—just in case it might be the hour when it happens."

"Well, I can imagine the Chicago PD wouldn't take kindly to having a killer on the loose in their city, especially one who slipped in under the wings of the FBI, sliced a couple of marshals in two, then chopped off the head of their star witness." Brognola's voice went grim. "Speaking of which, the executions have all the earmarks pointing to the East. I can't help but think of Withers and his Japanese friends in those pictures."

Bolan couldn't agree more. "I took a good look at the wound on the neck of the one marshal. It was a deep puncture, right through the jugular. A throwing star caused that wound, probably would have killed the man by itself. The assassin gutted him, either to make sure the job was finished, or maybe the marshal was going for his weapon. The way they were sliced open, the fatal blows were done by a long sword.''

"Ninja?"

"A pro hit that room. Yeah, ninja style. But he had help getting in. The ones I'm looking at are fighting real hard to keep up the front."

There was another long pause on the other end before Brognola said, "Listen, what we talked about before you left, I'm going ahead and putting together that package. With some help from our Stony Man wizards, of course. I'll be there, working around the clock. I've already done some digging on Osaka Worldwide. I'm getting real strong and very bad feelings on what I've turned up. A lot of what looks like borderline, if not shadowy business dealings, loose ends all over the globe, but enough slippery pieces around Osaka for me to go ahead with a samurai package for you. I suggest you pack that sword."

"Chicago first."

"Do that. And good luck. One more thing. Your Lebanon terrorists know you. I'd suggest you keep some distance. You get pegged by the Beirut half, well, there goes your cover."

"There will be enough agents and marshals and enough confusion among the ranks on both sides that it shouldn't be a problem."

"Just the same, watch yourself. I'll be waiting to hear from you."

Ending the communication, Bolan gave long and

grim consideration to what he'd seen so far: dirty law, assassination, some connection to killers from the East. And Bolan had seen the deadly work of a ninja before. There was no question in his mind what had happened in that slaughterhouse, who had fulfilled the lethal contract. But what was really in the wings? the Executioner wondered. What was the Japanese connection? Why did it appear the Japanese might be interested in helping to free Iraqi terrorists? Or had they come to America to assassinate them? If so, why? Was Withers maneuvering the terrorists into position for execution, then taking the egg on his face, later shrugging his shoulders, proclaiming he didn't have the first clue?

One troubling question after another kept boiling through Bolan's mind. Questions with no answers, riddles with no clues.

Bolan had seen enough tainted badges in his day to know a dirty lawman when he saw one. Make no mistake, he thought, Withers was as tarnished as they came. In fact, Withers was worse than the savages he was sitting on, using the law to hide behind. How many, though, supposedly upholding the law of the land, were involved? You could bet serious money had changed hands in a city infamous for graft and corruption for this conspiracy to reach its critical mass. For damn sure, all sense of honor and duty had been forsaken by dirty law. Withers was going for himself.

So was Bolan.

But in the name of honor and duty.

Then there were those winds blowing in from the East, winds of treachery, shifting all the time, wisps of foul smoke as fleeting and invisible as the killer who had assassinated Muftazi, executed two U.S. marshals.

The Executioner had a full plate, and he was ready to invite the savages to dine with him, see them choke on their own blood and guts.

TURNBULL AND MARKINSON on his flanks, Withers strode across the grounds. The three FBI special agents were shadows beyond the interlacing fingers of white from the compound's lights as they marched toward the prison structure. Withers wanted to personally give the Iraqi chiefs the final word. He didn't need any screwups, any panic on their part, not when he was less than twenty-four hours away from flight and freedom. A million here, a million there, another quarter mil to pick up. Spread it around between six guys...well, it wasn't bad but it wasn't great. Could be that a few of his own men might get caught in the cross fire of battle, up his piece of the take. You never knew.

At the moment, though, Withers had more than money concerns on his mind. Problems were mounting all over the place, turning tighter by the minute the knot of tension in his belly. First there was Belasko, a tight-lipped guy Withers couldn't figure out. He was smug, looking as if he thought he knew something, throwing around cryptic little remarks, checking everything and everyone out, trying to give the impression he was just along for the ride. He wasn't even all that upset, it seemed, that the informant he had flown out here to pick up had his head lopped off, and under what sure as hell would have looked to Withers like suspicious circumstances. Whatever, Belasko sure didn't have the soft look of anybody who did his time behind a desk, much less Washington. No, there was nothing soft at all about the guy, more like something icy, menacing almost, as if he'd pulled the trigger a few times, faced it down. Go figure. What the hell, tomorrow it would all be a memory.

Or would it? Detective Ben Hanlin's hard words ran through Withers's head as he closed on the cell holding Zabir and Abriz. The cop had fallen just short but hinted that if he didn't get some answers about Muftazi's execution, he'd be at the *Chicago Tribune* first thing in the morning, shouting loud enough to wake J. Edgar Hoover from the grave. No problem, cooperation with Chicago Homicide, that was the name of the game. Withers pledged to the grizzled hardball detective he wanted some answers himself; he had two dead marshals to answer for.

Okay, separate investigations, but working together. Teamwork. Beautiful stuff. Throw enough smoke around, and nobody was going to see the truth until it was too late. Even had the mayor on his side, pulling for the FBI to get the job done. He'd convinced the state's attorney to hold the trial in the Daley courthouse. It would be a better vantage point for his snipers to monitor the streets than from atop the Federal Center. Man-oh-man, were they all going to look stupid or what? All his pieces had fallen into place, everything maneuvered perfectly into position.

Withers had put a couple of his own men on sentry duty. It was the night before, after all, and he wanted to make sure nothing happened to his payload. Marshals were either in the farmhouse, seething over the news of the killings or catching a restless night's sleep in the makeshift wooden quarters down the road leading to the compound. Complete privacy was what Withers needed right then.

He keyed open the door. Inside they came alive, swinging off the cots, drilling into him those hate-ravaged stares Withers had come to know so well. Turnbull and Markinson watched the compound from the doorway.

"Listen up," Withers told the Iraqis. "It goes down tomorrow night. You'll know exactly when. Follow orders, and you'll get out of this country in one piece. Fuck with me, or try to do something cute, I'll shoot you dead on the spot. You shower in the morning. My men will be there with you. Pass the word along." Withers took a few moments to let his gaze pierce each Iraqi. Finally he showed them a cold smile. "You might think about acquiring a taste for sushi."

Withers slipped into the doorway, then turned, figuring one last word of warning was in order. An expression of deadly calm fell over the FBI agent's face.

"One last thing. When this is finished, if I ever lay eyes on any of you ever again, no matter where I am in the world, I will kill you without any hesitation. If I even suspect my name or the names of my men are coming out of your mouths anywhere at any time, trust me when I tell you I will hunt you down. I will find you. I will kill you, I will kill your families, your dogs, your camels." He waited a moment to let the threat sink in, to let them know he was the man in charge of their lives, their immediate destinies. "Now, get a good night's sleep. You're going to need your rest. And may your dreams be filled with many beautiful geisha."

Withers rolled out of there, feeling alive with hope. Forget Hanlin—Chicago PD could be dodged. And Belasko? Well, the Justice Department's not so golden retriever was going to be one of the first casualties. No way would there ever be any noose around the neck of Mark Withers.

Hell, even with the Justice Department looking over his shoulder, things were still shaping up his way.

So far smooth sailing.

It was just about show time.

## CHAPTER TEN

By FBI design they were to spend most of the next day nailing down the final preparations. Dark shades on, Bolan stuck to the joint-task-force team like glue, hanging back on the fringes of the group but listening to Withers carefully. The soldier took in his surroundings. A blue sky seemed to sit nearly right on top of the Sears Tower, the John Hancock Center, the IBM and Amoco Buildings, the entire mountain wall of steel, concrete and glass dwarfing man and machine alike on Lake Shore Drive.

Bolan stood on the Lake Michigan waterfront with the FBI agents and U.S. marshals. They were grouped at the Navy Pier where seven Huey choppers would touch down, off-load the law and the lawless into waiting vans and unmarked vehicles. Bolan got some more quick bearings. Beyond the domed ballroom at the east edge of the pier, a barge could be seen chugging down from the north. Sailboats sluiced across the calm waters of Lake Michigan, grabbing the last bit of good weather before fall rolled into the icy bitterness of winter. West, citizens were in the parks beyond the pier, biking, jogging or eating a late-morning lunch. And the giant Ferris wheel was taking citizens and tourists up for a bird's-eye view of the skyline. By all outward appearances, it was just another day in the Windy City.

But that unseen firestorm was sweeping in. More and more Bolan didn't like what he was seeing or hearing, and certainly didn't like what churned in his gut. So far there was no mention by Withers of air cover or police boats patrolling the lake or the river. No hint even of security beyond the immediate perimeter around the Daley Center.

Dark thoughts swirled, fueling ominous instinct in Bolan. This entire on-the-spot brief was a smoke screen, a ruse for some sinister plan; he was sure of it. But what? Where? When would it happen?

He then caught Withers scowling at him before the SAC informed them Chicago PD would have streets blocked to any traffic while they were moving west on Grand Avenue. Having noticed the presence of only a lone steamship docked at the pier, Withers explained the facility was going to be shut down in a few hours by order of the mayor. No boat traffic around the pier after 1400 hours.

The dry run began.

While he rode in an unmarked Plymouth with Agents Markinson and Smith, Bolan listened via radio as Withers went over the logistics. Escorted even now by police squad cars, they turned south on Michigan. Just the way they were doing now, Withers said, the caravan would roll between the Wrigley Building and the Tribune Tower. Marine snipers with M-40 A-1s with ten-power scopes would be in the top-floor windows, along the rooftops of the Wrigley and the Tribune. It could pose a security problem, but Chicago PD and National Guard units were going to handle any unruly crowds at the plaza.

If it looked as if it would turn ugly on the plaza, Withers announced he'd have to call down some of his rooftop snipers to lend a hand in crowd control. That alone started the warning bells going off with siren force in Bolan's head, but he kept silent. First, a howling mob demanding blood, pushing and shoving to get at the terrorists, could prove a distraction for whatever Withers might be planning. A leak by Withers or one of his men to the press? Second, moving snipers to ground sounded more like some dark strategic move to shave the odds in Withers's favor instead of bolstering forces for crowd control. The man was making it sound good, security tight, everything covered.

No sweat.

Bolan had more than enough questions he could fire off at Withers, but he decided to let the man reel himself in for the catch.

Looking around, pretending he was more interested in the scenery and the street life bustling between the canyons of buildings than in what Withers had to say, Bolan watched the surging crowds along Michigan thin out when they crossed the Chicago

River, then turned right on Randolph. Withers said more snipers would be in position on the rooftop of Marshall Field. Hell, the whole area around the Daley Center was covered: snipers on the county building, monitoring Randolph and Washington, more marksmen atop the Commonwealth Edison Substation, still more M-40 A-1s tracking for suspicious movement from the Wabash Building. More showcasing, Bolan decided.

More smoke.

They disembarked at the plaza. A lot of wide-open ground was all Bolan saw. Too much. And with a vengeance-hungry throng of irate American citizens on standby? Looking around, Bolan spotted the Picasso being worked on by some pigeons who obviously weren't art lovers. All around him Bolan saw citizens, surging in and out of the Daley building: well-dressed and heeled women, guys in suits with briefcases, the usual sign carriers protesting some cause or other. Their group, Bolan noticed, was catching a few curious looks. It was clear with all the official lettering on their jackets they weren't a sight-seeing tour.

Withers pointed up at the roof of the thirty-one-story courthouse. Still more snipers would be in position up there. Nothing cute, nothing fancy—they were going in the front door.

Bolan caught Withers studying him.

"Something bothering you, Agent Belasko?"

Withers asked, pushing his dark aviator shades up his nose. "Maybe we're boring you?"

"This all looks and sounds well and good," Bolan said, feeling the eyes of the group drilling into him, some stares a little more penetrating than others. "You're covered going in, but only from the north. What about everything in all other directions? What about roadblocks, barricades on Wells, Van Buren, other surrounding blocks? How about setting up a radar net monitoring all air traffic around the city? What about contacting the FAA, find out about any commercial or noncommercial flights in and out of the Chicago area, maybe even coming down from Canada?"

Bolan was thinking about the executions. The ninja, he was sure, had been dropped on the roof by chopper, then picked up. Clockwork. It was the only explanation why an invisible killer could come down the wall of the high-rise, scale back up to the roof, then vanish into thin air.

Withers played it off, chuckling. "What's your problem, Belasko? You think maybe a bunch of MiGs are going to come swooping down on the city? Maybe a fleet of gunships are going to land on top of this building, where they will whisk that bunch of scum to safety?"

A few of the FBI agents joined Withers in a grim-sounding round of low laughter. None of the marshals found any of it the least bit amusing. Bolan just looked at Withers, measuring the man even more. At first he thought the SAC was trying some sarcasm or cynicism on him, putting up a front that nothing could go wrong. But Bolan now detected something threatening in the FBI man's whole demeanor. Withers was cracking hard under some dark stress. Bolan had asked some hard, point-blank questions, and Withers wasn't about to present any solid answers.

"Listen, Agent Belasko," Withers went on, "I'll have a miniarmada of Hueys on standby at the Navy Pier. They're all the radar net I need. Now, any other questions?"

Bolan said nothing.

"All right, then, let's move on. We'll do a walk-through inside the building. I'll hand out assignments inside. Get some lunch after this, then we'll assemble at the compound. One last briefing at 1900 hours, then we're airborne at 1930 sharp. Court is in session at 2200."

Still hanging back, Bolan let the others move across the plaza. It was feeling more wrong to Bolan with each word that came out of the SAC's mouth. He caught Withers looking back over his shoulder.

"Would you care to join us, Belasko? Or maybe you'd like to go back to your hotel room and take a nap?"

Bolan hesitated, catching the scowl tighten on the FBI man's face, then fell in. He was going to link up, all right. And if what he suspected was going to happen played out, justice was going to get served.

Hard justice, Executioner style.

A SINKING FEELING of doom settled on Mahmud Abriz's shoulders. Chained hand and foot, marched with his comrades toward the grounded Hueys, he felt a strange elation of fear mixed with hope. He gazed at the FBI man, Withers. Was the man being truthful about the breakout? He had better be straight, Abriz decided, or the Iraqi would start singing himself.

Shuffling through the deepening shadows of the setting sun and into the dust blasting up from the rotor wash, Abriz took a hard look around at a small army of American lawmen. They wore grim expressions, a fever pitch of hate directed at him. He could sense their vengeance demanding his blood all around him, an invisible wall of raw emotion. Those M-16s they held against their shoulders had Abriz believing many of the marshals could be crazy enough to unleash a rain of lead at any second, sudden execution, the same instant death he had seen on the street in Beirut.

A tall shadow beyond the ring of lawmen suddenly caught the Iraqi's eye. Peering through the swirling grit, he tried to get a fix on the figure in sunglasses and dark jacket. It was a flash of a shadow beyond the scope of his vision, but there was something about the way the man stood, something bold, deadly even. Before he could get a good look at him, Abriz was shoved into the belly of the chopper. He tried to look back over his shoulder, but FBI agents and marshals were blocking his view, lawmen barreling into the chopper, barking at him to grab a seat.

Abriz stared through the doorway, trying to see between the marshals. It was no use. Still...

No, it couldn't be. He tried to recall the shadowy figure he'd just seen, tried to put a face on it. It was only a fleeting glimpse, but the shadow stood, looked, even from a distance, cloaked by flying dust like...the big American commando.

Abriz decided it had all happened too fast to be certain. He had other things to worry about.

And dread.

The hour of truth was upon the Death Brigade. Silently Abriz implored God for deliverance from his enemies.

BOLAN STOOD HIS GROUND beyond the rotor wash. Grim, he watched as the shackled terrorists were loaded onto the Hueys. Only moments earlier he'd caught Abriz looking right at him. It had happened too fast, with too much grit obscuring the Iraqi's view, but Bolan had seen the Iraqi freeze long enough to wonder what he was seeing. It could prove interesting if the Executioner were to take a seat right next to the mass murderer, look him right in the eye, cock a half grin, ask him how he liked coming back to Chicago. Well, it wasn't going to happen. Of course, if any of the terrorists recognized him, he would outright deny any allegations of involvement in Beirut. He had to. He was going after bigger fish right then.

"You want to get with the program, Belasko?"

The SAC was clenching his jaw, giving Bolan's hardware and duffel bag a good scowl. The soldier had already gotten his assignment, but Withers seemed to feel a repeat message was in order. More nerves fraying on the man's part, Bolan sensed.

Judgment night.

"You'll fly in the last chopper with Smith and Markinson," Withers told Bolan. "We touch down, you'll stay with them. You'll be picking up the rear. What's in there?" he asked, jerking a nod at the duffel bag.

"Reassurance," Bolan said.

Scowling, Withers treated Bolan's blacksuit with a suspicious look. "What's up, Belasko? You look like you're more ready for Halloween in that commando getup. Only thing missing is some black greasepaint to complete the camouflage." Withers took a moment to scowl again. "Look, cowboy, I trust you're taking all this damn seriously."

"Deadly."

Withers seemed confused, maybe even more suspicious. "Get in the chopper, Belasko."

Bolan hesitated for a moment, watching Withers stride for the chopper holding Abriz. The SAC gave his watch a hard and longer look than seemed necessary, as if urging the hand of time to either speed up or freeze. Yeah, Bolan sensed the wheels were already spinning in the man's head. How come, Bolan thought, it all felt as if it would soon come to some grinding, deadly halt? The Executioner also checked his watch: 1930. Right on schedule, according to Withers.

It was then Bolan noticed Withers and other FBI agents were boarding the gunships with large black duffel bags. None of the marshals carried anything but themselves and M-16s into the fuselage of each chopper. But the FBI agents held their luggage tight to them, didn't seem about to let it go. Additional firepower, or something else? But what?

Bolan grabbed his own duffel with its Uzi and spare clips for the subgun, Beretta and .44 Magnum Desert Eagle. As soon as he hopped into his designated gunship, the Huey lifted off. He found his escorts, Markinson and Smith, already seated among a half-dozen terrorists, none of whom Bolan recalled from Lebanon. Both agents gave the Executioner a quick look, their expressions hard behind their sunglasses. And both agents also had black duffels. Bolan took his seat.

Moments later they were airborne for the Windy City, for the trial of the century.

Feeling drawn like iron to a magnet to some savage, unknown destiny, Bolan looked through the open doorway.

Beyond the gunship the Executioner found only darkness, falling with a rapid, clutching hand over the land of Lincoln.

AT EXACTLY 1930 HOURS Harisomo's wheelman had maneuvered the black Chevy van into position over the manhole cover on Dearborn. Shasiko Fukiyo hit the flashers, alerting traffic behind them he was having some sort of difficulty.

Time, diversion and cover were Harisomo's only concerns. Quickly he slid open the precut floorboard, slipped the iron bar through the hole in the steel cover below and lifted it. One by one, eight ninja assassins, swords over their shoulders, plunged with tigerlike grace into the sewer below. Each man vanished into the black hole with a satchel carrying cowl and mask. Those satchels were also stuffed with grenades, submachine guns and spare clips.

A horn bleated from behind them, but Harisomo was looking intently through the windshield. North at the corner of Dearborn and Washington, a phalanx of police cars and uniformed lawmen was erecting the barricade. They might think they were securing the plaza, Harisomo reflected, but they were unaware of the horror about to drop over them, spring up from every corner, pinch them in and annihilate any and all resistance. Yes, an invisible and invincible army was on the march. Their mission would either be a blinding and stunning success, he knew, or they would die in the streets of Chicago.

It was all moving ahead perfectly, a precision machine of death and destruction maneuvering into the folds of oncoming darkness. Even then, more of his assassins were slipping into position near buildings around the courthouse, soon to make their way to rooftops where snipers were watching the streets, but going in only when it began. Of course, it was all extremely risky. Should any of his ninja meet with unexpected resistance, they would have to act swiftly and decisively, take the opposition.

Harisomo couldn't resist the cold smile he felt stretch his thin lips. At that very moment still more samurai involved, either Japanese or Iraqi, were hard at work, laying the final trap. Initial reconnaissance had pinpointed holes in security in the NBC Tower, the Rookery and Union Station, while other duffel bags or briefcases filled with powerful explosives were being planted in rest rooms or casually left in the lobbies of the nearby hotels. Still other targets had been selected up Lake Shore Drive. Vehicles, including several cabs from local companies where his men had taken jobs as hacks several weeks earlier, would soon be parked on crowded streets: up Michigan Avenue between the canyons of buildings marking the Magnificent Mile; on Hubbard and Grand Avenue; in parking garages and along the streets of La Salle, with the heaviest and deadliest payloads reserved for Wacker and Franklin, for Dearborn and Randolph, and Dearborn and Washington. And very soon several vehicles would suddenly break down, on the Loop, on the Stevenson Expressway, vehicles packed with either dynamite or C-4, to be activated by a radio signal.

Not even Chinatown would be spared. Right then,

Harisomo knew two of his men were in the middle of dinner at the Emperor's Choice, two others dining at Hong Min. When they were finished, they would get up, pay the bill, but leave beneath the tables briefcases packed with C-4. Same thing would happen at Cook County Hospital, but with a couple of his people moving freely about with phony ID, every movement, quiet and casual. Every samurai had a specific assignment and was on the move, soon to link up.

Getting in, though, was only half the battle, he knew.

Escaping would prove the ultimate challenge to his samurai skills.

Harisomo showed his wheelman a grim, determined smile. The horns behind them began to blare now with relentless impatience.

The ninja assassin dropped into the hole and covered the lid. The hour of glory or utter defeat was upon them all, but Harisomo was prepared to die.

Even in death he would find a samurai's glory and honor.

IT WAS 1941 HOURS when Ali Mussalah completed the first half of his assignment at 860-880 North Lake Shore Drive. Looking at his watch, he smiled. He knew something about the war in the Pacific the Great Satan had waged against imperial Japan. It didn't escape him that he was right then at the very minute of the hour coinciding with the year the Japanese had annihilated Pearl Harbor. Coincidence or fate when he had on impulse marked the time? he wondered. Maybe it was simply the will of God, he decided, guiding him to destiny.

Finished now with his task, he gave his unit smiling approval, admiring his work. The third-floor apartment overlooking Lake Michigan was a spiderweb of connecting detonator cords. From all points of the compass, including the ceiling, wire connected five hundred pounds of C-4 to the time-delayed hellbox. Planning and a little bit of luck had landed him the apartment six weeks earlier. The same could be said for Muhammad Talik, who was at that very moment completing the same task in the other glass tower of the apartment complex.

Checking his watch again, he set the timer and flipped the switch to activate the box. Everything, he had been told, had to happen at once. And what would happen here would prove catastrophic. There were enough explosives in the units of both towers to quite possibly bring the entire structures crumbling down in twin titanic balls of fire.

He wished only he could be there on North Lake Shore Drive to behold the awesome majesty of his work.

Quickly he slipped the M-16 with attached grenade launcher over his shoulder and shrugged on the loose-fitting black leather trench coat. After stuffing his pockets with a mix of fragmentation and incendiary grenades, he left the apartment to meet with Talik in the lobby.

In just over one hour, destiny would unleash its supreme justice on the infidels.

WHEN THEY TOUCHED DOWN on the Navy Pier, Withers ordered the marshals to get the prisoners out and into the vans. Moments later he had only the pilot and copilot to deal with.

"Shut it down, then get outside to give us a hand."

He waited until they did as ordered. Alone, he unzipped the duffel bag, took out a block of C-4 and attached it under the bench, against the fuselage wall. Inside the bag was a mini-Uzi, plenty of spare clips and a dozen frag grenades, not to mention most of the money. From there on, it had to go down by the numbers.

He knew it would. Everyone involved had bet their lives on it.

In the other choppers, he knew his men were either hanging back or boarding the gunships after they cleared them out, likewise attaching blocks of plastique. Of course, Turnbull would have to be left on the pier with the remote-control box. It was shaving his force, since Withers knew he would need every man, every gun available, but he had to make sure the Hueys were blown clear out into Lake Michigan. Other than a roving police chopper or two, there would be no air cover.

Only evacuation.

Only freedom.

A chunk of cash would stay in the sedan with Turnbull. After completing his part of the operation, Turnbull would then move into ground zero. He would bring the Osaka briefcase with him, which Withers had lightened by a few hundred thousand. As incentive, Withers had promised Turnbull a fifty-grand bonus to complete his task at the pier. Whether Turnbull made it, well, that was up to the man's own tenacity and determination. Withers already had his cut, with more to come.

Hopping out of the gunship, the SAC swept into the tense flurry of manhandling prisoners into the vans.

BOLAN WAS GROWING more suspicious by the minute. For some reason, Markinson was still inside the gunship, alone. Moments later, as the prisoners were herded into three separate vans by U.S. marshals, Bolan saw Markinson emerge from the helicopter. The FBI agent was zipping up his bag. Shades off now, Markinson was looking around the pier with concern all over his face. Down the pier Withers was barking out orders. Doors on unmarked units were slamming shut. Six Chicago PD units, lights flashing, would be the vanguard. Due west, the lit skyline of the Windy City cast an ominous sheen to the swirling glow on the pier, almost turning night into day.

But a cold and terrible darkness was steadily swelling inside the Executioner.

"Let's go, Agent Belasko," Markinson called.

Bolan found the short, stocky FBI man holding open the front door of the unmarked black Plymouth as Smith piled in behind the wheel.

Removing his shades, Bolan strode toward his designated unit but made a beeline for the back seat. Opening the door, he caught the anger flash into Markinson's eyes.

"Front seat, if you don't mind," Markinson said.

Why was the guy pushing it? Bolan wondered.

"I think I'll take my moment of silence in the back seat."

The agent hesitated, a trace of scowl on his face. "Have it your way."

Bolan intended to. Sliding in, he found Smith treating him to a look in the rearview. If Bolan didn't know better, he would have sworn he read guilt or shame shining like a beacon in the man's gaze.

The Executioner shut his door. Right away he caught the strong and unmistakeable whiff of fear.

The odor came from up front.

## CHAPTER ELEVEN

Bolan sensed their mounting agitation, their fraying nerves stretched taut as piano wire, the deeper the caravan rolled down Michigan. The smell of fear was becoming almost a vile stench, and the soldier even spotted the first telltale signs of sweat trickling down Smith's forehead. If Bolan didn't miss his guess, he figured Smith was set to hyperventilate—or confess.

It was going down.

Bolan was all fire and steel, braced for any sudden, threatening move, ready to whip free both Beretta and Desert Eagle in the blink of an eye.

That it could come this far was incredible, even to him. But the conspiracy was there; he could feel it, smell it in their fear in the hot confines of the unmarked vehicle. Too many times he had seen that the savage will of animal man could make anything possible. Especially if it was a cop masquerading his badge of honor and duty in the pursuit of personal gain.

Still, the law was something to be cherished and honored. Across the endless miles of his lone crusade against the predators of the unsuspecting and the innocent, Bolan had always gone well out of his way to keep from bringing down the final hand of doom on even a dirty badge. But he would let Withers call the play, then he would act accordingly.

Before he knew it, they crossed the Chicago River. Bolan kept grim sights fixed on the flashing lights of Chicago PD units leading the way. More warning bells sounded as squad cars peeled off at the Old Republic Building, falling back of the caravan. Slowly they kept rolling south on Michigan. Everything around Bolan looked dark even though the windows of towering buildings were lit. Worse, pointing ever more to a breach in security, citizens were out in force on the sidewalks and streets, with crowds marching ahead of the caravan. On both flanks of the caravan, uniformed policemen, some in riot gear, were all over the street, getting into shoving matches with citizens. Obviously the word had spread like wildfire.

"Death to the Iraqi murderers," someone shouted.

"Kill those bastards," another screamed.

A cauldron of human rage was bubbling over in the streets of Chicago, and it was set to explode.

WITHERS HOOKED the mike back on the radio console. The angry mobs had been pushed back just as the caravan rounded the corner on Randolph and began to roll down the facade of the massive department store, Marshall Field. Withers observed the barricade at Dearborn and Randolph. Chicago cops and National Guardsmen in helmets and flak vests were holding back the surging mobs, but they were mere fingers plugging up the holes in a dike set to burst. Checking his watch, counting down the numbers, Withers then gave it all another thorough assessment.

There had to have been a dozen or so squad cars, blocking the intersection and lining the plaza down Dearborn. The way to the east edge of the plaza had been cleared by police and guardsmen. Beautiful. Almost without exception Chicago PD and guardsmen were tied up with crowd control. Not to mention the gaggle of reporters and cameramen, newshounds from all over the city squeezing into the act.

At that moment Withers knew the other strike teams were coming in from the west, the south. Some would melt into the frenzied throngs. Others would hold back after the initial onslaught, as planned, then just explode onto the scene. It looked the perfect setup, the howling, vengeance-fueled mobs just what he needed to pull it off, maybe seal their escape route with human shields. Hell, he had practically called the citizens of Chicago in with anonymous phone calls to the *Sun-Times* and *Tribune* yesterday. Now he was looking at a lynch mob. Outstanding. It had given him the perfect excuse to bring down his snipers, leaving only a skeleton crew of marksmen on the surrounding rooftops. Crowd control—that was the name of the game, people. Preach some teamwork, let everybody on both sides,

FBI and marshal alike, know he was just one of the boys. So let's bring the murdering Iraqi bastards to justice.

Again Withers got on the radio, ordered the vanguard Chicago PD units, two vans and three unmarked cars full of marshals, to join the barricades.

Shave the odds in his favor a little more.

Once the units moved on, he told the driver, a marshal named McCoy, to stop. Suddenly Withers felt his heart pounding in his ears, adrenaline dammed up like a raging ball of fire in his belly. Damn, but those hellboxes in the pockets of his jacket were starting to feel real heavy. There was no stopping now. It was in motion, and he was at the threshold.

McCoy hesitated but slowed the van, then parked. They were right beside the Delaware Building. Ignoring McCoy's odd expression, Withers looked beyond the barricade, waiting for the first of three black suicide rollers to show. Earlier his agents had parked their unmarked units at the barricade at Dearborn and Randolph, and Dearborn and Washington, left them there, packed with C-4. Mere moments remained before blasting death and chaos sliced through the ranks of unsuspecting lawmen.

Just then, beyond the dizzying swirl of all those flashing Chicago PD lights, Withers glimpsed the dark shape of the van down Randolph.

Mentally Withers began the countdown.

"You mind telling me what's going on, Agent Withers?"

Suspicion was in McCoy's voice, but Withers was on the radio, monitoring the frequency to tune in to the van with Thomkins and the unmarked car that was seconds away from becoming Agent Michael Belasko's hearse.

"Why bring down most of the sniper teams?" McCoy asked, an edge to his voice. "Why spread our people out so thin?"

Withers hit the button on the mike, said, "Do it."

"Withers, I want to know what the hell is going on."

Gaze narrowed, sucking a deep breath into the fireball in his gut, Withers looked over his shoulder. Through the iron grille he gave Abriz a look, smiled, then nodded at Agent Ledbetter.

Withers met the angry eyes of McCoy. "The end of your law career is what's going on," he said, swiftly drawing his Beretta. A millisecond of shock bulged McCoy's eyes, then Withers fired a silenced 9 mm parabellum slug through the marshal's vented mouth. While the killing shot blew out a ragged tuft of McCoy's skull, cracked a neat hole through the window behind a slick finger of crimson, Ledbetter unloaded six, maybe seven or eight rounds into the heads of the three marshals in the back. Consumed with the furious drive to seize the advantage, Withers couldn't tell how many rounds Ledbetter was pumping into their skulls.

The agent kept pounding home overkill until he emptied the Beretta's clip.

As Withers grabbed his duffel, blood and brains were washing a gory rug over the terrorists. No sooner were the marshals thudding off the walls and pitching in a tangle of twitching limbs than Withers was out the door, hellbox in hand.

Moving for the second van, hearing the muffled cracks of Thomkins's weapon barking out the executions of the marshals inside, Withers glimpsed the suicide roller coming at the barricade. A shadow leaped from that van, hit the street, rolled and came up firing an M-16 assault rifle.

Withers hit the button of the first hellbox. For a heartbeat he held his ground, watching as he lit the night with a fireball that seemed to go screaming up the side of the Daley Center. A moment later a line of explosions then marched through the barricade as fuel tanks ignited. Severed limbs, mangled scarecrow figures of cops and guardsmen and smoking sheets of razoring metal rained on the plaza.

One barricade was down, gone without even a hint it ever existed.

As SOON AS he heard Withers say "Do it," Bolan reacted instantly to what he strongly suspected was coming next.

Markinson was quick, but he wasn't fast enough. The Beretta cleared the agent's jacket, but Bolan was already springing forward, clamping one fist over

Markinson's wrist in a viselike grip. Following up as the Beretta spit flame and thudded lead into the roof, Bolan locked his forearm around the agent's neck. Eyes of rage and fear stared back at the Executioner as Bolan struggled to haul the guy over the seat while smashing the Beretta into the roof.

"Goddammit, shoot the bastard, Markinson!" Smith bellowed, his voice sounding squeaky with panic, nearly drowned out by the thunder of explosions rolling from down the street.

Stuttering autofire and the roar of the erupting explosions beyond the Plymouth filled Bolan's ears with a hellish din. Grappling with Markinson, he thrust the Beretta away as it spit out potential death inches past the soldier's ear. Behind Bolan the windshield pebbled under the barrage. Still more rounds pounded into the roof or tore into the back seat, spraying cushion and foam, with glass and stuffing hitting the Executioner in the side of his face.

With rage-powered strength, Bolan dug his forearm deep into Markinson's neck. Out of the corner of his eye, the Executioner then saw Smith bring out his own weapon. In the heat of the death struggle, the solder's only concern was keeping the flaming Beretta away from him even as Markinson clutched the weapon with fierce determination. Markinson's not letting go of the Beretta became Agent Smith's death knell.

As Smith twisted, drawing target acquisition on Bolan with his 9 mm Browning, the Beretta spit doom in the FBI man's face at point-blank range. Smith took the mangler right between the eyes, his head snapping back with such brutal force the hammering blow shattered the driver's window.

Bolan smashed Markinson's wrist on the roof, turning the hand into useless broken meat. The Beretta fell to the floorboard as Bolan began to drive sledgehammer blows into Markinson's nose and jaw. Distant screams and shouts penetrating his senses, Bolan cut off the guy's own screams with a rain of devastating punches. Still Markinson twisted, clawing for Bolan's eyes, the agent coming up high in the seat, an enraged bull of a man.

Suddenly the windshield imploded. A gale force of glass shards and countless slivers hurtled past Bolan, but his human armor took the razor's edge of the bombardment. Again, without warning, the soldier found himself tasting Markinson's blood, saw ragged holes blossom on the agent's torso. Before he ducked for cover, Markinson jumping around while absorbing the lead tumblers, Bolan spotted Withers. Dead ahead, the FBI man was striding for the unmarked car with a mini-Uzi spitting flame.

The Executioner had also glimpsed something small and egg-shaped flying for the Plymouth.

Grenade.

Snatching up his arms satchel, Bolan burst out the door.

Bullets whined off the Plymouth for another stretched second, but the Executioner was already racing for the cover of several vehicles near the stone behemoth marking the Delaware Building. Already a human stampede was charging from the plaza, spilling down the sidewalks on Randolph. Relentless staccato bursts of autofire and distant rolling thunder echoed down the stone canyon around Bolan.

Down Randolph and Dearborn, and at the plaza, all hell had broken loose. Chicago was under siege.

Before Bolan knew it, the concrete around him was ripped asunder when the Plymouth took to the air on a blazing tongue of fire. The soldier raced to the nearest vehicle, diving to the ground behind a tracking line of bullets and flying debris. Exploding glass overhead and sparking metal told Bolan he'd barely reached his intended cover.

ALI MUSSALAH AND Muhammad Talik led eight of their Death Brigade brothers up the south edge of the plaza. Beyond the police barricade now, Mussalah and his men melted into the frenetic mob. Curses and shouts assaulted Mussalah's ears from all directions. Everywhere he found the infidels swearing vicious oaths against Islam and Iraq. The howling lynch mob demanded blood, some screaming the death penalty was too easy for the Iraqi bastards. Well, Mussalah intended to give them exactly what they hungered so badly for. But it would be their own deaths he would feed to their bloodlust.

With all the chaos on the streets surrounding the Daley Center, it hadn't been hard at all to keep pace with the roving crowds surging for the plaza. Scouring the rooftop of the Daley Center, he spotted only three snipers. He gave the other rooftops a quick surveillance. Same thing. The bulk of snipers had been called down at the last moment, just as he'd been told would happen. The hard part would be the policemen and the guardsmen. All those helmets and body armor...well, a few well-placed grenades, go for the legs or groin with his M-16, chop them down, leave them bleeding to death in their own pools of blood. And the suicide rollers would hit the other barricades, with one vehicle loaded with dynamite soon to plow into the crowd.

Feeling invincible, believing their destiny was blessed by God, the Iraqi pointman checked his watch and began the countdown. He took up the spearhead behind a huge man with a mop of curly blond hair, his belly jiggling with each curse ripping from his mouth. Mussalah caught a whiff of alcohol, and his gaze flickered over the blond man's sign. It read Torch The Iraqi Murderers Of Women And Children. A grim smile touched Mussalah's lips. He nodded at his men. Slowly the ten Iraqis fanned out in a line behind the screaming mob.

Then, just as he anticipated, an explosion shook the ground beneath Mussalah's feet with the force of an earthquake. A stunned hush fell over the crowd at the sight of the titanic balls of rolling fire uprooting the barricade at the north edge of the plaza, followed a moment later by shrill female screaming.

Everything down there, man and machine alike, was all but vaporized, launched up the side of the Daley building.

All that death and destruction was a beautiful sight for Mussalah to behold.

Almost in unison, just before the human stampede started, Mussalah and his brothers swept their M-16s from beneath their coats and began to unleash death into the mob from behind. Raking their flaming assault rifles back and forth, they scythed several dozen men and women in a matter of seconds. The Iraqi firing squad, unflinching, hosed down anything that moved with searching and unforgiving streams of 5.56 mm hellstorms. No one was spared the lead flesh-eaters that drove them, spinning and crying and riddled with bloody holes, into one another. Mussalah took special pleasure in spraying the blond man's brains all over his sign.

The mother of all freedom fights had begun.

"EVERYBODY IN THE choppers. Let's move! There's trouble at the plaza!"

Turnbull repeated the order, holding the mike in his hand, hunched in the open door of the sedan. He started the engine, watched as the flyboys and the skeleton marshal crew on hand boarded the Hueys. Of course, no SOS had come over the radio, but they didn't know that. As soon as they were in the choppers, Turnbull flipped the switch to activate the hellbox. One radio signal was homed in to those

C-4 blocks in seven birds. They were sitting ducks, and no one would even know what hit them.

Turnbull thumbed the button and watched the fireworks.

Seven peals of ear-shattering thunder sounded in flashing, screaming unison. A fireball the size of a giant steamer, with geysers of shrieking flames shooting as high as the Sears Tower, boiled over the Navy Pier. Fragments of fiery hulls and unrecognizable black lumps of human beings were launched maybe a hundred yards out to water. Those blinding fireballs kept rising for what seemed to Turnbull like an eternity, incinerating everything in their consuming hunger.

With a screech of rubber, Turnbull was in flight. Whipping the sedan down the final stretch of dock, the agent flinched as wreckage came hurling after him. Even as he put safe distance between himself and the hellstorm, he still felt the gale force of its ferocious slipstream, with concussive shock waves roaring out to touch him. Hell, the whole city felt as if it would come down around him any second.

It just might, he knew.

Something then flashed in the corner of Turnbull's eye. Looking north up Lake Shore Drive, he spotted the twin fireclouds erupting from the base of what looked like two all-glass towers. One of those buildings came down in a horrendous volcanic spray of glass and fire while the other structure toppled in a sideways slide for Lake Shore Drive.

Turnbull hit Grand Avenue on smoking rubber. God help anybody in those buildings, or unfortunate enough to be driving by when the sky fell on them, he thought, unable to keep the cold smile off his lips.

Chicago was burning.

STANDING ON THE PLATFORM of the Randolph-Wells station, Hadj Massouk caught the faint distant sound of thunder. But he was concentrating more on the headlights of the El as the train rumbled down the tracks than on the opening explosions of the freedom fight. As passengers shuffled toward the edge of the platform, looking around now with some surprise and concern on their faces, Massouk casually walked away from the two large suitcases he left near the bench. Quickly he made his descent down the steps and, hitting Randolph, broke into a run, pulling out the hellbox.

And set off nearly one hundred pounds of C-4. The brilliant flash of the titanic fireball made him wince even as he smiled. Looking back, he couldn't help but admire with awe and pride the sight of twisted sheets of the platform along with countless mangled bodies raining to the street. Everything came crunching down, bouncing all over Randolph, with walls of smoke billowing in all directions, the sky overhead lit with the volcanic eruption's blinding flash. Then hideous cries blasted the air around him, the shrill pleas of the shocked, the wounded or the dying almost making him laugh out loud. A shattering heartbeat later it then felt as if the earth were opening up beneath him as severed train cars plunged for Randolph, crushing several passing vehicles beneath the elevated tracks.

Massouk reached his black van as fire kept boiling on behind his shadow, turning night into day with its raging illumination. He hopped inside and sped away, feeling one hundred percent justified in his vengeance on the Great Satan. Now he could laugh.

HASSAM FALIJ HIT the flashers, slowing the van as he pulled over, then stopped on the narrow shoulder of the Stevenson Expressway. He waited until the other van carrying six of his Islamic freedom fighters passed, rolled a dozen or so yards up the expressway, then also parked. No flashers this time.

Six silhouettes with AK-47s and RPG rocket launchers disgorged from the vehicle. Falij exited the van, lugging his own RPG. Traffic was moderate in every lane, but it was the Amoco tanker he had passed a mile ago that he searched the expressway to find.

His behemoth target loomed to the south. As his brothers cut loose with long, savage volleys on passing vehicles, Falij lined up the sights on the fuel tanker. Vehicles downrange began to put on their brakes, sliding in crazy zigzag patterns all over the place, horns blaring, alive with the panic-maddened hands of occupants at the sight of wreckage quickly piling up.

Falij triggered the warhead, watching the streaking tail of smoke and flame, followed by rolling thunder as the rocket slammed into the tanker. The initial explosion was deafening in itself, but it was instantly drowned by a towering inferno of whooshing flames. And that fireball spewed ignited waves of gasoline all over the highway, incinerating lesser vehicles before turning them into mushroom clouds of fire.

As the flaming tanker slammed to the highway in a rolling slide that crushed still more vehicles, Falij and his brothers of the jihad piled into the van.

One last thing remained to do. Falij took the hellbox and detonated his abandoned vehicle. Two hundred pounds of C-4 hurled yet more carnage and mayhem across the expressway.

"Death to America!" Falij heard several of his brothers shout.

He smiled as they raced away from the wall of flames, explosions and rending of metal and shattering of glass that kept piling on the wholesale slaughter. Downrange he even glimpsed the sight of people, torched by the tidal wave of cascading fire, streaking from the fiery ruins of vehicles. It was the breath of Paradise, he thought, falling with righteous wrath over them.

Yes, he thought, death to their enemies. It was a pity. So many infidels, so little time.

So few bullets.

## CHAPTER TWELVE

Anarchy reigned supreme inside the Loop.

Death ruled the night.

One human wall after another was fleeing the inferno, a pell-mell crush of panicked citizens sweeping past the Executioner. They were running for their lives, all right, seeking safety at Wabash or charging for the corner of Michigan and Randolph. Some couldn't wait that long, opting to bust in glass down Marshall Field with anything they could get their hands on. It quickly became apparent to Bolan they were either seeking refuge in the dark bowels of the department store, or maybe adding a new dimension to the madness.

Looting.

At the plaza Bolan spotted ten men in long trench coats, mowing down anything that moved with blazing M-16s: police, National Guardsmen or citizen, even children, it didn't matter. Hot rage boiled in the soldier's gut over the sight of the indiscriminate slaughter.

More explosions ripped through the news vans or

squad cars taking up position around the plaza, Bolan glimpsing the steel eggs flying through the palls of smoke rising up the facade of the Daley Center. Still more hellbombs, chugging from M-203 grenade launchers attached to stammering M-16s, pounded through the hastily erected defensive perimeter down Dearborn. Chicago PD didn't stand a chance against that kind of firepower.

It was mind-boggling slaughter and chaos, but it was exactly what Withers wanted—no, needed—to pull off his conspiracy. Pour it on, hard, fast and final. Keep moving, keep killing. Use innocent targets for diversion, maybe even as shields for escape. Now that Withers had started the conflagration, though, Bolan couldn't help but briefly wonder how he planned to end it. Escape was the ruthless FBI man's obvious goal. But how? Where?

Whatever, Bolan grimly intended to track down the man and his doomsday legion wherever they went, chase them straight to the gates of hell if that's what it took.

He wouldn't have to go far. The whole night was on fire, with twisted wreckage and countless corpses already littering Randolph, the plaza, Dearborn. Squad cars were bursting through the barricade down Randolph but were blown back by sizzling warheads. Through the din of stammering weapons, pounding explosions and the screaming of the wounded and dying, Bolan caught a muffled, distant roar. Searching the western sky, he saw a ball of fire flare up at some point beyond the State of Illinois Center, followed by a terrific screech of metal. Was the elevated train also a prime target? No doubt the strike force had planted explosives at strategic sites, with landmarks right now going up in flames all over the Windy City. More diversion, more horror.

It was going to prove one monumental task, Bolan saw, to track down Withers.

Already two vans holding Withers and the terrorists were racing for the east edge of the plaza. One by one the bodies of the executed marshals were dumped onto Randolph. The number of pencil-tip flames stabbing through the side doors and passenger windows told Bolan that Withers had unchained and armed some or all of the terrorists.

Uzi poised to fire, Bolan broke cover. Right away the stampede spotted the lone man with Uzi boil out of the smoke and flames swirling around the Plymouth's blackened shell, and fled from him. He put the citizens out of mind but silently wished them a safe and fast exit from the hellgrounds.

Quickly the Executioner inspected the battleground. Seven marshals had been shot in the head at point-blank range. Death masks of shock and horror stared up at Bolan, some of those faces all but obliterated by obvious overkill. Sickened beyond righteous fury over Withers's treachery, Bolan stripped a marshal of his jacket and shrugged it on. At the moment everyone out there was fair game, anyone armed a potential target. Bolan didn't need Marine marksmen sniping at him from the rooftops, or cops barreling onto the hellzone, shooting first, asking questions later.

But the rooftops above Bolan were strangely quiet.

A moment later, moving in for the plaza, he discovered why. Out of nowhere bodies were rebounding off the street, then a severed head struck the pavement to Bolan's right flank.

Looking up and fanning the overhead gloom with his Uzi, the Executioner found dark-garbed shadows sliding along the edge of the Delaware Building, figures in hoods and masks. Steel was flashing from up there, chopping through any snipers. Without hesitation, not even wondering any longer about the sudden appearance of the ninja force, Bolan triggered his Uzi. He caught two of the killing shadows with a quick burst. Silently they spun, teetered on the edge, then dropped over.

Combat radar locked on for any hint of threatening movement, Bolan caught sudden movement from behind while checking his flanks. He whirled just as two ninja seemed to fly through the smoky wall that ringed the Plymouth. One charged the soldier with his sword raised above his head, the other holding back on a mini-Uzi.

Nose-diving from the tracking line of 9 mm lead, Bolan came up in a kneeling stance, triggering his Uzi subgun. Downrange both ninjas were propelled back into the fire by Bolan's sustained burst of flesh-shredding lead.

After giving the battleground one last hard search, the Executioner darted across Dearborn and into the inferno to turn up the heat.

GIVING THE ILLUMINATED dial of his watch one last look, Harisomo led his force out of the sewer.

The war was under way. It was now time to do their part: move in, annihilate.

Every ninja had been ordered to fight to his last breath or die where he stood, even if death came by his own hand.

That included the Iraqis. And if they had any problems with seppuku, Harisomo would gladly help them achieve the final glory.

Sword out, he crept up toward the targeted barricade. Dead ahead the Dearborn-Washington barricade was the second-to-last stand of law blocking the retreat from the plaza. Of course, reinforcements were soon to appear, but even then the combined ninja-Iraqi force was closing in. Having driven or walked in during the confusion of the mob descending on the Daley Center, they would all link up and begin the savage fighting withdrawal. Harisomo expected casualties, but he knew his ninja would go down to the last man or disembowel themselves if threatened with capture or otherwise unable to carry themselves to the evacuation site.

Right on time, he saw the black van streak past him, racing up from the First National Bank on the corner of Madison and Dearborn. Ahead he caught the voices of panic as Chicago police were shouting into their mikes. A moment later they spotted the rampaging vehicle zeroing in on the heart of their barricade. Even at a distance Harisomo saw their eyes popping with terror as they realized death was an eye blink away from taking them.

Rolling doom plowed into the barricade with one tortured rending of metal and flying glass.

Having already dropped from the van, the Iraqi terrorist hit the street. Coming out of his roll, the man was up and triggering his M-16, one-handed, while he blew up the van with the touch of a button.

Ear-shattering moments later, leading his ninja assassins into what was left of the enemy, Harisomo began mopping up with ruthless precision. Some of the police had survived, and were dodging the fiery wreckage that was pelting Dearborn or banging off the stone walls of buildings on both sides of the street. Beyond the barricade another battle was now raging, Harisomo saw, but he put his mind to the task, steel to flesh.

On his flanks his assassins began to rake the shattered barricade with submachine-gun fire. Groans of wounded men in pain became death gurgles. Closing on a run, Harisomo put his sights on a cop who was wobbling to his feet, gun drawn. The pistol started to flame when Harisomo took to the air, somersaulting high above the policeman. Landing on the roof of the police car, Harisomo drove the edge of his sword through the cop's neck from behind. The sight of steel cutting through flesh like a hot knife through butter never failed to mesmerize Harisomo, but only for the briefest of moments. The slightest hesitation now in the heat of battle meant certain death.

Scorching flames licking for his exposed eyes, Harisomo threw himself into a triple somersault over the several units left intact. Hot lead from three police guns at the far end of the flaming wall sizzled past his face, but he came down behind them, landing with catlike grace. They died in shock and terror, their expressions clearly telling Harisomo they didn't know what had hit them.

Behind new targets now, the ninja assassin skewered the two policemen with disemboweling thrusts that angled up beneath their flak vests.

Just as he anticipated, enemy reinforcements showed.

So did Iraqi rocket teams.

SWAT vans, four in all, roared up Dearborn but were annihilated by Iraqis chugging out payloads from the squat MM-1 Multiround Projectile Launchers. As wreckage hammered to the street, the Iraqi death squad rolled toward whatever survived the explosions. There were a few SWAT officers still breathing and seeking to fight from down there, Harisomo observed, but they didn't last long.

Iraqis charged the SWAT units with blazing autofire and chugging MM-1s, pouring on lead and hellbombs that added more death to the night, scything more flesh to pave the way for their escape. Still

Harisomo glimpsed a few of the Iraqis go down, riddled with bullets. But the SWAT teams were gone, almost as soon as they showed.

And, of course, he also anticipated casualties. However it played out, death in battle was always the highest honor for any samurai. No capture, no surrender here.

Harisomo glanced at his watch. There remained just under twenty-eight minutes to make the evac site, and counting. It would be close.

BOLAN SECURED COVER at the left front of a WGN news van. Cameramen and reporters stared up at the Executioner with unseeing eyes, their bodies so ripped apart it was hard to tell if flying lead or razoring shrapnel had taken them down in the opening moments of the attack.

At the northeast edge of the plaza now, Bolan was steeled to make his move. Everywhere he found the dead and the dying; everywhere flaming wreckage marred the plaza with fresh corpses.

Scanning on, Bolan found the bulk of police and guardsmen were strewed in death all over the plaza. Another quick search revealed the discarded sniper rifles of Marines who had been torn apart by bullets or grenades, called down, he knew, at the last moment and into the waiting deathtrap.

Countless civilians were also sprawled all over the plaza, or littering Dearborn and Randolph in twisted crimson heaps. Many surviving citizens were hastily retreating across Dearborn, though there were groups of men and women, either hugging the ground or huddled together, in isolated pockets. Paralyzed by terror, they held their ground, as if covering their heads or embracing each other would save them.

It didn't.

Through the drifting clouds of smoke, Bolan saw the trench coat shadows grabbing up hostages.

Down Dearborn a half-dozen Chicago PD units held the line in the final defense against the savages. Lawmen held their Berettas in a two-handed Weaver's stance, firing steady streams of lead at the two vans in the middle of the plaza. They scored two enemy dead before a standoff entered the picture.

''We've got hostages!'' one of the Iraqis shouted, the muzzle of his M-16 pressed into the temple of a teenage boy. ''Drop your weapons or I kill the boy!''

Putting down his Uzi subgun, Bolan drew the .44 Magnum Desert Eagle and held it in two-fisted readiness. Other Iraqis, he saw, were reeling in human shields, sliding for the waiting vans. It was risky, but Bolan had no choice. Somehow he had to seize back the initiative from the terrorists. At the moment surprise would be on his side.

The guns of Chicago PD went silent. Radio units were crackling from that line of squad cars, throwing eerie static across the plaza. Chicago law had mikes in hand, barking desperate messages to their precinct.

No matter what they did now, Bolan knew it wouldn't be enough. They could seal the city with soldiers and tanks, but Withers and his savages had already seized the upper hand. And they were gaining momentum with each passing moment. With Chicago on fire, every available lawman and firefighter would be needed to put out the flames, tend to the wounded.

Down Dearborn, Bolan heard, then saw the next killing ground. Fireballs mushroomed up the sides of the glass and stone canyon. Autofire, then screams, sounded from that direction, but the din of battle went silent moments later. Peering hard down Dearborn, Bolan thought he spotted more dark specters of ninja flying through the air with flashing steel.

First the plaza.

Bolan drew target acquisition and started to unload one peal of .44 thunder after another.

The lead Iraqi was already inside the van with his hostage, but Bolan's line of doom exploded three enemy heads into pink clouds. No sooner were those headless Iraqis dropping than their hostages scurried from the line of fire. One citizen tried to play hero, slashing an elbow into his Iraqi captor, but was toppled with a 3-round burst of 5.56 mm lead through his back.

A sudden squeal of rubber from behind drew Bolan's attention, and he saw the black van barrel off Randolph. With no chance to stop the vehicle, he could only watch for a split second as the runaway van streaked for the line of squad cars. Once again lawmen opened up with their Berettas. Realizing they were hemmed in, and faced with suicidal maniacs, Chicago PD realized the only way out for anyone was sudden death, a fight to the last man.

The Executioner turned laser-focused sights on the driver who had disgorged himself from the van. A roar from Bolan's hand cannon sent the terrorist sprawling, but not before he completed his suicide mission by hitting the button on his hellbox.

With the rolling thunder of the Desert Eagle fading over the plaza, the van slammed into the Chicago PD units. On impact the vehicle erupted into a series of flashing fireballs. Riding those shrieking waves of fire, lawmen were blown across Dearborn. Jagged slabs of wreckage took to the air, hammering the plaza, even clipping a few innocents, sending them screaming across the trembling concrete.

Moving out, Bolan angled for fiery wreckage to the left of the vans. Autofire then raked the air, slugs ricocheting off the ground beside the soldier as the enemy tried to pinpoint his position. Taking cover near the lapping flames, he saw two more hostages hurled into the van. Two Iraqis were left exposed.

Bolan triggered two quick .44 Magnum rounds. Blood sprayed the van a heartbeat before the Executioner's victims thudded into metal, and he glimpsed a familiar face poking out the passenger window.

For a fleeting moment Bolan locked stares with Withers.

"Go!" the rogue agent roared.

Bolan cranked on some Uzi heat, but Withers was already pulling his head back, the tracking 9 mm rounds exploding the side-view mirror, cutting a smoking tattoo across the passenger door.

"Talik! Hurry!"

On the run, with one eye searching the flaming ruins for an intact vehicle, Bolan spotted an Iraqi limping for the van. A quick search by the soldier turned up one squad car, miraculously unscathed by the explosion. Bolan sighted down the Desert Eagle and fired.

The wounded Iraqi almost made it to the safety of the van—would have if his head were still attached to his body.

A groan of agony greeted Bolan as he ran for the squad car, where he found a uniformed officer stretched out in a pool of blood by his unit. Glazed eyes sought him out. The lawman was mere moments away from giving his final breath to duty.

"What...what happened? Is...this the end...of the world?..."

Rage tore at Bolan as the officer let out one final rasp of air.

Yeah, Bolan thought, the end of the world. All around he saw the dead and the dying, heard the wail of distant sirens.

Everything was on fire.

There were plenty of wounded all around the Executioner, civilian and lawman alike. But he had to put them behind, hope the best for them.

Chicago was at war, and the Executioner wasn't taking any prisoners.

Clenching his jaw, Bolan saw the vans racing down Dearborn toward the wreckage and the wall of flames that stretched across the street. Leathering the Desert Eagle, the Executioner hopped into the squad car, hell-bent on shoving some personal Armageddon of his own right down the throats of the enemy.

WITHERS COULDN'T BELIEVE what he was seeing. One moment Mussalah had his hand out, screaming for the Iraqi to run, and the next instant most of the guy's head was removed from his shoulders. Just like that, gone in a cloud of exploding brains and blood.

It wasn't so much the killing shot that disturbed Withers.

No, it was the triggerman.

Belasko.

As he snarled the order for Ledbetter to keep moving, Withers couldn't help but brave another look at the plaza. There he saw the tall shadow with an Uzi subgun and a hand cannon climb into the only police squad car left untouched by the van's explosion. Withers cursed. Belasko wasn't any Justice Department flunky. No, the guy was something else, something that had been sent to Chicago for the express purpose of rooting out the conspirators and nailing all parties involved.

Fuck Belasko, whoever, whatever he was.

Withers had to get out of Chicago.

Still the rogue agent couldn't help but see the bright side. It danced through his mind that Markinson and Smith were out of the picture. Figure in their untimely demise, and that made his piece of the pie twice as sweet. Oh, well. Things happened.

Visions of unexpected gain aside, the FBI man gave the Iraqis a sober look over his shoulder. He had armed almost every one of them, but was worried by the rage he caught flashing through their eyes. There was a kid back there they'd snatched, a woman and some middle-aged guy, all three hostages petrified, shaking like wet dogs. Withers figured a few words of encouragement to the troops were in order, to get that team spirit cemented.

"Stay with the program. A few more blocks and we're all home free." He softened his voice a little to pep up the hostages. "You people, just do as you're told and you'll get out of this in one piece. Disobey me, and I won't hesitate to kill you."

He wasn't sure that was enough. The hostages looked set to collapse from terror, and the Iraqis still looked angry.

"Stop the van," Withers barked at Ledbetter as he saw the dark-garbed ninjas and a few Iraqi stragglers with assault rifles and rocket launchers boil out the smoke and flames of the devastated barricade. One last look over his shoulder told Withers that Belasko was in hot pursuit in his squad car.

Heart racing, filled with a sudden fear of failure, Withers sought out and found Harisomo, fixing on the telltale sign of the jagged scar that appeared just above the ninja's mask. With the Japanese force costumed like that, Withers couldn't help but worry for a moment about them getting IDed later. But they were in motion, right at the final stretch toward evac and freedom. Just a few more blocks.

"We need our rear secured," Withers snapped.

It was then he spotted three more of their team's vans barrel around the corner of Adams, cutting a smoking swath past the Dirksen Building, battering through all the wreckage.

"Go," Harisomo ordered. "I'll take care of it."

Would he? Withers wondered. The ninja was all over the street, growling orders. But it was a few Iraqis and only two of his ninja assassins that Withers found Harisomo assigning to cover their retreat. Precious seconds passed while Harisomo and most of his ninja force piled into the vans. Obviously they were concerned only with getting to the evac site.

The van lurched ahead. A second later Withers braced himself as Ledbetter rammed the van through the flames, hurling wreckage all over the street.

Withers could almost taste freedom now, coming through the window. A spirited rush of the future hurled straight into his face from all that fire in the wind.

Best of all, he was retreating from the flames, the croaking of the wounded and the dying. He was leaving them behind for his shot at tomorrow.

TAKING THE SQUAD CAR south on Dearborn, away from the plaza slaughterground, Bolan got a quick look at the escaping vans. Three blocks downrange he glimpsed those vehicles as they turned right on Jackson.

Then the Executioner was forced to cut the wheel hard to the right, spotting the shadows rolling out of the flaming wreckage piled against the facade of 33 North Dearborn. The enemy unleashed chattering assault rifles meant to decapitate him where he sat, but it was the fleeting glimpse of an RPG-7 that Bolan was more concerned about. Ducking a nanosecond before the windshield and driver's window exploded, the soldier found a point of cover between two fiery hulls. Braking hard, he sluiced the cruiser deep to rest behind the heaps of smoking debris. Enemy guns went silent right then, but he knew they were on the march to check their handiwork.

Ramming a fresh clip into his Uzi, the Executioner barreled out the passenger door. Moments later the squad car began to shudder under the impact of more thudding lead. Clearing the ring of tracking autofire, Bolan crept between two tongues of fire, away from the terrorists. Suddenly he saw them freeze up, packed tight now around the squad car.

A wink of dark lightning, Bolan sprung up on their flank. Holding back on the Uzi's trigger, the soldier greeted them with a deadly surprise. Under his relentless stream of doom, they screamed, spun and toppled, three sacks of bursting inhumanity.

Bolan started to move for the discarded RPG when a shadow came flying over his squad car. A quick burst from the Uzi spun the ninja in midflight, sword flying from his dead hands. Bolan detected yet another shadow to his flank. Darting ahead, the soldier heard, then felt, the slipstream of autofire graze the back of his shoulder. Sliding behind a wall of fire, he came up, searching the flickering haze across the street. One moment he had the ninja in his sights, but in the next instant the assassin had vanished.

From all directions shrill sirens sounded, but they were still far off, beyond the Loop. Right then, it was only the lawless Bolan was concerned about.

The soldier gave a hard search downrange, moving ahead, between dense banks of smoke and cordite. In the pause of battle, crackling flames filled his ears with a near deafening noise. Even the sky above him seemed on fire, with rippling waves of glowing light casting a ghostly curtain over the Loop.

Chicago was in flames.

Crouched, Bolan kept moving on—just as the ninja raced up on his flank. Pivoting and loosing a 3-round burst, the Executioner sent the assassin flying backward, sliding down the street. The ninja slithered away, crabbing farther down Dearborn. Blood spilling from the man's legs told Bolan he had a prisoner.

It had been a hasty, nonlethal burst, but the Executioner would get some answers.

Slapping a fresh magazine into the Uzi, Bolan

headed for the ninja. No sound of pain, not even a groan, emerged from the dark-garbed assassin who suddenly, incredibly found the strength to bring himself to his knees. Dark eyes burning with anger and determination stared back through the tendrils of smoke, seeking out the Executioner.

Bolan was less than a dozen yards from the man when the assassin slid a short sword from his sash. The Executioner cleared the smoke, lengthening his strides, but knew he couldn't stop what was about to happen.

The ninja's eyes actually lit up, and Bolan would have sworn the man was smiling behind his mask. Before he could get his hands on the short sword, the ninja bowed in the sacred ritual act of seppuku, then drove the sword deep into his belly. There was still no sign of pain in the ninja's eyes, even as he sliced his stomach open, going hard to the right. One thrust up, and the ninja plunged on his back.

Dead. Suicide.

For some strange reason, seppuku even made sense to Bolan right then.

None of the enemy was going to allow himself to be taken alive.

So be it.

Quickly Bolan retrieved the RPG-7, finding its warhead still intact. He was in the commandeered unit and racing for the corner of Dearborn and Adams moments later.

Something then clicked in Bolan's head as he

briefly reflected on the night kill in River North. He didn't know how or why it flared over him, but a strong suspicion grabbed hold of his combat senses as he rounded Adams.

The cruiser felt like a magnet at his control, guiding itself into the night, for the Executioner knew where Withers and his savage horde planned to evacuate.

It was their only logical way out of Chicago.

# CHAPTER THIRTEEN

When Withers found their point of departure under siege, he became alarmed. Once more he felt the hand of failure drop squarely on his shoulder. Right then, icy fingers seemed to dig straight down through his writhing bowels. Luckily the sensation lasted only a few seething moments. Withers reminded himself that any hesitation now spelled disaster, any thought of failure meant doom. No way was he going to fail.

While Ledbetter hit the brakes at the edge of the plaza on Jackson and Franklin, Withers took in the new, and final, battlefield. A SWAT team and Chicago PD were all over the place. A few vehicles were in flames, the Wacker lobby entrance smoking and on fire, with a sea of glass and rubble all over the plaza. With all the bodies strewed across every point on the compass, down Jackson, Franklin and Wacker, it was hard to tell which side was winning. Obviously, though, the bulk of the strike force had made the evac site. Beneath the umbrella of firelight, Withers even spotted Turnbull, crouched behind the sedan at Wacker, the man's Beretta 92-F flaming away, catching a man in a SWAT jacket downrange.

Suddenly Withers felt compelled to give the landmark of their escape a hard look.

Unless you were blind, you couldn't miss it, Withers thought, gazing up the dark steel-tubed gargantuan that speared toward the sky. He tried to behold it in one eyeful, staring up the glass facade, now winking with flashes from the firefight on Jackson and Wacker, but it was impossible.

They were going 110 stories up. Forget the sky deck on floor 103; they were going all the way to the top of the Sears Tower.

It was set to go. Key security men had been greased, with paid inside plants in maintenance and utility. Those hyperspeed elevators were just waiting to take them soaring toward the pinnacle in eighty seconds flat if his source was right. All of them knew the way, their escape route already mapped out from the building's floor plan. Having gone over it several times during group or private briefs, the way up and out was mentally locked in. Withers had even done the scenic tour a few days earlier. He'd been just another sightseer on the sky deck, no one the wiser that he was there on recon, prepared to set Chicago on fire. Well, he was back now.

"Anybody afraid of heights," Withers growled over his shoulder, "better stay put."

Ledbetter knew the drill and kept up the furious pace, hitting the gas. Withers watched, waiting until the van was midway across the plaza. Someone in a helmet got bulldozed off the windshield during the short run. With blood smeared across the glass, they rolled on, right into the boiling clouds of smoke pouring from the lobby arcade entrance. The toughest leg yet was dead ahead, Withers knew. If those elevators were shut down, or if they stopped suddenly on the way up, well, that's what the hostages were for.

It gave Withers reassurance when he saw the mob evacuating from the target site, the FBI man knowing the elevators were operating even as the building was under attack. History did repeat itself, he thought. Just over two months earlier the world's tallest building had been hit by a terrorist's bomb, and only two weeks ago the skyscraper reopened to the public. Now this. A second and final seige, and they would be gone. Strike hard again, while the city was still reeling from the previous attacks.

The advantage, Withers knew, was with him and his strike force. Unlike the Chicago police, SWAT, even military that could be called in, Withers and his people didn't give a damn about innocent civilians or landmarks. Brutal aggression was their blazing torch to ultimate victory.

Freshly loaded mini-Uzi in one hand, duffel bag with the loot in the other, Withers was out of the van and barking orders to his people. From the other vans, he found the ninja, a cloaked Mongol horde streaming across the plaza, armed to the teeth with swords and Uzis. Turnbull even made it to his side, Withers saw, and couldn't help but feel a little disappointed, his partner toting the briefcase with the Osaka logo. Well, small details like the briefcase he could sweat later, Withers decided. Maybe a thorn like Turnbull would even have some unforeseen accident, do a swan dive for the street from almost fifteen hundred feet up, leaving behind, of course, the briefcase. Sorry, pal.

Right now it was time to roll back the heat.

Withers grabbed the kid as the strike force surged into the smoke wall and thrust the muzzle of his mini-Uzi under the boy's chin. Withers got a kick out of the fear in the kid's eyes, grew more confident of victory with each step.

"We've got hostages, assholes!" Withers shouted at the line of SWAT and Chicago PD. During the lull in the firefight, he caught the groans of men in some serious pain, spotted a few of the wounded crawling through pools of their own blood and leaking guts, trying like hell to secure cover behind what was left of their vehicles. Withers felt steel go up his spine, proud as hell over how devastatingly precise the operation had gone down.

Backing toward the smoke wall, glass crunching under his feet, catching the crackle of flames from the lobby, Withers sought out the SWAT commandos. Their M-16s were quiet, but he had to keep it that way.

"You—asshole," he snarled at one of the SWAT

commandos. "The lobby will be mined with enough C-4 to put a hole in this place big enough to make you worry about it coming down." Out of the corner of his eye, Withers saw the Iraqis moving inside to place the charges. "If I see you decide to make a grandstand play, I'll blow you clear out to Lake Michigan. In fact, get on the radio now, spread the word."

The SWAT commando hesitated, forcing Withers to bark the order again. A stretched second later the FBI man heard the man relaying the message over the radio. He then met Harisomo's gaze as the ninja slid up beside him. Withers found Abriz and Zabir in tow, in one piece. They were fanning the line of lawmen with M-16s he'd plucked from dead marshals, the Iraqis looking itchy to cut loose for the hell of it. Still more Iraqis with RPGs and MM-1s were securing the rolling phalanx. Better still, a couple more citizens had been snatched on the way across the plaza, with more civilians disgorging, screaming, out of the pouring smoke to spill onto Jackson, adding still more confusion to the chaos.

Covered by his human shields, Withers heard Harisomo suddenly take charge. The ninja growled they would ride up in different elevators, Zabir and Abriz sticking with him on the express. Withers was set to protest splitting up but knew he could get to the roof just as quickly, maybe faster than the ninja. Either way, they had to link up at the sky deck, take the stairs all the way. Togetherness. The Iraqis Withers knew as Mussalah, Massouk and Falij, along with a cadre of their Death Brigade brothers, were ordered to lag behind until the charges were placed.

Withers found Turnbull still on his flank. "I take it everything went off without a hitch?"

"Clockwork," Turnbull replied. "Fish bait in the lake."

"Outstanding."

Before he completely disappeared into the roiling smoke, Withers caught a glimpse of one cruiser, streaking from the east on Jackson. He felt his heart skip a beat. No lights flashed, but he made out the dark shape as the tall man stopped near the plaza's edge, got out and crouched. The figure was nothing more than a distant shadow, and with all the smoke it was impossible to get a clear fix on the face. But Withers knew who it was. Cursing, the FBI man felt Harisomo's angry stare boring into the side of his head.

"What?" Harisomo rasped.

"Belasko."

"Who?"

"A pain in the ass."

"Belasko?" Turnbull echoed. "How the hell did he survive?"

"Forget him," Withers barked.

Harisomo wheeled on the Iraqi rocket teams, thrust his sword in the direction of the SWAT vans and squad cars and ordered, "Destroy them!"

The Iraqis unleashed a wave of destruction on

what was left of the SWAT team and Chicago PD. Before the fireballs scythed through the line of defense and wreckage was hurtling all over the plaza, Withers was plunging into the smoke, heading for the lobby.

For the home stretch.

SAVAGE AND CIVILIAN alike were scrambling to save themselves. A new hellground loomed before the Executioner at the end of his short but hard run west on Adams, down Franklin then up Jackson. He had ridden from the Dearborn killzone, homed in on the sounds of battle, opting for entrance on Jackson, where the din of autofire sounded less furious but only by a few notches. It didn't satisfy him the least finding his instinct had played out again, full cycle.

At the moment the only plus, Bolan found, was that the mass exodus from the Sears Tower seemed to be over, with only a few stragglers pouring through the smoke and cordite, stumbling their way for Wacker. Waiting until the last possible second, so that innocents wouldn't get caught in his line of fire, Bolan moved out from his cruiser, Uzi in hand, the RPG slung across one shoulder.

The enemy pulverized still another wall of lawmen and their vehicles into flying and flaming scrap. With the plaza shaking beneath his feet, Bolan charged into the smoke and began to take out any of the enemy who got caught in his sights.

The soldier took down three right off with steady

3-round Uzi bursts, ventilated two more terrorists as soon as they wheeled toward him with brief stutters of autofire. The real danger would come inside the lobby, he knew. Beyond the thick curtains of smoke, he saw flames dancing from several areas in the lobby. At that point the Executioner was certain Withers would do whatever it took to get him airborne—even if that meant setting off C-4 charges all over the Sears Tower, perhaps mine the elevators.

An armed shadow racing toward the obliterated lobby entrance became Bolan's target of opportunity. A raking stream of 9 mm parabellum rounds chopped into the man's knees. Screams lanced the air, but Bolan was all over the guy in the next eye blink, drawing, then sighting down the .44 Magnum Desert Eagle. It was an Arab face, the soldier found, staring back up at him with hate and agony.

"Where are they going?"

Defiant, the Arab spit at Bolan's feet.

The Executioner aimed the Desert Eagle in a rocksteady grip at the guy's crotch. Some of the rebellion left the terrorist's face.

"You can take it quick or I can make it last," the soldier said in an ice-cold voice. "Turn you into a eunuch, then I'll amputate an arm."

The terrorist hesitated, then snarled, "To the roof. Long live Iraq. Praise God." He made a move to unleather a hideaway gun in an ankle holster, but it was a feeble attempt.

Bolan fired one .44 hollowpoint round, taking him

permanently out of play. A delayed explosion rang out, then wreckage rained around Bolan. Sirens were closing on the Sears Tower from all directions. The Executioner knew he didn't have long to finish matters by his own hand.

He charged into the smoke, flames dancing all over the lobby. Inside he found them, sprinting across the sprawling lobby arcade. Bolan put his sights on a group of Iraqis piling into an elevator. They hadn't taken hostages. It was as near perfect as it would get.

The Executioner dropped to one knee, the RPG-7 filling his hands. The terrorists were squeezing into the elevator downrange, some of them even taking the time to hug each other, clasp arms, exchange triumphant smiles and laughter. The soldier sighted on the packed elevator, then braced himself to finish their party with a bang. Even if the door closed on them, he would still send them for the ultimate ride.

At the final instant before he squeezed the trigger, the Executioner met the gaze of an Iraqi. The terrorist spotted the rocket launcher and started to hit buttons in a mad panic, his eyes bulging with sudden terror as the warhead streaked across the smoke-choked lobby. When it flew right through the closing doors at the last split second, the ensuing explosion sent razoring waves of metal, glass and shredded body parts on a screaming tongue of fire.

Bolan raced for the bank of elevators and was inside a car, door hissing shut when the lobby erupted, shaking the floor and walls with rolling seismic tremors.

But the Executioner was already soaring, even as the walls trembled and lights threatened to blink off. At this point the Executioner had to bet fate would throw a little luck his way.

AS SOON AS HE SAW the others go into the express elevator, Ali Mussalah ordered his brothers to stop mining the lobby. There was no time now. What the FBI man didn't know wouldn't hurt him. Mussalah wasn't going to be left behind. Besides, the staccato bursts of weapons fire on the plaza told him reinforcements for his enemies had arrived.

There was a sudden mighty peal of thunder from somewhere in the swirling clouds of smoke across the lobby, but Mussalah forced visions of more SWAT commandos out of his mind. Most of his Death Brigade brothers had already gone in the elevator with the FBI man and the ninja, soaring for the sky deck. There would be a short run to the roof, then freedom. For a second Mussalah wanted to find some insult in being ordered to stay behind to secure their rear, but the Iraqi suddenly found himself nearly euphoric with relief, dizzy with the ecstasy of victory. The blood of countless vanquished enemies was all over his hands. Their brothers were unchained, freed from the Great Satan. In a few short moments they would fly from there, return to their homeland, heroes of the revolution. Yes, Mussalah was riding an adrenaline high, the likes of which he had never known. The mere sight of Falij, Massouk and thirteen of his Iraqi brothers further told him their mission of glory had been a stunning success. But they could celebrate later.

Reaching the roof was all that mattered. Boarding those choppers was the final critical phase.

Still, as they piled into the elevator, Mussalah couldn't help but hug Falij and Massouk. All around him the others were chuckling in grim mirth, praising God, laughing. It was a moment of triumph.

Mussalah was reaching for the bank of buttons when he saw a tall shadow emerge from the boiling rings of smoke and cordite, the figure striding midway across the lobby. He dropped to one knee and lifted an RPG-7. It was incredible.

No, it was horrifying! Mussalah couldn't believe what he was seeing—worse, knew what was doomed to happen. Beyond terror now, he started pounding buttons, trying to close the door. Suddenly the smell of fear pinched into his senses. The doors started to close, but the warhead was streaking right at them.

As if it had a life of its own, the warhead cleared the closing doors by mere inches.

Ali Mussalah never knew what hit him as he was vaporized by a screaming ball of unforgiving fire.

WITHERS, TURNBULL and Ledbetter trailed the strike force up the stairs. Checking his watch, the young hostage locked in one arm, Withers held his spot as

Harisomo gave the order and one of the Iraqis blew the door with an RPG warhead. They were two minutes late for evac, delayed at the sky deck when they were met by security guards. They mowed down any resistance there, blasting their way for the roof. Throngs of citizens ran screaming all over the place, and the Iraqis cut down a few hysterical women who wouldn't get out of the way. Ninja lopped off some heads, hurling aside like so much garbage all but one hostage. Harisomo guarded Abriz and Zabir as if they were worth more than all the gold at Fort Knox. Strange how the Japanese seemed prepared to offer their own lives to ensure the continued survival of some terrorist trash, but Withers cared only about liftoff. Either way time was up. Even with precious minutes consumed below, killing on the run, he still figured their fighting withdrawal should have been sealed when he'd set off those C-4 blocks in the lobby. Funny, though, how there hadn't been much more than a faint rumble, going up the elevator shaft when he'd thumbed the button, dying too quickly. There should have been enough charges set to shake the walls clear up the sky deck.

A vision of Belasko wanted to dance through his mind, out of nowhere. But if the guy had entered the lobby when he'd hit the button, well, Belasko was going back to D.C., human hamburger so diced and shredded you could put what was left of him in a sandwich bag.

Hauling the kid, Withers followed the strike force.

Before the FBI man knew it, he was on the roof, catching the sound of freedom, beating rotors sweet music to his ears.

"Beat it, kid," Withers snarled, shoving his hostage away.

Heart pounding, blood surging through him with excitement and fiery adrenaline, Withers spotted the six sleek Bell JetRanger choppers, lowering for the northwest edge of the skyscraper. Harisomo held a radio, barking orders to the pilots. Withers couldn't understand Japanese, but he read the situation well enough. With all the wind gusting over the roof, there was no way the choppers could touch down. Rope ladders were dropping from the open fuselage doorways, those fragile ascents to departure whipping furiously all over the place. It would be a tough, dangerous climb to those choppers. With the howling wind slicing with Herculean strength over the roof, getting thirty or so men up those ladders was going to prove a monumental chore. Withers had come too far now to be stopped by a little wind.

But no sooner were the Iraqis and ninja scaling the rope ladders, swaying like miniature dolls all over the place, than trouble started.

First one of the Iraqis lost his grip, or nerve. Whichever, Withers would never know. But the guy was plunging, screaming like a banshee. Soon he was out of sight, riding free fall for impact on the street below. It was a fifteen-hundred-foot drop that would burst him like ripe fruit, spread him clear across the Chicago River, Withers knew. Damn tough luck for that guy, but it was the second problem that snared the FBI man's unwavering concern.

Forging into the wind and rotor wash, Withers spotted three choppers, flying hard from the west—one Huey and two Chicago police choppers.

"You on the roof," a voice boomed like rolling thunder from the sky. "Throw your weapons down...."

Withers didn't have to relay the obvious orders. From his flank Iraqis with RPGs and MM-1s started to rake the sky with sizzling warheads. The wind proved an unnerving factor at first, with hellbombs blown off course, plummeting for the sea of lit buildings stretching like an endless winking carpet beyond the skyscraper. A little adjustment, and the rocket teams finally scored three brilliant flashes of erupting fireballs. For what felt like frozen and mesmerizing eternal moments to Withers, the sky above the Sears Tower was ablaze in a glowing band of fire, with the flaming hulls looking suspended in midair.

Then it turned ugly in the next flash. Withers felt a scream of terror on the tip of his tongue, felt helpless as he could only watch, brace himself. One of the burning hulks was seized, as if grabbed by giant invisible hands in the wind, and hurled toward the skyscraper. Magnetized for sudden inevitable doom, it seemed, the wreckage plowed through two of their evac choppers. Before he could nose-dive for any kind of cover, Withers was driven to the roof. The roar of fireballs was deafening, but it was the pain, lancing and burning through his side and legs, that clutched him in terror in the next instant. Looking up through a haze, as fire dropped from the sky, hammered off the roof or slashed with hellish force off the northwest face, Withers saw Turnbull hurtled over the edge by the blast. A brief shrill cry, and Turnbull was gone.

Withers tasted blood on his lips. He found Ledbetter stretched out before him in a pool of blood and greasy innards, the guy having taken the ground-zero blast head-on. Staggering to his feet, finding metal strips impaled in his side and legs, Withers was then hit full in the face by something fluttering wildly around his head. Adding to his horror, he found both the duffel bag and Osaka briefcase torn open.

Money was swirling all over the roof, sucked up by rotor wash or hurled over the edge.

Mark Withers bellowed, not so much in primal pain, but in utter frustration and mindless rage.

SOMEHOW TOTAL DISASTER was barely averted.

Harisomo was helping Abriz up the final rung of the ladder, hurling him into the helicopter just before the sky was ripped asunder. Before Harisomo knew it, the skyscraper and the antlike figures of vehicles and flashing lights far below seemed to mesh into one collage of exploding color. Shock waves hammered the fuselage, threatened to throw the chopper into a tailspin. The Japanese assassin grabbed the door handle, fought with all the strength at his will and command to keep himself from plunging to his death. Somehow the danger passed. One moment they were angling straight for the wall of the Sears Tower, and the next instant they were banking away, up and gone. The pilot had just proved himself worthy of the highest samurai honors, Harisomo decided.

Wide-eyed, tasting fear in his dry mouth, Harisomo wheeled. Abriz and Zabir were safe, along with five of his own ninja. If the others made it, well, that had to be their own concern.

Harisomo ordered the pilot to keep going, then moved into the doorway. The wind was tremendous, shattering his senses with its merciless icy rush. It was all Harisomo could do to hold himself upright in the doorway. Even as they achieved distance from the Sears Tower, he still felt the far-reaching concussive force of the unexpected midair collision. Moments later the sight of descending balls of flaming wreckage quickly became small bonfires in the ninja's sight. Debris ricocheted off the sides of the skyscraper, then descended on downward spirals for whatever was on the receiving end of their crushing weight. Something else was happening on the roof, also. Harisomo wasn't sure, but he thought he saw one lone figure charge the blind side of the surviving force attempting to evacuate. One weapon was in the hands of that figure, spraying any and everything that moved, climbed or tried to fight back. One man? How could it be? No matter, they would all fight to the last man down there, no capture, no surrender.

Slowly Harisomo shut the door.

Everyone was on his own.

BOLAN WAS ALMOST through the door and onto the roof when he heard the tremendous series of explosions. For a dangerous moment it felt as if the skyscraper would topple, the stairwell swaying beneath Bolan's feet, threatening to kick him down the steps.

Beyond the door he caught the screams of men in agony, or shrill cries grabbing the wind for a moment, then fading rapidly. The latter he assumed were the sounds of men falling to their deaths. Something had gone right for a change, and the enemy was having a nightmare of a time getting off the roof.

Whatever was happening out on the roof, Bolan intended to make things far worse for whatever remained of the terrorists and traitors.

Uzi in hand, Bolan hit the door. The boy came out of nowhere, yelped when he saw the Executioner. "They take anyone other than you out there with them, son?" The boy hesitated, petrified, and Bolan said, "Hostages."

When the boy shook his head, the Executioner told him, "Get down the stairs and stay put until I come back." Bolan gave the youth room to get by, then he was on the roof.

Above a flaming behemoth that went over the

edge of the roof in a slow-motion roll, shadows were flying in the wind, fighting nature and rotor wash to climb the ladders into two choppers. A faint whapping bleat took Bolan's attention in the next moment. To the east, soaring above the skyline, he spotted two bullet-shaped choppers vanishing beyond the city lights, out to Lake Michigan.

Bolan grimly focused on the surviving forces and began to unleash streams of 9 mm parabellum manglers at the shadows scaling the ladders. Two, three, then four of the enemy cried out, riddled up the back with lead flesh-eaters. They dropped from sight in a free fall for the street. Scanning the roof, Bolan found only a handful of survivors. Before they even knew he was charging up their rear, the Executioner hosed them with merciless subgun fire.

Alerted to the new danger on the roof, the last two choppers banked away, following in the slipstream of the vanguard. Two figures clinging to the ladders were then sent plummeting for the streets of Chicago, flung from the sudden jolt of the choppers they had so desperately sought refuge in.

Closing down on beds of flaming debris, the angry winds shrilling in his ears, the Executioner rammed a fresh clip into his Uzi. Something groaned from the shadows along the wall. It was then Bolan saw the money, flying all over the roof, a paper hurricane. Some of the bills were ignited by crackling flames, whipping all over the place like flaming bats.

It was also the moment Bolan saw the fury-ravaged expression of Mark Withers seeking him out from the shadows.

"It's over, Withers."

The FBI man struggled to stand but collapsed. Bolan saw the blood soaking the man's stomach, sides and legs from the flying shrapnel of downed choppers.

"Hey, fuck you, whoever you are," Withers rasped. "You can kindly kiss my ass, you can kill me. You think this thing is over?" Withers choked on his blood, then gave a strange laugh. The guy was holding hard, Bolan knew, and glancing at the mini-Uzi near his feet. No, the FBI man wasn't about to go quietly. Not now. Not ever. But the Executioner, stopping several yards shy of the last enemy survivor on the roof, would let Withers call the play.

"Let me tell you, Belasko, this thing is bigger than any one of us," Withers said. "Whatever happened here tonight, I can tell you no one's going to stop the next phase."

"You forgot to mention one detail." Bolan chambered the Uzi's first round. "I'm still breathing."

Some new depth of demonic rage seized Withers. "Who the hell are you?"

"I'm one of those 'heroes' from Beirut you mentioned."

Withers appeared stunned for a tight moment of utter disbelief. His jaw hung open, but money then slapped the traitor in the face. It seemed to be the final insult that propelled the FBI man into suicide.

Withers glanced at his blood money, some of it going up in flames right before his eyes, then went for his weapon. Cursing, the FBI agent stood, swinging his mini-Uzi around, but Bolan was already holding back on his subgun's trigger.

The Executioner stitched the man from crotch to sternum. With the mini-Uzi flaming, Withers rode the stream of lead through an obliterated section of wall, then over the edge of the roof.

A trailing scream came from beyond, then Bolan stood alone. Crackling flames and howling wind pounded his senses for long moments. The Executioner stared through smoking pieces of jagged rubble along the wall, which had been demolished by downed choppers, over a city on fire. In every direction he saw clouds of rising smoke reaching for the sky. Whole sections of the city appeared to be awash in flames. There were countless flashing lights everywhere, looking like mere pinpoints, from his sweeping vantage point.

Even Bolan was numbed by the carnage stretching over the Windy City. And Withers was right about one thing.

It wasn't over.

Why the Japanese had risked their lives, even jeopardized their nation by their ferocious kamikaze assault to free Iraqi terrorists on American soil, was beyond Bolan.

But the answer was across the Pacific, hidden somewhere in the Land of the Rising Sun.

The briefcase with the Osaka logo snared Bolan's eye. He grabbed it up and drilled an Uzi burst through the case, erasing the samurai logo. He alone would gain any obvious clues as to where this night in Chicago was headed. Once gone from the roof of the Sears Tower, Bolan was intent on making a long-distance house call.

Far to the west, Bolan saw the choppers headed for the Sears Tower. The cavalry was too late. Even then, looking east, he couldn't find any sign of the enemy choppers over the black and seemingly infinite expanse of Lake Michigan. And he could be sure they had planned their escape with as much thought, and would act with as much ruthlessness to get out of the country, as they had already displayed.

Slowly the Executioner walked away from the edge, from the jarring sight of a city on fire.

For the moment the enemy could taste victory. But in the coming days, Bolan would seek them out, hunt them down. There would be no refuge for them. Victory now, but they would soon choke on the vomit and blood of defeat.

Moments later Bolan heard the choppers coming in, but he was already stepping out of the wind. No matter what tomorrow brought, he would never shake the feeling of those icy winds, rife with the feel of raging death high above Chicago. Ultimate justice was ahead for someone, he determined. In the screaming winds above the flaming streets of Chicago, the Executioner believed he could hear the cry of the savaged innocent, crying out for a blood debt.

# CHAPTER FOURTEEN

*Japan*

He stood not quite five and a half feet tall. But that morning, when Misimoto Harisomo strode the bustling corridor of the top floor of Osaka Worldwide, he felt larger than Godzilla.

Gliding along the plush carpet, he couldn't resist a glimpse of himself in a floor-to-ceiling mirror. He was dressed sharply in a silk gray suit jacket, slacks and Italian loafers. Expensive, yes, but not pretentious, since his lord and master wasn't one for unnecessary displays of wealth and power. Harisomo couldn't help but feel proud of the way he looked, believing the aura of power and privilege encompassing him like a halo was the angelic visage of triumph.

One final glance revealed his raven black hair swept back, a touch of gel on the sides. Chiseled features and burning dark eyes stared back at a face that could have been carved from the edge of a sword. Truly he wore the imperial image of the victorious samurai. A vision of triumph, yes, certainly a mystery that made the unsuspecting Osaka employees wary, even afraid. Of course, the jagged scar slicing down the side of his face did little to make others feel at ease, but that was also to be worn, a badge of honor. And, of course, no one on the twentieth floor, outside his lord and master and Miji, knew the truth. Either about the scar, or his duty as assassin for the divine-wind samurai.

Harisomo couldn't help but feel some contempt for the Osaka employees. He received their looks and bows with indifference, striding on. Envy and resentment shadowed the bland faces of men, while curiosity, admiration, even lust flickered in the eyes of secretaries or lesser-ranking females. Indeed, he knew he was in stark contrast to the harried employees. He was samurai, after all, above and beyond the world of the merchant. All around him they scurried, a human termite colony, rushing to the ceaseless clatter of computer keyboards or fax machines while he charged headlong into the sudden threat of death all over the world, paving the road for the coming supreme majesty of a new Japan.

A beautiful young woman's deep bow and her fleeting look of keen interest then softened Harisomo's edge. Even though they were mere mortals, they were still vital cogs in the Osaka Worldwide juggernaut. Indeed, the smell of power swirled around him with an intoxicating aroma. It seemed to hover even in the sweet air of perfume, cologne and the perspiration of frenzy. It could be breathed in like a narcotic, galvanize the workforce to greater achievement, heights loftier than Fujiyama. At that moment he could be certain multimillion-dollar deals were even hanging in the balance of victory or defeat.

Marching on, he finally acknowledged a curt bow or two from Osaka male employees. Soft moon-shaped faces stared back at him with uncertain expressions even as frantic eyes were consumed with the business of the merchant. Two or three executives he recognized, men who knew he was head of Osaka security. He understood the hard looks they cast him. After all, he had the blessing of his lord to delve into all areas of the empire's business, here and abroad, even investigate the personal lives of employees if his lord demanded. It was he who had uncovered Ashiba's secret homosexual life, his shame and his conspiracy with the Yakuza. It was he who had also cleaned up the mess in the accountant's office, disposed of the body, then laid the necessary trail to cover Ashiba's sudden disappearance. The honor, of course, had been given to Miji to take the dog's head. Soon it would be discovered Ashiba had been murdered by a jealous lover.

Sweeping past the clustered bays or open doors with executives pouring in and out of their offices, he reached the end of the corridor. On cue, his lord's secretary was up and bowing, then grasping the gold dragon doorknob of the teakwood double doors.

Being summoned here by his lord was a gesture of respect and honor in itself. It was rare these days that Lord Osaka ventured into the city. The Yakuza was everywhere. Not that Lord Osaka was afraid of mere gangsters; it was the teeming madness of Tokyo he didn't care for. And business was for his merchants, Lord Osaka neither having time nor interest in money matters. The financial empire could take care of itself. Affairs of commerce and money were for subordinates.

Harisomo drew in a deep breath, his heart racing. This was his moment of glory.

It had been, what, a little over three days since he had returned from America? After landing by jet on their private airstrip near Fujiyama, then securing the Iraqis in a bunker at the Osaka castle, Harisomo had reported to his lord. At first Lord Osaka hadn't seemed impressed by the stunning success of his victory in the barbarian wasteland of greed. His lord's silence warned Harisomo that he was waiting to see if any traces of the battle in Chicago would point his way. Harisomo understood infinite patience, caution, prudence.

Still Harisomo couldn't help but feel a cloud of potential disaster building on the horizon. In the wake of the kamikaze attack, nothing other than outrage was sounded by the Americans, their bellicose threats aimed mostly at Iraq. So far no signs of Osaka involvement had trailed him to Japan. Even the madman of Baghdad was denouncing the attacks, his PR puppets denying Iraq had anything to do with "the tragedy of Chicago." Perhaps America should look to Iran. Clever, but how long would it stand up? Or perhaps the Americans were simply biding their time, tracking down clues, plotting a course of action against Japan. But what could they do? No trace had been left behind. Or...

He suddenly recalled the briefcase with the Osaka logo he had left with the FBI man. It had been a simple act of arrogance on his part to leave behind what now could become evidence. No matter, he decided, an informant in the States had confirmed the deaths of Withers and his men. If anything had turned up regarding Osaka, he would have already heard the incriminations pointing toward Japan. Strong denials might eventually have to be issued, but Harisomo could almost be one hundred percent certain none of the combined samurai force left behind in Chicago had survived to shed any light. Yes, there had been a madness about the FBI man and his agents that told Harisomo they, like his ninja and the Iraqis, would never be taken alive.

There was no time for looking back, for searching every shadow for potential traps, for fearing conspiracies within conspiracies. While the Americans considered possible actions against Iraq, if any, and with the respective embassies of Japan and the United States going back and forth in a war of words, Lord Osaka had ordered the Iraq matter had to move ahead. Not only as scheduled, but actually accelerated.

Harisomo glided into his lord's suite. There was nothing fancy inside, a desk, leather-backed chairs, couch, coffee and conference table and surrounding chairs. No ornaments, decorations or even prints. The suite was austere, even by Western standards.

The door closed with a quiet whisper, and Harisomo found himself alone with Lord Osaka—and Miji.

Right away he felt the breath lock in his chest, as he stared at the most beautiful woman in the world. Why did she always affect him like that? Her poise, her grace, the softness in those brown eyes never betraying the coldness that lurked beneath her petite but exquisitely proportioned frame. Those full cherry-blossom lips he hungered so badly to taste. Small, delicate hands that could give pleasure, he believed, and hands that had shed much blood. She was a contradiction, a mystery that Harisomo for years had so desperately wanted to unravel. How he wanted to take those small hands in marriage. Was today the day, perhaps, that Lord Osaka gave his blessing? Would that be his reward? Harisomo couldn't help but gaze at her for another moment, wanting to will his heartbeat to slow, wishing his blood would stop racing with a sudden fever pitch.

Somehow Harisomo found the will to look away from her. He saw Lord Osaka with his back turned, staring out the floor-to-ceiling window. Hands clasped behind his back, Harikami Osaka remained unmoving as stone in his plain dark suit jacket and slacks.

Harisomo moved toward the desk. Miji bowed and the ninja returned the gesture. Finally Lord Osaka turned, also bowed, and Harisomo returned the bow with deep and heartfelt respect.

A smile ghosted Osaka's lips. "It would appear that my congratulations to you are in order, as well as overdue. I hope you understand my being remiss these past few days in not telling you how you have honored myself and the house of Osaka with your duty as samurai. From this day on, I look upon you as I would a son."

A son? With sheer will Harisomo choked down the emotion welling in his soul, forced back the mist building behind his eyes like fire. Out of the corner of his eye, he glimpsed even Miji viewing him with a new look. Was it respect? Admiration? Desire? At that moment Harisomo felt he couldn't trust his senses. For so long his beautiful Miji had treated him with the cool demeanor reserved for business associates. At times Harisomo had believed Miji even resented the trust her father bestowed upon him. No, he could never replace the two sons Lord Osaka had lost, would never even imply such a dishonorable notion.

Harisomo bowed. "As your humble servant, forgive me, if I cannot find the right words to express what this moment truly means to me, my Lord."

"Your service to me has spoken more clearly and honestly than any utterance of mere words." Osaka paused, the moment electric with tightly leashed emotion, then cleared his throat. "However, this is no time to slow down, or be swayed to change direction." He nodded at a manila folder on his desk. "I trust you have read this file on the American, Michael Powers?"

"Yes." A respectful silence followed, then Harisomo continued, knowing his lord was asking him for his opinion. "If I may be so bold, I do not trust this sudden interest by any Westerner in our affairs. Especially now, in light of all that has happened. The proposals for mergers in America by this man's Milo Incorporated, for his further proposals to establish casinos here and in Hawaii, I am beyond suspicious—I am even outraged at his seeming impertinence, the mere assumption that we would be interested in what he is offering. I believe we should send him, at the worst, a definite no. At best, stall him until we have had time to research the man."

Osaka nodded, his expression stoic as always but with a flicker of something dark and dangerous in the eyes. "Under different circumstances, I would agree."

Harisomo kept his face blank, even as confusion rippled through his heart. What was his lord saying?

Father glanced at daughter. The ensuing silence became a roar in Harisomo's ears. Knowing what was next, Harisomo waited for Miji to speak.

"I, too, am honored to congratulate you on your success, on your duty, thus far," Miji said. "From this day on I will pledge you my undying loyalty and devotion in the divine wind." She bowed. "I will wait for you in my office."

Bowing, Harisomo watched her sweep past him without another word, another look. Now he was more perplexed than ever, finding her words warm but gauging her tone cool. Wait for him? Why? What was going on? What did her mixed blessing mean? Pain lanced his heart. Then she was gone, as silent as the flutter of a falling leaf. It would be better to commit seppuku a thousand times over than to endure such heartache, such uncertainty, no hint of anything possible between them other than their allegiance to her father and Osaka Worldwide. Nothing more than an oath to continue their work as assassins of the divine wind. But what had he expected?

"I see the profound bewilderment in your eyes, Misimoto. I also see your torment. I warn you now, be strong!"

Harisomo fixed an unwavering gaze on his lord. It would be unseemly, but he longed to plead his worship for Miji to her father, try to sway his lord to appeal to his daughter to accept his heart, indeed, to take his soul, his blood. But as samurai, he could never do that.

"You must be as steadfast," Osaka went on, injecting some steel into his voice, "you must remain as strong as the divine wind that crushed the Mongol hordes at sea when Kublai Khan attempted to conquer our nation. Make no mistake here, my son, it is no folly, no mere eccentricity on my part when I gave you the honor of your circle's namesake." Osaka softened but for only a moment, his eyes wandering over the scar on Harisomo's face. "Yes, I know how you came by that scar. I have never forgotten. Nor has my daughter. Because of that alone, I can never turn my back on you in any matter."

Again a flood of wrenching emotion swelled in Harisomo's belly. He wanted to touch the scar, remind Lord Osaka how it was he who had defended Miji's honor that day, so long ago, in a country inn. He, the son of a poor rice farmer, who had rushed to Miji's side when a dishonorable cretin had dared to touch her, shame her with his unwanted barbarian advances. How he had gone straight to the barbarian, full of righteous fury. It flashed through his mind as if it were only yesterday. The knife had streaked out of nowhere, slicing across his face, so deep the slash exposed gleaming white bone. Blood then poured in what seemed like a river off his chin, and a flash of rage had seized him, knowing he would be disfigured for life. With all the fury and skill honed from years of training in all the martial arts, he had taken the assailant, as quick as lightning would strike, snapping his neck like a dry twig.

"I remember, too, every minute of every day as if it only happened hours ago," Osaka continued.

"How I brought you into my home. How you came to call me teacher, while I made sharp as the edge of the sword all your skills in the dojo. Yes, I saw the undying light of the warrior in your eyes. Like the true samurai, you were obsessed with the honorable pursuit of what you could be. Now you are here, before your teacher, in near glory, having almost arrived at perfection." Osaka paused, a moment's sadness fleeting across his narrowed gaze. "Yes, I had hoped all these years to call you son-in-law. Be patient. Fulfill your duty, remain faithful to your destiny. Miji is Miji. Like yourself, she is samurai. If it is meant to be, then it will be. Now, I do not wish to speak of my daughter again in these terms. Concentrate solely on the task before you."

Harisomo bowed, knowing better than to speak again.

"I sent this man's envoy back to America. I have arranged for you and Miji to pick up this Michael Powers at Narita in just a short while. If this man is a fraud, then we will know in short time. We must proceed as normal. Our enemies number more than the Yakuza. Perhaps this Powers is an American agent of some type, this business proposition of his people a ruse to uncover the truth. But we will treat him as an honored guest. Miji will explain anything else you wish to know on the way to the airport." Osaka paused, then added, "Be careful. The Yakuza has been too quiet these past few days. You can be certain the leaders will not let go unavenged the blood of their clan. I can feel them out there, circling us like sharks.''

Harisomo returned his lord's final bow. Dismissed, he left the suite quickly, barely able to control the tangled web of twisted emotions writhing like restless vipers through his being. This should have been a day of ultimate honor, even tribute. Now it was back to business as usual. Worse, now this sudden news of a foreigner coming to them, one who could be full of hidden agendas, treachery. Resentment wanted to flare up in him, but Harisomo caught himself, knowing Lord Osaka always knew the way. Still there was a dire rumbling in Harisomo. It was all happening too fast. Lord Osaka was pushing too hard. Suddenly Harisomo's frustration was hedging toward fear of the future, then anger at the past.

Duty, he told himself on the way back down the corridor, yes, and patience. All of his service, even the blood he had shed to defend Miji's honor, would not be in vain.

He was samurai, after all. He could conquer any situation, master any man, defeat any enemy. A gangster of the Yakuza, or foreigner, it didn't matter.

Before reaching the elevator bank, he caught one last glimpse of his face in the mirror. This time he winced at the sight of the serpentine slash marring his face forever. But right then the fleeting reflection of the disfigurement seemed to strike his soul with a sudden brilliant flash, a revelation of himself. No, he would never again do something for Miji, not even his lord, without getting what was due him. He was samurai, and he was worthy of honor, tribute. He had come too far, done too much, risked everything. Soon, very soon he would ask Miji for her hand in marriage. If she refused him...

Well, Misimoto Harisomo was owed.

ONLY HARIKAMI OSAKA needed to know the true reason he had called for the brief meeting in his office. Of course, he wanted to congratulate his second-in-command, acknowledge his gratitude to his adopted samurai son. And naturally Harisomo was owed his honor. That alone was the problem.

Thinking about Harisomo and Miji, there was no doubt in his mind that his adopted samurai son had acted with selfless courage on that day so long ago. Even still, Osaka had always known but kept the truth about that day locked in his heart. And the tragedy was that Harisomo believed he was owed the life and the love of his daughter. Always had, always would.

Events were all rushing toward collision, which was why Osaka had come to his office. For days something cold and tight deep in his soul was telling him this day would be the last time he ever came to the building of his empire.

And last night the fever had told him he had to act quickly, decisively. Time was running out; he could feel it as strongly as anything he had ever known. Death was coming. But to whom? Who were his true enemies? The Yakuza? The Americans? Perhaps even the Iraqis?

Standing at the window, his gaze fixed on nothing, Osaka suddenly wondered why he felt so alone. Crushing, twisting, swarming Tokyo lay before him. In Japan, where space was a cherished luxury, where the size of a room was measured by the number of mats, one learned to live alone in one's self, accept, even nurture to a degree, personal pain and disappointment. Loneliness for the Japanese, he knew, was their single greatest affliction. It was very true how a man could feel alone even in a crowd.

Right then, the space around him felt hot with the worst kind of pain—emotional pain, unfulfilled desires, love of an honorable man, the worship of a true samurai for his daughter that would never be consummated.

A stab of shame drilled into his heart as it then flickered through his mind that this should have been a day shared with his sons, a day when the ultimate triumph was within his grasp.

With heavy legs and sinking heart, Osaka went to his desk and opened the top drawer. He removed the case, opened it and gazed at the silk drawstring pouch holding the short sword. If he was found out, if they came for him, he would be left with no choice. But today wasn't the day to commit seppuku.

And what would his ancestors think of him if he was to suddenly take the sword and commit ritual-

istic suicide when the greatest hour of his nation lay
before him?

Osaka slid the drawer shut. He was hot with fever
all of a sudden, and the fever was telling him he was
on the verge of confronting the foreigner of his
dreams.

BOLAN WAS CLEARING customs and immigration,
heading for the arrival lobby in the north wing, when
he spotted the escorts sent to meet him at Narita. He
hadn't seen the first intelligence photo of his Osaka
contacts from Brognola, but instinct was flaring to
life even at first glance of the Japanese trio. Judging
their keen interest in those narrowed gazes of quiet
intensity, catching maybe a hint of suspicion behind
stoic masks, the soldier knew they knew who he was.

Or, he hoped, they believed they knew something
of Michael Powers, vice president of Milo Incorporated, home office in San Francisco, California.

Closing fast, Bolan kept sizing up the opposition—two men, and one beautiful woman no man
could not notice in any crowd. The mere sight of her
almost threw even Bolan off stride. It was an unfor-
gettable face of ivory-smooth texture, liquid almond
eyes and prominent cheekbones, not too sharp or
round. A cascading waterfall of silky black hair
framed a face that could have graced the cover of
any fashion magazine. She certainly didn't strike Bolan as any secretary, and he assumed the hypnotic
beauty was none other than Harry Osaka's daughter.

Miji. If he guessed right, then, according to Brognola's Intel, she would someday be the sole heiress to the Osaka fortune. With both Osaka sons having died from a strange fever of undetermined origin years earlier, she stood to inherit a conglomerate so vast and so varied, the empire's net worth could only be guesstimated in the tens of billions of U.S. dollars.

True professional that he was, Bolan hid his surprise, mentally cooled the sudden rush of heat in his belly at the sight of such a mesmerizing beauty. He raked a quick look over a short, smartly dressed Japanese man who stood just behind the woman. Closing the gap, Bolan spotted the livid scar on the man's face, a face with features that looked as sharp as a razor's edge. But beyond the scar there was something in the man's eyes that triggered the Executioner's survival instincts. From savage experience in battlefields all over the world, confronting every type of enemy on earth, Bolan read the unmistakable look of a cold-blooded killer in the scar-faced man's stare, which he was attempting to pierce through one Michael Powers. Visions of ninja killers on the streets of Chicago suddenly wanted to lock onto Bolan's thoughts.

The soldier found the third member of the party no slouch, either, and likewise impossible to ignore. Bolan figured the giant topped out at nearly seven feet tall, three hundred pounds. The giant had all the size of a Sumo wrestler, but Bolan detected nothing but bulging, granite-hard muscle beneath his silk jacket and slacks. The bald dome and the pinheads of burning dark eyes made the giant appear even more formidable upon further scrutiny.

On the flight over, the Executioner had had long hours to mentally digest all the Intel on Harry Osaka and his empire put together from the wizardry of the Stony Man computer net. Coming in on the 747, catching an eyeful of snow-crowned and imposing Mount Fuji, soaring over neatly manicured green fields on the outskirts of Tokyo, he experienced a coldness of determination he hadn't known in some time. Even still, during that momentary stretch of solitude in his first-class seat, he had felt strangely at home, at peace even in the land of the samurai.

Japan. An ancient land with a history bulging with legends and myths. A land of holy shrines and temples, monasteries and the castles of shoguns. Where a shroud of eternal mysticism cloaked the land, and spirits were believed to dwell even in nature, from the wind to seashore rock. Where numerous active volcanos jutted from the four main islands comprising the archipelago could spew agonizing death at any moment. Where seismologists predicted Tokyo was long overdue for the next great earthquake, which could kill three million people.

And, finally, but certainly not least or last, the unique history of the samurai still pervaded the culture.

Not to mention Japan was also home of the ninja

assassin, the invisible supermen who were a relatively young creation—three hundred years, at best—of samurai tradition, but who had their birthplace in ancient China.

Undoubtedly the Land of the Rising Sun could be intimidating to the uninitiated, the skeptical, the ignorant. Not so Bolan. This was the earth of Bushido, and he understood the way of the warrior as few ever had.

The problem would be the role he was adopting as businessman. But that was the double-edged sword he would have to wield.

During two days of briefing and working on his game plan, Bolan had pointed out to Brognola all the holes in the setup. Sure, Milo Incorporated was a legitimate business, manufacturing and distributing the latest in computer technology. Sure, the company had agreed to cooperate with the Justice Department, give Bolan his bogus stature as vice president. Brognola had even talked the President into holding off on any military action against Iraq, put aside any thought of intended probes into the Japanese connection or possible trade sanctions against Japan until Brognola could get his man in place.

Still, if the Osakas dug too deep, they could soon uncover the phony paper trail, topple the hasty erection of dummy corporations Brognola had set up as possible mergers, poke gaping holes in proposals for leverage buyouts of world-renowned American companies marked by their three initials.

Only a few days ago Justice Department agents, using the same cloak-and-dagger business approach, had asked for and been granted a meeting with Osaka heads. The scheme was to introduce proposals for mergers, even suggest contracts for the construction of casinos. They had played it low-key, not pushy, and Osaka had taken the bait. That alone signaled Bolan that Harry Osaka was perhaps suspicious of sudden interest in his conglomerate, wanted a face-to-face inspection of one Michael Powers. Now two of those agents were in Tokyo to assist Bolan. They were holding his Beretta 93-R, .44 Magnum Desert Eagle, an Uzi submachine gun and Ka-bar fighting knife, combat blacksuit, webbing and pouches, all smuggled in via diplomatic pouch. With the phone number and address of their hotel in West Shinjuku mentally locked in, Bolan would rendezvous with those agents later.

Yet any way it was cut, it was all extremely dicey. There were enough holes in the story to bring it all crashing down around Bolan's head in the blink of an eye or a flash of steel.

Before he made it to the trio, Bolan quickly sifted through the drill.

Before leaving Stony Man, Brognola had answered Bolan's questions on his role with two words. *Get creative.* Thus, in short, Bolan was immersed in role-playing, at which he excelled. However it played out, he intended to make the ruse work to his advantage. In short time Harikami Osaka would have to see right through him. Suspicion should lead to some action on Osaka's part, and hopefully the man would somehow tip his hand as the mastermind behind the Chicago apocalypse.

For very few answers had been forthcoming since the Chicago disaster. There had been no tangible clues, other than the briefcase with the Osaka logo that Bolan had defaced, no ID on the dead ninja, not even a solitary enemy survivor. Local and federal law had found the evac choppers blown up into scrap near the Canadian border. No doubt, the terrorist force had escaped by jet after destroying their choppers. For damn sure, they seemed to have vanished without a trace. The FBI had no leads on whoever had helped the terrorists get into and out of North America.

There was nothing Bolan could do to change the firestorm that had swept Chicago. Now was all that mattered, getting answers, either by role-playing or by striking out for a hard probe of Osaka Worldwide—anything it took to root out what he strongly suspected was Osaka's role in the ferocious kamikaze attack to free Iraqi terrorists. The reason for the attack Bolan would wrench out in due time.

"Michael Powers," the woman said as Bolan stopped before the trio. It was a statement instead of a question. "I am Miji Osaka." She bowed. "Welcome to Japan."

Bolan returned her bow. The Executioner had a passing knowledge of the Japanese language, knew enough not to embarrass himself. During the flight he told himself he wouldn't speak Japanese, knowing the Osakas might see it as a way to impress them or ingratiate himself to the clan. Still, he sensed he had arrived at some critical threshold to many unanswered questions. It was time to lift a few eyebrows before turning up the heat. "Pleased to meet you," he said in fluent Japanese, then went on. "And thank you. I am both honored and grateful you and your father would so graciously spare the time to see me."

Bolan caught a fleeting glimmer of surprise on all three faces.

Up close now, Bolan decided his first assessment of them was slightly off. There was no curiosity in the eyes, not even a trace of suspicion. Rather, the soldier sensed a silent but seething deadliness about these three, as if they were mentally honing their swords, eager to cut him to ribbons at the first hint of treachery or deceit. It even struck him as somehow strange, perhaps even quietly lethal, that Miji Osaka was the first to speak. It was all coming across as very un-Japanese to Bolan, the men waiting in silence behind the woman.

"Allow me to introduce the head of Osaka security," she said, indicating the scar-faced Japanese. "Misimoto Harisomo."

The head of Osaka security threw Bolan a curt bow, the Executioner detecting some resentment in the man's eyes as he returned the gesture but with a little more grace.

Finally Miji Osaka looked at the giant. "Kedo will take care of your luggage if you would be so kind as to give him your baggage claim."

Bolan bowed, then handed Kedo the receipt.

"It's only one duffel bag. Black," the soldier said in English, seeing a telltale sign of suspicion in their eyes. But the Japanese, he knew, however cynical or wary of outsiders, were never ones to pry or ask questions. Whatever seemed accepted at face value was privately dissected, measured. Beyond their quiet scrutiny of him, he knew they were wondering hard about Michael Powers. And the Executioner gauged conflicting views of him in their eyes—first resentment and cold leeriness in the eyes of Harisomo and Kedo, then curiosity and a flame of sudden interest in the eyes of the Osaka heiress. Strong signals were sent out, and Bolan was suddenly believing he was onto something dark and sinister.

"I know you have had a long and tiring flight," Miji Osaka said. "If you will follow us, please, we will do everything required to make you comfortable and relaxed."

When she held out her arm to indicate the way out of the terminal, Bolan locked a brief stare with the beautiful Japanese heiress. It was then he sensed he was way off about this woman, and the realization was suddenly driving hard and deep.

The Executioner was picking up something decidedly cold and deadly in Miji Osaka's eyes.

The Executioner knew a killer when he saw one.

## CHAPTER FIFTEEN

Fifty minutes later, rolling south in the limo on the expressway, Bolan sensed the shadow of danger stretching over all of them.

It was an all too familiar hand of impending doom the Executioner couldn't shake off.

The soldier's immediate problem was determining at whom exactly the threat was directed. Judging what he'd seen and sensed so far about his escorts, though, he could be sure the portent of trouble wasn't his imagination.

Nor undue paranoia.

Facing Miji Osaka and Harisomo, Bolan sat behind the glass partition separating them from Kedo. Kedo was proving himself a first-rate chauffeur, smoothly guiding the limo in the far left lane while bumper-to-bumper traffic shot past them like bullets en route for escape from the last judgment. Whatever else Kedo was, Bolan could be sure the man was as dangerous as he looked. When opening the limo's trunk at Narita to store his duffel bag, Kedo had pulled a Bushmaster autopistol in full view of Michael Powers. The giant had then showed Bolan a strange grin before holstering the elongated autopistol with banana-shaped 30-shot clip beneath his jacket. Business as usual, or some warning? Less obvious, Harisomo had swiftly removed a short sword from the trunk and tucked it in a sheath inside his jacket without glancing at Bolan.

It was the black Lexus, though, holding a steady five-car length on their rear, that snared a frequent glance from Bolan. The luxury car stayed far enough behind but close enough to flare the soldier's combat instincts. At the first tollbooth outside Narita, they had picked up the Lexus, moving in, Bolan sensed, like a shark scenting the blood and the fear of its prey. With its dark-tinted windshield, Bolan couldn't make out any faces or take a head count. Grimly aware that the heiress and Harisomo were measuring him in their continued silence, Bolan made a point of not letting his gaze stay fixed on the Lexus dogging them. The Executioner sipped his tea.

When clear of Narita's congestion, Miji Osaka had used the bar beside her to perform the tea ceremony. Even without reed mats, the woman went through the ritual, using the bamboo spoon and whisk on the emerald powder like a painter would bring to life a canvas with loving strokes.

Miji Osaka cleared her throat, a delicate sound that struck Bolan as the soft fluttering of a butterfly in a summer's breeze. "Would you care for more tea, Mr. Powers?"

The Executioner had already determined he wouldn't speak unless spoken to. If he didn't honor their traditions, if he came across as impatient or pushy, they would send him packing. He had come too far, sensed he was too close to the truth now, to blow it.

Bolan politely accepted her offer.

Once again he picked up a flicker of keen interest in the woman. Curiosity, suspicion or something else? While she took his cup and gracefully went to work, Bolan also caught a fleeting look of jealous rage on Harisomo's face. The scar-faced man met Bolan's eye for a moment, then looked away, seeming to take great care to hide any disturbance. Interesting. Bolan sensed Harisomo's protectiveness of the woman went deeper than business, but she didn't seem to be buying. The soldier knew he wasn't about to strike up any lasting friendship with the man, not that he cared. Maybe some mixing of business and pleasure was in the cards. Maybe his ace in the hole was to use Miji Osaka to shake the vipers out of the trees. Perhaps. Either way the dice were rolling. Undoubtedly the woman was sending out strong signals, which was very un-Japanese, and more than a little disturbing.

As he waited for Miji Osaka to make tea, Bolan took in the suburbs of Tokyo, which now cropped up in staggered white blocks of apartments. The deeper they went into the heart of the city, the more crushing and furious traffic became. Was it progress or madness? It was strange, either way, how the soldier understood them, felt so at home even in his role of deception. The Japanese lived in a city that would someday be utterly and completely destroyed by an earthquake. Yet they went about their business in a controlled frenzy, the wild but tightly leashed and raw energy of an uncertain people well aware they lived on the razor's edge of a catastrophe yet to be known to mankind.

Little did they know, but a seismic roller of a different kind was rumbling their way. If the Executioner's strong suspicions played out, then Tokyo would topple.

Miji Osaka handed Bolan his teacup, saying, "I feel an apology, an explanation, is in order, Mr. Powers. Forgive Kedo's display at the airport when he made a show of the weapon. You must understand, please, that it is necessary because of who we are that we protect ourselves. Lately we have had some problems."

Bolan decided that was his cue to turn it up a notch. "Yakuza problems?"

He watched both of them stiffen a little, knowing he'd struck a nerve, but it was Harisomo who spoke. "What would make you say that, Mr. Powers?"

Bolan kept his tone polite. "I have done some homework on Osaka Worldwide, Harisomo-*san,* as I'm sure you've done yours on me. It is no secret that Harikami Osaka is looking for sizable tracts of land on which to build entire casino cities. Traditionally such an endeavor has been left to .the Yakuza, who would deem such a pursuit by Osaka Worldwide as encroachment upon their sacred territory. Besides, and I hope you forgive me here if I seem presumptuous, but part of my proposal involves helping Osaka Worldwide attain its desire to build casinos.''

Harisomo cocked an eyebrow. ''Really. Understand this, if you will, Mr. Powers, since you seem to understand so much about our ways. We live in a nation where education is deemed as absolutely critical for the fulfillment of one's duty to his or her nation, where the education of mind, body and soul is deemed one of the most noble of pursuits, where street crime is almost nonexistent because we, in Japan, have an unwavering sense of honor and respect for ourselves, for each other and for our nation. We honor our tradition and have a keen and unforgetting knowledge of our history.

''I say this with great sadness, but, yes, it is most unfortunate our Japan has adopted some of the problems of the West. Yes, we have gangsters. Yes, we have cocaine and heroin here, which threaten to bring the West to ruins, but it is a poison used by those in Japan who are weak, who have no honor, no sense of tradition or duty. There are those of us, however, who wish to avoid the same looming disasters of the West.''

The man had said a mouthful to Bolan. In proclaiming his contempt and paranoia of Western influence, good or bad, Harisomo had merely heightened Bolan's suspicions.

Miji Osaka's tone was far more gentle. "Mr. Powers, I have seen you look past me with some concern. If we are being followed, then we are being followed. We have many enemies, yes, but our enemies are our concern. I say this to you with absolute honesty and unwavering faith. You are our honored guest. As long as you are with us, you are safe."

Bolan looked them both dead in the eye. He kept a polite tone, but his voice was edged with just the right amount of steel. "Believe me when I tell you— I believe you."

They seemed uncertain as to how to respond. Miji Osaka sipped tea, looking over her cup at the American with some undetermined fire in her eyes.

Bolan worked on his tea, feeling more than ever that he was about to arrive at the source of the Chicago apocalypse.

THEY MIGHT BE WEARING their masks of veiled smiles and reassurance, but Bolan sensed Miji Osaka and Harisomo were homed in for all hell to break loose.

When they entered the mouth of the parking garage at Osaka Worldwide, the attendant bowed to Kedo, hit a button inside his station and raised the mesh gate with an electronic whir.

Only two blocks earlier, Bolan had seen the Lexus peel off to melt into the congestion of a side street in the Shinjuku district. Coincidence or design? Whatever, he felt the tension thicken in the limo.

Harisomo and Miji Osaka exchanged a dark look. The scar-faced man said, "I did not see him here this morning."

Miji Osaka seemed to dismiss the cryptic-sounding comment by throwing Bolan a gentle smile.

Bolan felt his patience fraying. It could be days before he was granted or deemed worthy of a face-to-face with Harikami Osaka. Time was running out. Every subtle word between them, every veiled but piercing look, threatened to further erode his cover. Bolan had to find a way to speed matters along.

They descended deeper into the gloomy bowels of the garage. Before Kedo turned the corner of the ramp, Bolan noticed the gate behind remained up. Then the soldier glimpsed a shadow roll into the mouth of the garage. Something definitely felt wrong to the Executioner. Long lines of parked vehicles, either domestic or imported, began to fan out on both flanks of the limo. No vehicles passed the limo on the way down, nor did any vehicles go up or down from the adjoining maze of ramps, the soldier noted. It was the time of day when Osaka employees would be confined to their offices, involved in the daily grind of building the Osaka empire. Meaning they were alone in the garage.

And Bolan sensed a human volcano set to erupt. This was the same way it felt, he recalled, riding with Smith and Markinson in Chicago before it hit the fan. Only now the threat wasn't directly aimed at him.

Harisomo glanced around the murky recesses of the garage. It was then Bolan spotted the sleek metallic shape of the Lexus, two aisles over, before it vanished behind a thick column.

Another level down, rolling on, and Kedo stopped the limo. Bolan waited until the driver got out and opened the door. Miji Osaka indicated Bolan get out first, which he did. Stepping out, he caught a sound, a faint click that struck him as someone trying hard to quietly close a door. Bolan felt the beauty's soft flesh mold into his hand as Kedo went to open the trunk. Gently helping her from the limo, the soldier then picked up the faint sound of soft soles rapping on concrete. He noticed Harisomo lingering in the limo, glimpsed the shadow of the man reaching for some compartment beside him. What was going on? For damn sure, the soldier knew something was about to happen. Their apparent confidence did little to soothe the tension in his belly.

Miji Osaka glided past him, out into the open space between the rows of parked vehicles.

Kedo, the duffel bag in hand, walked toward Bolan.

And it struck like a bolt of lightning, just as Bolan expected.

The four shadows boiled up on the limo's rear, out of nowhere. No sooner did the opening rounds of automatic weapons start barking than Bolan swept Miji Osaka into his arms. Reacting solely on instinct, he hurled her inside the limo, ducking the sizzling stream of lead blasting out the back windshield and door window. The Executioner might have just saved the woman's life, but he was seized with instant and grim concern over his own neck in the next heartbeat.

Out of the corner of his eye, he found Kedo absorbing the initial savage streams of lead. As the giant twitched, riddled with spurting crimson holes, Bolan caught Harisomo, a blur of movement, bursting from the limo. Mini-Uzi flaming, the scar-faced man forged toward their attackers.

Bolan ripped the Bushmaster from Kedo's holster and hurdled over the hood of a red Mercedes, glass razoring for the soldier and lead thudding off the sports car's body. The soldier saw Harisomo's first target pinned to a concrete barrier in a convulsing crucifixion. It was overkill on Harisomo's part as he shredded the man, but the Executioner decided to let him have at it. The three of them were all targeted for oblivion. Bolan knew the only way out, to save them, was to strike back as quickly.

Crouched and darting ahead between the concrete barrier and the noses of parked vehicles, Bolan took down hardman number two with well-placed head shots, the Bushmaster chugging away in the soldier's double-fisted grip.

Surging on, he joined Harisomo in a pincer move-

ment for gangster number three. Relentless, Bolan
scythed the man with a marching line of slugs up his
ribs, arms and skull, but Harisomo found it necessary
to drive home still more overkill. With no chance of
seeing another sunrise, that goon was pinned to the
side of a Honda hatchback, ventilated and spewing
gore.

Number four beat a fighting withdrawal across the
stretch of no-man's-land. A sweeping burst of the
enemy's Ingram subgun sent Bolan to ground. Popping up, the soldier found the hardman nose-diving
on a long scarlet slide for a black Jaguar. The subgun
flew from the enemy's hand, clattering on concrete,
but the metallic noise was quickly drowned by his
moans of agony.

With the trailing echo of autofire in his ear, Bolan
broke cover, following the scar-faced killer to the
downed enemy. Scanning his flanks, Bolan found
them alone. He also saw Miji Osaka coming up hard
on his rear. There was a mini-Uzi in her hand, held
low by her side. And there was a new look in the
beauty's eyes. Bolan couldn't pin her expression,
which was torn somewhere between admiration, respect and deep suspicion.

Rolling up on Harisomo's rear, not looking at Bolan, she said with the same calm she had displayed
on the ride to Tokyo, "Mr. Powers, please, at this
moment kindly do not interfere. This is personal."

Bolan quickly discovered just how personal it was.
The livid scar on Harisomo's face seemed to pulsate

with rage and adrenaline. The head of Osaka security grabbed up the wounded man's arm, looked at the amputated little finger of the man's hand, then grunted, "Yakuza."

Harisomo flung the arm away as if it were garbage. He unsheathed the short sword and barked to the wounded gangster, "Roll over. Face me."

Soaked in a stream of crimson, the gangster did as he was told. Bolan held his ground behind Harisomo, Miji Osaka stopping behind the scar-faced man. At the sight of the fearsome blade, the gangster injected defiance into his stare.

With utter contempt Miji Osaka looked down at the gangster and growled, "You can die with honor, or go to God like a dog. This is your moment of truth. Call it!"

An eerie sense of déjà vu locked onto Bolan. He watched as the gangster somehow found the will to shudder to his knees and take the sword from Harisomo. The gangster bowed, plunged steel into his belly and ripped a deep thrust up, then toppled on his back.

While the gangster twitched in an oozing pool of blood, Miji Osaka turned and looked Bolan square in the eye.

"Mr. Harisomo will take care of this unfortunate incident from here on. We will proceed as normal. Please, Mr. Powers, follow me."

Bolan held his ground for a stretched second, ghosts of Chicago flaming through his mind.

Harisomo retrieved his sword and wiped it on the gangster's pant leg.

If there was any doubt before in Bolan's mind about the source of the Chicago apocalypse, it was gone.

A specter of terrible memory washed over the Executioner.

But he felt as cold as the steel of Harisomo's sword.

The Executioner knew he had arrived at the threshold of the truth.

The evidence was as immediate and compelling to the soldier as the life leaking from the gangster who had been forced to commit ritual suicide.


"THIS IS UTTER MADNESS. This is not the way we do business even with our own, much less a foreigner. I can only imagine your father's disapproval! I could only imagine his outrage when he hears of this!"

Miji Osaka vaguely heard Harisomo. She sat in the high-backed black leather swivel chair behind the desk of her nineteenth-floor office. She was lost in thought, nursing strange and unseemly desires, the slender fingers of her hands forming a steeple to her chin. Harisomo's ranting seemed to strike her from a great distance. The man who craved her body, heart and soul was practically storming around the office, railing off his suspicions and his distrust of the American.

His envy.

How long had it been since the attack in the garage? An hour? Two? Time seemed irrelevant all of a sudden. Ever since she had first laid eyes on Michael Powers, she had sensed there was something different about the man. Something dangerous lurked there, a caged tiger beneath the tall, dark, ruggedly handsome exterior. Who was he? What was he? So many questions, so little time. Either way she couldn't deny the flame in her belly. Indeed, what would her father think? It was very un-Japanese, even whorish to feel like some schoolgirl with a heated crush on a stranger, to feel drawn like a moth to the flame, to secretly maneuver a man toward a romantic encounter. But why did she feel it necessary to have this Powers? And for what exactly? Duty to her father? Herself? Uncover any hidden agenda the man might have? Sating of her sudden and inexplicable lust?

Whatever, it would make it all that much easier since he knew their ways, was polite and respectful to a fault.

Suspiciously courteous and knowledgeable.

The American was indeed a warrior, carried the soul of a samurai. It was about the only thing at that moment Miji Osaka could be sure of.

Again she mentally reviewed the attack. How the American reacted as quick as lightning, throwing her out of a line of bullets that would have certainly cut her down. Then he braved the gunfire, moving like some great jungle cat, hurdling himself over parked vehicles with Olympic ease, surging for the Yakuza assassins, delivering death, unflinching, as if he had done such a thing many times before. Of course, Harisomo had played no small part in the counter-attack, but she was consumed with visions of Michael Powers. Privately she stoked the fires of her intrigue, interest and desire.

The American was no businessman. Whatever he was, she intended to find out. With whatever it took. She was looking forward to dinner with Michael Powers, if that was even his real name. She could be sure the man wouldn't disappoint her, in any way.

"Miji? Are you listening to me? What can you possibly be thinking?"

Obviously Harisomo had gauged her reaction to the American. She finally acknowledged Harisomo with a cold eye.

"I am thinking we need to learn much more about Michael Powers."

"We?" Harisomo's breath rasped out flared nostrils. "How? By your having dinner with the American?"

"Is it my generous show of hospitality of having dinner with the man that troubles you so much?" Sensing his outrage like heat from a close fire, she added, "You do not wear jealous anger well, Misimoto."

Harisomo stiffened but got himself under control. "I am merely voicing what I am sure would be your father's concern—and objections."

"Really. Well, if you must know, while you were dealing with the police and keeping word of the attack from spreading throughout the building, I was on the phone with my father. He is deeply grateful to the American. And to you. I acknowledge your role in defending me, and I am grateful beyond words that you risked your life for me once more."

If he was appeased, Harisomo didn't show it. "I must believe your father is likewise suspicious. This man is no merchant. He has the look and the smell of a warrior who has shed much blood. Your father will see right through him. Does no one but myself find it strange that a mere few days after what happened in America, and on the eve of our concluding our business with the Iraqis, that this Powers suddenly shows up?"

Of course it had all crossed her mind. But there was too much at stake, too much she believed could be learned about Michael Powers, to blindly attack what appeared coincidence.

"What you say may or may not be true. But my father has left the matter to me. If there is some deceit at work on the part of the American, then I will be the one to find out."

A cruel smile slit Harisomo's lips. "Then there is something you would like to know. After paying off the police, I received a call in the limousine from one of our people. It seems that two of the men who came to Osaka several short days ago with all their grand schemes for leverage buyouts and heavenly visions of mammoth casino cities, well, they are staying in a hotel right here in Shinjuku.''

''And?''

''They had indicated to Osaka executives they would be returning to America.''

''Spare me the drama. Your point, please.''

''A simple payoff at the hotel, and it was discovered from phone records these two men made calls to Washington, D.C. More specifically to the United States Department of Justice.''

She hid her surprise even as hot fury welled inside her. Interesting. Well, if Michael Powers wasn't who he said he was, he would not only be her first foreign lover, but she would slay him by her own hand and deliver his head, a trophy, to her father for his treachery.

''I assume you intend to pay these two Americans a visit?'' she asked, changing the subject.

''Yes. While you are having dinner with the American.''

The woman scoffed, softly shaking her head. ''I suggest you put caution in your tone. You are wearing my patience thin. You know how much I despise the double standard of Japanese men. I am not like other Japanese women. As for whatever I intend to do with Mr. Powers, that is my concern, my affair. I can be sure all the times you have gone to America, you have on numerous occasions had 'dinner' with a beautiful blonde or brunette. Do not stand there and tell me that after all these years you have saved your love for me.''

A strange look shadowed Harisomo's face. For long moments he stood there, staring at the woman. And for a fleeting moment Miji Osaka felt her heart soften for this man. It was as if his spirit were slowly fleeing him through unseen holes in his body, never to return, she thought. The look of utter pain and confusion, of feeling betrayed, was a ghosting visage. But the raw emotion was as powerful as anything she had ever sensed from Harisomo. There was even a hint of mist in the eyes, but he pulled back the expression of agony, forcing it down, deep inside his soul in the next instant. With great effort she hid the compassion she suddenly felt for Harisomo.

''Why?'' he asked, sounding almost like a lost child who was too young, too naive to fathom all the injustices of the world.

She knew what he really wanted to ask, but couldn't because of his pride. *Why not me?* was the unspoken question raging in his heart. She knew the answer, but she would never tell him. Harisomo believed she owed him her love, her life.

''I don't know,'' was all Miji Osaka could say. ''I really don't.''

Another eternal moment, then Harisomo nodded, as if some great mystery was suddenly revealed to him in the ensuing silence.

''You know the importance of your father's meeting tomorrow. You know we are on the brink of perhaps world domination," he said, once again all steel, all fire.

"I know about the meeting. The rest my father is leaving up to you."

"Then you also know that Kedo was a great friend of mine, a warrior who gave his life for you." He paused, and when she didn't respond, he added, "When I return from Iraq, Kedo will be honored in death as befitting the traditional funeral rites of a samurai. Whatever you decide to do tonight—Miji, hear me now—I can forgive you in the name of duty."

She wanted to take offense at his arrogance but decided to let him play the spurned would-be lover. Her own duty called. Now was not the time for a war of hearts. Or was the depth of his passion for her that great?

"We will speak later," he said, bowed and left the office.

Alone, Miji Osaka once again became inflamed with visions of Michael Powers. Tonight, she determined, would be the night she either began what she hoped would be a long-lasting union between the two of them, or it would be the beginning of her destruction of the American. Either way she would get what she wanted.

She was Miji Osaka, after all.

## CHAPTER SIXTEEN

The day had already proved a heady experience, even for the Executioner, and Bolan sensed the night was about to culminate in an even more unexpected turn of events.

Sitting on the mat, facing Miji Osaka, the low table between them lined with bowls of raw tuna, sea bream, rice, caviar and chicken, Bolan warned himself to keep up his guard. He couldn't decide if the woman was charming or deadly. Whatever she was, whatever her game, Bolan found her a silent but gracious sorceress in her red silk kimono with black obi wound loosely around her slender midriff. Beautiful, yes, and somehow lethal, even in silence.

In her quiet way she had already informed him they were completely alone. Apparently the entire nineteenth floor belonged to her, complete with its own dojo, bathing facilities, offices. She said they could relax and enjoy the evening in complete privacy. She had also relayed her father's deep gratitude, his indebtedness to Michael Powers for his bravery in saving his daughter's life.

They ate in respectful silence, each waiting for the other to speak, neither wanting to appear intrusive or improper. When she offered more hot sake, Bolan accepted, enjoying the aroma of spiced and steaming food and the sweet smell of incense burning from sticks Miji had placed around the suite.

It had been nearly seven hours since the ambush in the garage. He'd had a steam bath and a massage, then been led to a room where he was told by his female attendants he could rest.

But there was nothing but a restless and raging fire for the truth in Bolan's heart. The fact that the attack hadn't been mentioned by Miji, nor had the police paid him a visit, told Bolan the Osakas probably owned some of the Tokyo law. Much as the Yakuza kept a handful of paid badges in their pockets, the powerful Osakas were targets for blackmail, extortion, even assassination. Their money would certainly buy them all the benefits of special police assistance when the need arose.

Finally, after long hours, he had been summoned by the woman to her suite.

Glancing around, using the chopsticks with easy skill on the sea bream, Bolan found the suite, like the woman, ablaze with contradictions, mystery and not so subtle clues to the warrior female inside Miji Osaka.

First the white marble Buddha. The floor-to-ceiling statue loomed near the drawn silk curtains aglow with the lights of the city. With candlelight flickering over the statue, the Buddha's obsidian eyes seemed almost alive, watching, waiting, judging. Numerous prints hung from the walls on all sides. They displayed everything from samurai in battle, to naked geishas bathing their shoguns, to a ninja in the act of raping a woman while who Bolan assumed was her husband was outstretched, close at hand, with his hands pressed over his crimson stomach. There was one print that covered the entire length of one screen, beyond which Bolan assumed was Miji Osaka's bedroom. Awash in the yellowish orange dance of candlelight, that particular print seemed to flash with a seething life of its own. It showed ships colliding into each other, helmeted warriors tumbling over the sides, plunging into thrashing waters. In the dark background of the print, streaked by a jagged finger of lightning, a faint white shroud loomed over the sea carnage. Just inside the painted glow, Bolan made out the specter of a face with eyes that were either laughing or angry; it was hard to tell. Either way the print was fearsome looking just the same.

Then there were the porcelain Kabuki and lion masks, as well as an array of weapons that hung from the wall. Crossed swords, a half-dozen nunchaku, an octagon steel *sai*. Everything, perhaps, but a few *shurikens*.

And last, but certainly not least, in the corner, just beside the burl-ash double doors, was a man-size statue of a black cobra coiled high in the air, fangs bared. Wrapped in the viper's tail was a mongoose with bulging white eyes and razor-sharp teeth, flashing in vain. Death grip. An image of Bolan playing the mongoose to Miji Osaka's cobra flickered through his mind.

Everything about the decor told Bolan this woman was gentle and spiritual, but equally serious about her fierce warrior heritage. However it was viewed, the soldier took these subtle clues as mounting evidence, betraying with each passing moment the origins of the Chicago breakout.

"For the first time, Mr. Powers, I sense some uncertainty about you."

Bolan showed the woman a gentle smile. "I would say I'm more intrigued than uncertain."

She returned the Executioner's smile, delicately wiping her mouth with a white silk cloth. "I feel comfortable with you, as I hope you do with me. I know that in Japan women are not supposed to be...forward with men. They are supposed to be subservient, know their place. In Japan a woman's highest honor is to be a mother, to be a loyal and faithful wife, to watch and guard the home while the man carves his place in the world. But I am my father's daughter. I am not spoiled, mind you. I simply understand and know who I am. I have supreme regard and eternal gratitude for the honor my destiny has blessed me with as Harikami Osaka's daughter. Life is short. It is the one principle that guides my every action. When I want something, I see no reason other than to go after what it is I want."

"What is it you want?"

"I am sure that much I have made obvious. But what I want right now is for you to tell exactly what it is you find most intriguing when you just looked around."

Bolan gave the silence a long moment of careful thought. He sipped his sake, his gaze finally settling on the large print of the ships colliding. She broke Bolan's eye for a moment, concentrating on her sake.

"The divine wind," Bolan said in a whisper he made sound near reverent. For a second she seemed startled, her eyes alive with fire. The soldier hid his own surprise over her sudden reaction.

She quickly regained her composure. "What?"

"The print on the sliding door. That's what fascinates me the most. I'm not sure if it's the candlelight...the way I'm feeling right now...graced with the presence of the most beautiful woman I have ever seen...but the print almost seems to move, to live, to want to tell the beholder about glory and honor, maybe even that there is cosmic justice. If I don't miss my guess, it depicts the attempted Mongol invasion of Japan. The Mongols twice attempted to invade and conquer Japan under the Khan. Both times an entire nation prayed for deliverance. Both times a typhoon destroyed the Mongol fleets."

She regarded Bolan with new appreciation, smiling. "Yes, how right you are. To this day Japan has not forgotten how the gods answered the prayers of a nation. God breathed a divine wind over the barbarians, crushed them all in a storm that left none of them alive. It is perhaps the one moment in our history that tells us we are unique, special in the world, a people of destiny. God saw fit to save the Japanese." She regarded Bolan with subtle but sudden renewed keen interest. "You seem to know an awful lot about us, Mr. Powers. I must be honest with you. I am not sure how that makes me feel."

"Miji, I am not here to intrude or interfere in personal matters."

"You are referring, of course, to Harisomo."

"The man...well, I can see he feels protective of you."

"You needn't be so polite. Harisomo is in love with me, but I do not feel the same for him." Briefly she explained how Harisomo came about the scar on his face, speaking with no disrespect, some feeling of loyalty, but mostly providing just cold, hard facts about that day in the country inn. "Because of his service to my father—regarding today—tomorrow he will be paid a very high tribute. Do you know who Yokitomo the Great was?"

Bolan dredged up his Intel from Brognola. "I read an article once about your father in a business magazine well-known in my country. In this rare interview your father granted, he said Yokitomo was one of the greatest samurai, if not the greatest warrior Japan has ever seen. Your father is a direct descendant of Yokitomo." He embellished the legend some with hints of knowledge about Yokitomo's mystic powers.

Miji Osaka smiled. "For several hundred years the sword of Yokitomo, believed blessed while he slept by the spirit of the same divine wind that saved Japan, has been safe in the treasure house of the Osaka Shinto shrine. Tomorrow my father will present Harisomo the sword as tribute. Understand, Mr. Powers, that my father can be the most generous of men, he can show undying gratitude for loyalty, reward honor for honor's sake. If nothing else, Harisomo is owed respect and honor."

Bolan nodded that he understood. For a dangerous moment he found himself unable to take his eyes off this woman. If what he believed about the Osakas turned out to be true, then he knew he would regret the future. Another time, another place, under different circumstances, he knew he would like to spend time getting to know this woman on a deeper level. But he knew what she was, even if he didn't have proof.

Miji Osaka was a killer. The heiress, her father and Harisomo were directly responsible for the slaughter that had taken place in Chicago. Instinct had never failed Bolan before, and that same gut feeling was telling him the following day would bring either his own death or tragedy for Osaka Worldwide.

A fire suddenly lit the woman's eyes. Gracefully she slid the table aside, seemed to glide over the short space between them on her knees. Staring into those liquid almond eyes, Bolan waited for her to come to him, to make the first move. Something told him he wouldn't be leaving her suite that night, probably wouldn't even be allowed out of Miji Osaka's sight. If that was the case, it would have to be sometime tomorrow before he could rendezvous with his Justice Department contacts, collect his weapons.

Bolan knew he had to accept whatever honor she chose to bestow upon him, take her hospitality in any form it was granted. And why not? It was another double-edged sword, but one he could use to maybe slice away the layers of mystery surrounding his mission.

The soldier knew the night would belong to them. Patience, he told himself. The next day would bring new challenges, fresh thunderheads of trouble.

SHAME AND RAGE propelled Harisomo down the hotel hallway. Images of his beloved Miji in the arms of the foreigner stayed branded in his mind as he approached the door to the suite where the American's two alleged business associates were staying.

Miji had inflicted the ultimate insult on him, the final disgrace. He felt spurned, rejected.

Betrayed.

Still he believed he could forgive her, clinging desperately to that last shred of hope that someday she would be his and his alone. What did it matter if she was with the American? After all, she had her own duty. Yet did that include a potential sexual liaison with a total stranger? His blood boiled. It was madness. Was she trying to tell him something? Finally saying without uttering the words that it would never happen between them?

Harisomo didn't want to believe that.

Still, she was with the American. Alone. Dinner.

Agony pierced Harisomo's heart. He needed action, relief right then, an outlet for his jealous rage.

The Americans would provide just the cure.

Harisomo gave the hallway a long look in both directions. Empty. All was quiet.

He lightly rapped on the door, conscious of the silenced Beretta 92-F in his waistband. He would get answers, then deliver justice the Osaka way.

"Who is it?" one of the Americans called from behind the door.

Harisomo stood close to the eyehole, head bowed a little, putting on a subservient face. "Room service, sir. Your dinner is here."

"About time," he heard the man growl. Harisomo had already checked with his man in the hotel's kitchen. The Americans were waiting for their evening meal.

The dead bolt turned. Harisomo took one last look around the hall, pressed close to the door and drew his short sword.

The door opened. A foreigner's face full of frustration appeared before Harisomo's eyes, but there was shock and agony carving that expression in the next instant. A single deep thrust drove tempered steel through the belly, tore upward to puncture the heart. The man was dead on his feet.

Harisomo surged inside the suite, closing the door behind him, already drawing the Beretta as his gutted victim plunged to the foyer. A sliver of a shadow came around the corner, a concerned voice asking what the noise was all about.

No sooner did the second American show himself than Harisomo shot him in the knee. When the man toppled to the carpet, Harisomo rushed to him, clamped a hand over his mouth to muffle the cry of pain.

Harisomo pressed the silenced muzzle against the man's forehead. Bulging eyes of fear and pain stared him back.

"I am going to remove my hand to ask you some questions," Harisomo rasped. "Scream or even raise your voice, and I will kill you. Nod if you understand."

The American nodded.

Harisomo removed his hand and stepped back. He listened for a moment while the American breathed hard in choked agony, checking the gleaming shards of his shattered knee jutting out of the torn pant leg.

"Who are you?" Harisomo asked.

"This is the way you do business in Japan?"

With a quiet sneeze from the Beretta, Harisomo shot the man in the arm. He yelped briefly, but Harisomo was already shoving the muzzle into the man's vented mouth, drowning any more cries.

"I know you called the Justice Department in America. One final time. Who are you? Who is Michael Powers?"

Defiance hardened the man's eyes. Harisomo slid the Beretta out of the American's mouth. Something told him the man was going to take the truth with him to the grave.

The American confirmed it, his voice all steel. "Go to hell. You're going to kill me anyway."

Harisomo nodded. "Indeed," he said, admiring the American's sense of honor and duty for a brief moment before shooting the man in the face.

Quickly he searched the suite, rifling through luggage bags, suit jackets. He found passports and wallets that IDed the dead men as who they claimed to be. Harisomo knew all about false documentation. There would be no concrete evidence here that they were agents of Western law.

In one room he found holstered 9 mm Berettas. Interesting. So his suspicions were panning out. It was their misfortune they had opted to leave the weapons behind, not wanting to draw suspicion from a mere room-service waiter when they opened the door.

Just beside the bed, Harisomo's intent gaze dropped on a large duffel bag, exactly the same size and color as the one Powers had with him at the airport. He opened the bag, was stunned for a moment at the weapons he found inside. Witnessing the American in combat in the garage earlier, instinct told Harisomo these weapons had been slated to fall into the hands of the foreigner who was having dinner with Miji.

No, Michael Powers was not at all who he said he was.

Smiling, wondering how Miji would react to this discovery, Harisomo zipped up the bag.

ARATA MITISUMA SAT at the head of the long black marble conference table, wondering how he was going to piece the family back together, fill the vacuum of the power structure now that his brother was dead. And his thoughts were also consumed with how he was going to slaughter the Osakas, redeem his honor.

For long moments he stared at his lieutenant, Mako Nagachi. Even though Nagachi sat as unmoving as stone, with no expression, Mitisuma knew the man with the sharp-featured face and the same sort of black, lifeless eyes as the shark after which he was named, was seething just the same.

Only two short days earlier, both of them had returned from business in Hong Kong, putting the final touches there on the shipment of cocaine that was to come down by freighter to the port of Tokyo. As he had stepped off his private jet, he had been informed the limousines his brother and his bodyguards had used to drive to the meeting with Osaka had been discovered by the police, abandoned and empty, just north of Tokyo. No bodies had yet been found. The police were baffled.

Arata Mitisuma wasn't confused at all. He knew all about Osaka's secret ninja circle of assassins, this divine wind. He was sure those same assassins had tossed the bodies of his brother and the others into the Sea of Japan, or ground them up at some remote farm to be used as fertilizer. Of course, the police didn't know that his brother had driven out to see Osaka, and Arata Mitisuma wasn't about to fill in any of the pieces of the puzzle. He had to take matters into his own hands if he was to save face with the other families.

The flashing neon jungle of the Ginza struck the drawn curtains, glittering shadows dancing across the conference room. The building was one of many legitimate Mitisuma businesses in Tokyo. This particular office in the Ginza District traded in Japanese prints, kimonos and other Asian artifacts. Most of the merchandise was hastily manufactured, cheap and worthless, but it grabbed up a good chunk of dollars from Western tourists, duped into thinking they were taking home some priceless memento of ancient Japan. It was the rest of the block, though, that Mitisuma owned, teeming with its countless sex shops, massage parlors and geisha houses of the Ginza, where he grew rich.

He traded in sex mostly, but for some time Mitisuma had been looking to branch off into gambling and narcotics. He wasn't as strong as some of the other families, but he was ambitious, paying off police and politicians, flexing muscle when necessary, even ordering a contract killing when he saw fit to expand his domain. This whole business, though, with the Osakas, had wounded his fledgling but growing empire. He had warned his brother to forget Harry Osaka; they didn't really need him. But his brother had foolishly hoped to merge with Osaka, use the mogul's name and money as a legitimate front to hide illegal activities. Foolish, yes, and stupid. Harry Osaka clung to tradition, saw the Mitisuma family as low creatures of no honor. But Arata Mitisuma clung to tradition just as fiercely as the Osakas.

Clearly vengeance was called for.

And the days ahead would determine much for Arata Mitisuma. Yes, he would personally bring the head of Harry Osaka to the leaders of the other families so they would see he was a force to be reckoned with.

Already he was planning the next, and what he knew would be the final, hit on Osaka. Just that afternoon his first attempt had failed. He had lost four good men. Worse, his paid policemen informed him there was an American in the picture, one who had helped with the killings. It was all striking Mitisuma as very strange. Certainly it all smacked of dishonor.

Mitisuma looked Nagachi straight in his dead eyes. "We both know what must be done. We will be patient for the next two days, maybe three, depending on the information I can gather from our two remaining sources inside Osaka. Then we will strike and crush this mosquito, this Harry Osaka, once and for all. We will remove this disgrace from the house of Mitisuma forever in blood debt. I do not care if we must leave a trail of bodies from the Osaka castle to his office in Shinjuku!''

For the first time since stepping off their jet, Nagachi's eyes came alive and a cruel smile slit his lips. ''After the failure in the garage this afternoon, you can be certain Osaka will not leave his castle. He will be well guarded by his ninja legion.''

Mitisuma nodded. ''Of course. I want every available man prepared for an all-out assault on the Osaka castle.'' He paused, already putting the pieces of the hit together in his mind. Nothing fancy really. Drive to the outer perimeter, move in, storm the walls. Kill any and everything that moved. Some payoffs to the police would be required later to keep the bloodletting from pointing his way.

''It has been what,'' Mitisuma said, ''three hundred years or more since the shogun's samurai last attacked the Osaka castle? Legend has it the shogun's samurai were slain to the last warrior by one Osaka, Yokitomo. Well, the castle remained intact even as the Osakas were chased clear across Japan. This time, though, there will be no magic sword to defend the Osakas. This time I will cut the head off Harry Osaka personally. I will even have his daughter raped before his eyes while I burn both his castle and his Shinto shrine to the ground.''

If Mako Nagachi was smiling before, he seemed now on the verge of practically erupting into laughter. ''What you mentioned about the daughter...may I be so bold as to implore you for that honor?''

THE HEAT OF THEIR PASSION was just starting to cool on his body when Bolan slipped into the kimono Miji had left for him. He swung his legs over the edge of the futon and saw her shadow in the candlelight, just beyond the sliding door.

Only moments earlier the phone had rung, taking her out of the bedroom, into the suite. Intently Bolan listened to the exchange. Miji said *''Hai''* over and over. It didn't sound good to the Executioner. No, it wasn't so much the lack of words that troubled Bolan; it was her tone. In just a few short moments, talking to whoever was on the other end, her voice had gone quiet but as cold as steel.

Suddenly the soldier felt an urgent need to get out of there, to find an excuse that would allow him to get to his contacts.

Finally she ended the conversation, but didn't return to the bedroom. Bolan watched as her shadow faded beyond the sliding door. Braced for anything, he quietly padded for the open space in the door and found a spot of semiconcealment. Standing in the shadows, he spotted her. She was kneeling in her red kimono before Buddha, her hands clasped in prayer.

Clearly she was disturbed about something. Bolan had to suspect she had just received some bad news. But what troubling news? About whom?

Whatever, Bolan sensed she knew. If she indicated knowledge of his acting job, pressed it with all the danger he knew she possessed inside that beautiful body, then Bolan would have to act accordingly, with whatever the moment called for.

He looked away from the woman and moved a few feet inside the sliding door. He was sitting on a time bomb; that much he knew. But the only thing he could do was wait for her reaction.

What the Executioner didn't expect was to find her, standing no less than three feet away from him, in the next eye blink. Bolan hid his surprise, even as he felt his gaze narrow from the sudden tension and anger he felt coil in his belly at her sudden appearance. He had taken his eyes off her for only a few seconds, yet she had come out of nowhere, as silent as a ghost. Or a ninja assassin. Okay. Just like that, Bolan knew what he was faced with. He made a mental note to watch his back more closely in the future when around this woman.

"I apologize. I gave explicit orders not to be interrupted tonight."

He smiled easily at her even as he measured her. She sounded fine, but there was just enough of an edge in her voice to warn him something had changed. And it had to do with the phone call.

"Why don't we return to bed." Gently she took

Bolan's arm. "Tomorrow is going to be a long day for you. I have been informed you will be meeting with my father in the morning."

Behind her gentle facade, Bolan detected something dark and seething. If he didn't miss his guess, he would have sworn she was looking at him as if she felt betrayed by him.

Something warned the Executioner it might be wise to sleep that night with one eye open.

## CHAPTER SEVENTEEN

Two silent, grim-faced men came for Bolan well before dawn. Earlier Miji had excused herself, telling Bolan he could clean up in her suite before leaving to meet her father at the Osaka castle. It had been a warning not to leave. Bolan sensed the woman was going to play it to the bitter end.

For Bolan strongly suspected she knew the truth, or something of the truth, about him. After the phone call her entire demeanor had changed. Cool friendliness masked the hungry tigress in her eyes, but Bolan sensed she wanted his flesh, and for her own pleasure of a different sort. The killing kind.

She had slept or feigned sleep during the rest of the night upon returning to bed after the mysterious phone call. The whole time lying next to her, the Executioner drifted off just at a level of consciousness where he could rest but stay alert for any sudden movement by the woman or anybody else.

The soldier knew he had arrived at what the woman had told the gangster in the garage was a moment of truth. The Executioner had been around too long and seen too much in his never-ending war not to know when his life was in danger.

Everything had changed, for damn sure, just like that.

Bolan had been marched to the garage by his escorts. Neither man had made an effort to conceal the hilt of his sword beneath the black leather trench coat, nor the dislike and distrust of the American in his eyes.

Now Bolan sat alone in the passenger well of a limousine, driven by his escorts to the Osaka castle. Before leaving the suite, the Executioner opted for a change of clothes from his travel bag, donning dark khaki slacks, black sport shirt and desert boots. Casual, and flexible to strike.

He couldn't see out the black-tinted windows to get a fix on where they were taking him. For all he knew, they could be driving him to some remote stretch of farmland or pull into the isolated gloom of an Osaka warehouse, open the door and go for his head with their swords. But he didn't think so.

Osaka was playing a human chess game, every move designed to win whatever it was the man sought to crown himself king with. Only Bolan believed he was being maneuvered to be staged, an Osaka puppet, with the string to be severed anytime by their samurai swords. From Miji Osaka's abrupt dismissal of the night in her own way, to the strange pickup, to his limo prison cell—it was all boiling toward critical mass. First, though, Bolan believed

Harry Osaka wanted to see the man who had helped save his daughter's life, this strange foreigner who had blazed into Japan, proving himself far more a samurai than anything remotely resembling a Western businessman.

Glancing at his watch, Bolan figured they were a good hour out of Tokyo, depending on traffic and the route his chauffeur chose.

How would the great Harikami Osaka receive him? Of course, if he was suddenly set upon, Bolan would have no choice but to fight back with every ounce of strength, determination and skill he possessed. But he didn't think Osaka would attack him suddenly, not without the man getting his own answers first.

This was all provided, of course, that Bolan had been found out. If they had discovered the truth, then how? With all of Osaka's vast resources, it stood to reason it wouldn't be a stretch to discover Michael Powers was a fraud.

Close to thirty minutes later, the limo stopped. Bolan waited until the door was opened. His samurai escorts stepped back, and he got out warily.

For a long moment the soldier felt as if he had been catapulted back into feudal Japan.

The Executioner discovered he stood at the gates to the Osaka castle. He gave his surroundings a hard look as one of the escorts grunted and nodded for him to get moving. Inside the gates Bolan found the walled courtyard empty. An eerie silence hung over the seven-tiered roof of the castle. The structure looked dark, even as it stretched for an azure sky, the morning sun having just cleared the tree line.

His escorts flanking him, Bolan was marched for the black maw of the ground-floor entrance. At the top of the steps one of the men gave Bolan's shoes a hard look and grunted.

After a moment's hesitation Bolan acknowledged their tradition and removed his shoes.

He was led into the main room on the ground floor. On the way in, he noted how the wooden floors squeaked. It was called Nightingale flooring, designed to creak to give the occupants advance warning of unwanted encroachment. He scrutinized the corridors, certain the entire castle was filled with trapdoors, drop points from the ceiling where intruders could be set upon and hidden compartments in walls. There would even be Judas slats in the ceilings and the walls, behind which either guest or intruder could be secretly observed.

Bolan was taken to a large room, where Harikami Osaka was already waiting.

The man was sitting on a tatami mat, with a vacant mat just in front of him. The empty space was close enough, Bolan thought, for Osaka to draw the sword inside the obi and deliver a swift, decapitating blow. Any sudden move, any hint of violence, though, and Bolan determined he would strike fast, no matter what. The Executioner counted six samurai with swords, three on each side of the room. All of them glared at the American.

Harisomo was on his lord's right flank, perched on his own mat. From his seat of honor, the scar-faced warrior treated Bolan to a look of pure hate. An air of simmering violence gripped the room.

Closing on Osaka and Harisomo, Bolan noted the spartan touches to what he suspected was the war room. Here feudal *daimyo* had most likely plotted battle strategy against rivals, or solemnly basked in the glow of victory. There were no prints, not even on the sliding doors, no flower arrangements or scrolls. A few rice-paper lanterns hung from the ceiling, now lit. This was a place where no distractions were tolerated, where the most serious of business was conducted, where samurai looked at only one another, measuring, judging, acknowledging honor or plotting revenge.

The Executioner stopped before Osaka, who stood and bowed. Bolan returned the bow, and his escorts also bowed to Osaka before silently departing the room. Harisomo didn't bow, much less bother to stand. If Osaka was offended by the scar-faced samurai's lack of courtesy, he didn't show it.

When Osaka indicated that Bolan should sit, the soldier took his place on the mat. The ensuing silence alone seemed to hold a roar of danger in Bolan's ears. At first Osaka didn't look at the Executioner, instead focusing on some spot in front of him, gracefully tucking his legs beneath him, choosing to sit in a long and thoughtful silence. When Osaka finally looked up, Bolan felt the full extent of his piercing stare. It was hard for the soldier to read the look. It was an expression torn somewhere between respect, fear and admiration. Those midnight black eyes seemed to Bolan to be probing his soul, seeking for hidden truths in his heart. Either way he knew he was being gauged in the silence, Osaka weighing the pros and cons of some life-and-death decision.

Several moments later something peculiar happened to Osaka. The Executioner hid his surprise when he detected a sheen of sweat beading the man's face. What was he seeing? Bolan wondered. Was the man burning up with fever? Brognola's Intel was complete with Osaka's strange medical history of high-grade fevers that would have claimed the lives of normal men. There were even reports of a faint white glow that often radiated from the man's face when he was in the throes of fever. Now Bolan was witness to what appeared to be a soft glow, or a shroud burning from Osaka's granite-hard visage. Moments later the glow—if that was even what he'd seen—vanished. Potentially unnerving, yeah, if Bolan didn't know what he did about Osaka.

Osaka cleared his throat. "Mr. Powers, I would first like to express my deep gratitude to you for your bravery in saving my daughter's life yesterday."

Bolan acknowledged the tribute with a short bow. Out of the corner of his eye, he saw Harisomo stiffen, the fury like a burning beacon in the scar-faced samurai's dark, narrowed gaze.

"I have already rewarded Harisomo-*san* before you arrived for his part in defending my daughter's life," Osaka stated. "My reward to you will be truthfulness."

Osaka paused. "Likewise the only gift you will honor me with will be your own truthfulness. Do you know what a moment of truth is, Mr. Powers?"

"I heard the expression used by your daughter yesterday."

"Indeed. A moment of truth is fleeting, a few brief seconds, where a man reveals his true nature while his soul is balanced between life and death, on the very threshold of the here and the hereafter. It is a moment where either honor or dishonor is exposed to the naked light of impending death, death being the only pure form of truth there is. It is a moment, needless to say, that is captured for all eternity. It is the moment when a man goes to God with honor and purity of heart, or he goes groveling, a dog to its master, attempting to excuse his sins and dishonor to the same God."

If there were any doubts before about the threat of imminent violence, Bolan knew they were now dispelled. The warning tone from Osaka and the angry eyes of the samurai boring into him clearly told Bolan his own life was now poised on the sword's edge of extinction.

The Executioner also concluded that Harikami

Osaka was insane. Insane in the way of a man who allows evil to twist and trample the truth in order to suit and fulfill his own selfish desires and ambitions. Wrong then became right, right became wrong, and every act was deemed justified or worthy in the eyes of the wrongdoer. It was perhaps the most dangerous sort of evil the Executioner had ever seen, the cornerstone on which all other evils were built. And Bolan had never been a believer in atrocities glossed over, even excused by reason of insanity.

Osaka drew in a deep breath, then exhaled very slowly. "It would appear a thorough background check on you, Mr. Powers, has held up, told me you are who you claim to be."

Bolan kept his stoic expression a mirror of Osaka's.

"I ask you now, in this moment of truth," Osaka said, "as one warrior to another, are you who you claim to be? More precisely are you Michael Powers, American vice president of Milo Incorporated?"

Looking Osaka dead in the eye, Bolan answered, "No."

Strangely there was no reaction on Osaka's face. "You are not a businessman?"

"No."

"An agent of the United States government?"

"No. Not officially."

"Then what are you?"

Bolan paused, then said. "Death."

Osaka's eyes lit up for a second as he stared long

and hard at Bolan, appearing uncertain as to how to proceed. "Really. If that is true, do you realize that because of your deception, I could either kill you myself or order you killed this very moment?"

Bolan heard the ice in his own voice. "That may or may not be true. But God pity the man who tries to shed my blood."

Osaka grunted, then nodded, as if he understood completely.

"Some most interesting developments have transpired since you arrived here yesterday, Mr. Powers. I am unsure at the moment whether you are blessed with good or bad karma. Perhaps I will leave that entirely up to you by your answers." Osaka nodded at one of his men, who left the room.

They waited several moments in silence. Bolan heard, then saw, the samurai return to the room. As the soldier looked up, he saw a large black duffel bag in the man's hand, which he dropped beside Bolan. Adrenaline racing through his veins, the Executioner found the bag open, revealing his weapons inside. There was little doubt in his mind how the bag had been taken.

"Yes, Mr. Powers, your two so-called business associates are dead," Osaka stated. "I believe those two were with the American Justice Department. I also believe those weapons were destined to fall into your hands."

Bolan said nothing. It took all his power of self-control to keep from going to Osaka's sword, wield it and take them as they came.

Osaka's gaze narrowed. "Had you attempted to lie to me just now, your head would already be rolling across the floor. Since you had enough honor to begin to come clean with me, you have stolen yourself some precious time. How much time is up to me and what I decide to do with you. I ask you now. Are you with your Department of Justice?"

"I already told you. Not in any official capacity."

Osaka paused, a thin smile ghosting his lips. "So be it. Then you are death. You have come to Japan to assassinate me."

Bolan ignored the man's cynical tone, deciding to push his luck. "Since we're both rewarding each other with the truth, Osaka, maybe you will answer some of my questions."

"Very well. What is it you wish to know?"

Bolan directed his question as much to Osaka as he did to Harisomo. "Chicago. Was it you who sent assassins there in the slaughter that freed those Iraqi terrorists?"

"Yes."

"Why?"

Osaka seemed to ponder something for a moment. "I'm sure there are many things you already know, or think you know about me, Mr. Powers. Do you know, when I was but a child, I survived what you Americans did to us at Nagasaki?"

"Is that what this is all about, Osaka? Revenge?"

"Yes. Revenge. It gets no more simple, no more pure than that."

"A lot of innocent people died in Chicago. If what you say is true, then what about their right to revenge?"

"A lot of innocent people died at Hiroshima and Nagasaki, Mr. Powers. Do not be so narrow in your view of humanity."

"Not at all. To me, life is life, wherever it is. Right is right, wrong is wrong. Gray is nothing but a shade of darkness in the human heart."

"You deny me my right to vengeance then for my own people?"

"I once heard a man say that war always ends the way it does for a reason, that it ends the way it should, ends the way it was meant to end. You might conclude in those words that maybe...the divine wind of a cosmic justice guides humanity."

Osaka regarded Bolan carefully. "How right you are, Mr. Powers. A divine wind does indeed steer the human race toward its destiny. As for what happened half a century ago, well, it is said that not even God can change the past. But man can certainly atone, not only for his own sins, but for the sins of others. Repentance by vengeance. Redemption by way of the sword."

The Executioner had no doubt now his first analysis of Osaka was frightening in its accuracy. Feeling Harisomo's stare take on a new depth of fury, Bolan then met the scar-faced man's eyes. Something was churning in Harisomo's mind.

"It was you on the roof of the Sears Tower," Harisomo stated. "It was you who killed the others."

Ice in his voice, Bolan said, "I was the last one off the roof—alive. And it's been you, hasn't it? You're the one doing all the killing."

Harisomo's eyes were ablaze with sudden rage. "Yes. It was I who took the lives of those two marshals, the Iraqi and your two Justice Department conspirators. Just as I will take your life!"

Just like that, it was going to blow up in Bolan's face.

"I say you allow me to kill the foreigner now, my lord!" Harisomo snarled.

The scar-faced man drew his sword, but only slid the blade several inches out of its sheath.

Osaka said nothing. It struck Bolan the man was going to let the killing begin.

The Executioner tensed to spring for Harisomo, as steel slid farther from the samurai's scabbard.

It was past the boiling point now, the Executioner sensed.

It was set to explode in madness.

## CHAPTER EIGHTEEN

"No! This is not the right time, Misimoto. Both of you, retake your places."

Bolan held his ground, leaning toward the duffel bag, poised on the razor's edge of potential bloodletting. Osaka barked another order for everyone to return to his place. Finally Harisomo sheathed his sword and sat. Still standing, Bolan was wondering about his weapons, if they were locked and loaded, when Osaka answered his question.

"I am not a fool, Mr. Powers. Your weapons are not loaded. No matter how quick you think you are, by the time you are able to load them, you would be nothing but a torso. I would have your head impaled on a stake in the courtyard before the last drop of blood flowed from whatever was left of your body."

The threat of erupting violence passed, but the danger lingered, a living force of smoldering rage around the Executioner. Bolan took his seat.

"I have just made a decision about you, Mr. Powers," Osaka announced. "You wish to know what this is all about, why I risked everything to free my

Iraqi allies from your American justice. Well, in just a little while you will be making a long journey to the land of the country you Americans despise and almost bombed back into the Stone Age.''

Harisomo cast his lord a doubtful look, but Osaka headed off any objections, lifted a hand. "Silence. My decision is made and it is final. This American is a warrior, a man of honor. I will not see him set upon like meat for wild animals. His time to die will come, an honor I will leave entirely to you.''

Finished with Harisomo, Osaka settled his piercing stare on Bolan. "Yes. I am sure you know about my brief oil endeavor in Iraq. I have personally met with Saddam Hussein, several times. We both share the same views. We both feel the West is no longer suitable to control the world, either by the sword or in the affairs of merchants. But we can't wait for your country to destroy itself. A most cherished shipment, one which Saddam is eager to receive and will pay me two billion American dollars from his pilfered oil money, is about to leave for Iraq.''

A chill went down the warrior's spine as the unthinkable boiled up in his thoughts. "Let me guess," Bolan said. "You're helping Saddam go nuclear.''

"The Iraqis, Mr. Powers, have been on the verge of going nuclear, as you put it, for some time. For almost a year I have been shipping fuel rods, component parts for a light-water reactor, plutonium scrap from disassembled warheads from as far away as the Ukraine. Today a final shipment of weapons-grade plutonium and enriched uranium 235, plus nearly a thousand pounds of zirconium, will be flown to Iraq, to be personally picked up by Saddam. I will spare you the details. Let us just say that money can buy anything, including silence, especially loyalty.

"Three jets of Osaka design, I call Firehawks, about to be placed on the international market as a rival to your Learjet, will fly a route that has already been secured and established with the help of an Indian colonel, Malik Puhjdani. Harisomo knows the way, and has flown into Iraq with Colonel Puhjdani personally to make prior deliveries. I have allies, contacts all over the world. One-time enemies, such as the North Koreans, are even now my allies.

"When the Iraqis were captured by you Americans the first time and it appeared my deal was in danger of falling apart, I decided to speed matters along. The North Koreans saw fit to deliver the necessary uranium and plutonium. What you do not know, but perhaps your country's Intelligence agencies may suspect, is that Iraq has an underground nuclear facility. With the help of a team of physicists from North Korea and India I will be flying to Iraq. It will be a matter of perhaps a mere few months before Iraq may even have a half-dozen ICBMs."

"What's the point, Osaka? What benefit would you get from helping a madman like Saddam Hussein build nuclear warheads? If a war starts in the Middle East, there goes a large source of energy for your own country. The flow of oil from the Persian

Gulf might stop altogether. Japan needs all the help it can get from outside petroleum suppliers.''

"This is not about oil. This is not about money. This is about honor, redress for the crimes committed against my ancestors. I am neither concerned about a war in the Middle East, nor whether my friend Saddam will lob a warhead into Israel and turn that part of the world into a glowing cinder. Creating a potential nuclear holocaust in that part of the world is merely a diversionary tactic. You Americans will certainly concentrate all your energy on the Iraqis, on saving your ally, Israel. Then I move in."

"How do Iraqi terrorists fit into your picture of the big sword?"

Osaka's gaze narrowed a little over the anger in Bolan's voice. "Abriz and Zabir are close to Saddam. He appears to trust them one hundred percent. He informed me those two must be the ones to transact the deal. I was introduced to Abriz and Zabir several years ago. We began together our plan to get Saddam what he so craved. With their contacts, with their pledge to Saddam that it could be done, the groundwork was laid for this, the final delivery, many months ago. Abriz and Zabir, with their contacts in the Republican Guard, know the safest passage into Iraq and have prearranged the logistics for delivery. If I did not show with them, the deal might have fallen through. They are revolutionary heroes, after all, in the eyes of their countrymen, and Saddam will most certainly honor them upon their safe return.

"However, I also suspect that Saddam left the matter of freeing the jihad heroes up to Osaka, to judge for himself how committed I was. Now he will see for himself just how serious I am. As soon as the Iraqis were freed and flown here safely, I had Saddam alerted through my contacts in the Middle East. He is eager to finish the deal."

Bolan noticed Osaka was again sweating. Only now his eyes were burning with the fires of his twisted conviction.

"I was always suspicious of your motives, Mr. Powers. However, I feel as if I have known you all of my life. Indeed, I believed a man such as yourself would one day come to assassinate me. Your business proposals would never have been honored, at least not by myself. I suspect now they were fraudulent, designed to get close to me for your assassination attempt. However, I had to meet the man I had suspected would come for my head. You are very clever. You have the soul of a samurai and all the right instincts that set you onto my trail like a wolf onto the scent of blood. That and the fact you saved my daughter's life are the only reasons I spare your life, at least for the present."

Attempts at flattery only stoked the fires of Bolan's anger. Too many good people had died as the result of Osaka's madness. Make no mistake, Osaka could gloss everything over with talk of honor, justice and redress, but the man was nothing more than a killer in the Executioner's eyes.

"You never answered my question, Osaka. How would a nuclear war benefit you or Japan?"

"While you Americans are looking the other way, perhaps even dreading the end of the world as you know it, Osaka Worldwide will move in on your biggest corporations. Already I have leverage buyouts working. I see IBM, MGM, General Motors all toppling to Osaka takeovers. Should those executives not wish to do business with Osaka, then perhaps I will send a ninja messenger to call upon them in the dead of night while they sleep the fat sleep of the rich, nestled in the bosoms of their wives. A sword to the throat can be the strongest of persuaders.

"I will own America, its largest conglomerates— they will fall, one by one, pawns at my whim. Your monopoly in international commerce will give way to the new and imperial Japan. My nation will dictate all terms. Trade sanctions? Well, a few heads will be lopped off in the night. Embargoes? Same thing. Loose tongues prepared to poison my good name with accusations and double-dealing? Cut out by the very same samurai sword, to be nailed to the front door of his home or office.

"Yes. You look at me as if I am insane. But who is going to stop me now? We of Osaka are unstoppable, indeed, have already proved we are invincible, that we are warriors of a divine destiny. You have already witnessed in Chicago what we are capable of." He paused, then added with the ghost of a smile, "Perhaps a further demonstration is necessary."

Bolan tensed as Osaka grunted another order for his samurai to leave the room. Long moments of silence hung thick with electric tension as Bolan met the piercing stares of Osaka and Harisomo. Shadows then fell over Bolan's back. Turning slightly, he found two young Japanese men, marched by the samurai to Osaka. Clearly terrified, both men bowed to Osaka, their bodies shaking so badly Bolan thought for a moment they might faint from fear.

Osaka looked at the Executioner. "These two traitors have shown their dishonor, their treachery. They have infiltrated Osaka, but they work for the Yakuza. Only last night they were seen in the presence of a hated enemy of mine, accepting their blood money."

Bolan knew what was coming next. Obviously so did the two men quaking before Osaka, both of the deemed traitors looking on the verge of begging for their lives. But like Osaka, they seemed to understand the concept of a moment of truth. Somehow they composed themselves to accept their fate.

Osaka stood, but didn't draw his sword. Once again Bolan detected what he believed was the faint shroud of light around Osaka's face. But the would-be shogun was no longer enraged. In fact, Bolan was almost amazed at how calm, almost serene Osaka appeared. The man didn't even seem to be breathing. But Bolan could be positive that, as a Zen practitioner, Osaka adhered to the rigorous daily exercises of the Zen master, where breathing, divine emptiness of the soul, was everything.

What caught Bolan by surprise was that Osaka didn't use his sword to kill one of the two men. Suddenly Osaka's hand speared into the chest of one of the alleged traitors. There was a soft squishing sound, followed by a sucking noise, as Bolan saw Osaka's hand disappear past the wrist into the man's chest. Before the victim even had time to react, Osaka wrenched his heart out. His face a death mask of eternal horror, the traitor crumpled to the floor, a boneless sack. Very little blood pooled around the man, but with no heart pumping blood, that was to be expected. Bolan never had any doubt about how dangerous Osaka was, but he didn't think he had ever crossed a more determined, more fearsome opponent.

"This is the heart of deceit, of dishonor," Osaka told Bolan.

"You, put your hands out and take this!" Osaka ordered the other man. Trembling, but looking relieved now that his life would be spared, the man held out his hands. Osaka then placed the flesh in the traitor's hands. A samurai quickly moved to Osaka with a cloth.

As Osaka toweled off the gore, he told the traitor, "Go back to Mitisuma and present your lord with that. Tell him the same fate will be delivered upon his head and the rest of his gangster family if I even hear a whisper of a rumor that he is plotting his vengeance against Osaka."

The traitor bowed and nodded while he was whisked away by a samurai.

Osaka retook his seat on the mat and settled his gaze on Bolan. "If you return from Iraq, Mr. Powers, then I will know that it is over. I will know my karma beyond any doubt. It will be my own moment of truth."

Harisomo stiffened at the challenge.

"Your bag with its weapons shall remain right here in this room," Osaka said.

Harisomo stood, bowed to Osaka, then told Bolan, "On your feet."

The Executioner didn't move right away. For a second the soldier pondered going for broke. Then he caught himself in the last instant, poised to suddenly lash out but grimly aware there was too much at stake to risk it all right then.

The source of potential Armageddon waited, thousands of miles to the west. Reason dictated Bolan stay hard, instinct telling him his time would come to strike.

Bolan was going to Iraq. He might have gotten the truth, but the war was far from being over. He decided the worst mistake Osaka had ever made in his life was letting him live.

Slowly the Executioner rose as several samurai approached him from the rear. Dismissed now, there was no bowing.

Without looking at Bolan, Osaka said, "Mr. Powers, kindly tell Saddam I send him my warmest regards and fond wishes for good health and good luck."

The parting shot, Bolan thought. So be it.

The Executioner told himself he was coming back to Japan. No matter what it took.

MAHMUD ABRIZ FELT electrified with unbridled jubilance. It was all he could do to sit still in the limousine as they pulled into the gigantic hangar of Osaka Airlines. He wasn't sure if he wanted to laugh out loud or weep with joy. Even nearby Mount Fuji, with its summit swathed in white mist, looked so truly majestic to Abriz, he imagined the blue sky perched on the summit was full of laughing, singing spirits, all praising the emerging victory of this Iraqi-Japanese alliance.

Ultimate triumph over the Great Satan was within the grasp of the Islamic world.

Certainly for the Iraqi leader of the Death Brigade, this was the end of a long and nightmarish ordeal that had begun with the fiasco in Beirut. But in a few short hours, half a day at best guess, he and his brothers would be landing in Iraq, there to be greeted with open arms by a personal visit from Saddam.

The Death Brigade leader sat with Zabir and six other brothers of the jihad. Faces beamed, eyes were ablaze with triumph, joy all around him. Abriz felt like a proud father to his brothers in the holy revolution. It was indeed a great day to be alive. They were going home, heroes.

They were conquerors, he believed, even in the eyes of the Japanese. It didn't seem to matter to Osaka and his samurai that they had almost blown the deal with their venture into America. What was done was done. Now was all that mattered. They had to show the samurai they were worthy of their honor.

Not only had the Japanese rescued them from a fate worse than death at the hands of the infidels, but the samurai had even treated them with utter graciousness, kindness almost, feeding them well, assuring them they would not have to wait much longer in the bunker. Patience. Everything was set. Saddam knew.

And the Suitcase from God was already loaded, he had earlier been informed by Harisomo. Yes, it was ready to fly to the bosom of his beloved Iraq in one of those three beautiful sleek superjets the samurai proudly called Firehawks.

The deal was done.

Surely God had blessed him with his own unique and divine destiny.

Abriz waited until the driver opened his door. His thoughts were consumed with glory. He was owed the world and all its riches. Every honor, respect and tribute worthy of a hero would be bestowed upon him by Saddam. Abriz was the new savior of the

Islamic world, after all, the spearhead of new Muslim conquest.

He was smiling as he saw the flurry of activity all over the hangar. More limos disgorged his brothers, and the two Indians stepped out, men who had been instrumental in securing the route across the Indian Ocean. From there they would fly right over Iran, all but blanking out radar screens along the way with the Osaka state-of-the-art radar scramblers. Harisomo had told him so. And so far Harisomo had proved himself nothing but a victorious warrior, a genius in strategy and tactics, on and off the battlefield. With that charisma of a natural born leader, he was a warrior who knew the hearts of men around him better than they knew themselves. This bold new samurai was full of confidence, untouchable, invincible.

They were natural allies, Abriz told himself.

Abriz could no longer contain himself. He started to hug his men, all of them quickly clasping arms, embracing each other, praising God. Finding a dozen samurai, armed to the teeth with submachine guns, assault rifles with fixed grenade launchers and those fearsome swords, Abriz wished Harisomo would arm him with at least one of those assault rifles. He would love nothing more than to step off the jet when they touched down, wielding his own rifle like the returning triumphant conqueror he was.

What a glorious day.

The future belonged to him, Abriz thought. No, the world would belong to him.

He was walking toward the lead limo, laughing eyes fixed on Harisomo, when his mood evaporated into confusion and cold fear. Just like that, it felt as if he had slammed into a wall. Freezing in midstride, Abriz watched, stunned, as the tall, dark-haired man with a face like death, with a nightmare visage from his not so distant past, emerged from the limo. How could it be? No, it was impossible!

It was the tall American commando.

Abriz felt his heart ready to explode from his chest, seeing the American just standing there, pinning him with that same death's-head stare he had seen in Beirut and beyond.

"Do you know who this man is?" Abriz demanded.

"We know all about this man!" Harisomo snarled, one hand falling over the hilt of his sword, appearing braced to head off a sudden lunge by Abriz for the American.

"What is going on? This is the man who captured us in Beirut!"

Abriz watched in utter disbelief as Harisomo glared at the American.

"It would seem you have been a very busy man, Mr. Powers," Harisomo said.

"Not busy enough," Bolan replied.

Abriz thought the unthinkable. He was being set up, betrayed on the eve of his greatest victory.

"I demand to know what is going on here," Abriz roared.

"I suggest you get control of yourself," Harisomo urged, the steel of a warning in his voice. "This man is my prisoner. We know who he is."

"Do you?"

"Yes. He will be flying with us to your country. There I shall decide what to do with him. Either way he is living on stolen time. I urge you, Abriz, to attempt nothing foolish. We have the situation under control."

Abriz shook with fury. His mind raced with fragmented pieces of a dozen terrible scenarios. Capture. Death. Betrayal. No, it couldn't be. Somehow the American had infiltrated the ranks of Osaka, and they had found him out. It was the only logical conclusion. The way the American held his ground, tight, wary but still measuring his surroundings with those eyes burning with tightly controlled violence... perhaps the Japanese did have the situation under control.

It helped Abriz resolve the matter when Zabir laid a hand on his shoulder.

"Let it be. We have trusted them this far."

"We must leave. In the first jet!" Harisomo ordered the Iraqis.

Abriz continued to stare angrily at Bolan, then couldn't resist the urge to show his former captor a smile. It came to the Iraqi's mind that maybe this wasn't so bad, after all, having the American go to Iraq with them.

Suddenly Mahmud Abriz determined he would find a way to kill the American himself. Just as he started to head for his assigned jet, one last vision of glory burned into the Iraqi's mind.

Abriz saw himself carrying the severed head of the tall American into the presidential palace, a tribute to Saddam, from one revolutionary hero to another.

LOOKING OUT the starboard window of the cabin from his position near the cockpit, Bolan used the rapidly shrinking summit of Mount Fuji as a gauge for their direction. They were flying due south on the opening leg, en route for the long run to Iraq, to deliver Armageddon to the most insane and evil dictator since Hitler.

With humankind closing down on the next century, the Executioner knew the nightmare scenario of an outlaw country such as an Iraq, Iran or North Korea going nuclear was a reality the free world was going to have to face. With all the arms dealers of every nation running wild to hawk their wares, with huge amounts of money floating all over the globe on international black markets, it was no stretch for a powerful and connected few to get their hands on plutonium scrap from warheads, supposedly disassembled under so-called new arms agreements.

Osaka had proved that to Bolan.

And it was a grim reality of the worst kind that Bolan now had to crush.

Starting at the end of the line with Saddam Hussein.

Mentally the soldier put together what he knew of the flight's logistics. Earlier Harisomo had boasted some about the Firehawk's capabilities, but hadn't given much firm detail on the superjet's specs. Nor had the scar-faced samurai told Bolan the exact route or how they would get into Iraq. Given what he'd seen so far, it wouldn't be much of a stretch, Bolan supposed, for Osaka's samurai to pull off the secret international flight, provided most of the run was clandestine. According to Harisomo, the Firehawk's top cruising speed was eight hundred miles per hour, and it could climb to thirty thousand feet. There was sophisticated radar-jamming equipment on the speedy birds, allegedly capable of even sending deflecting signals to U.S. AWACS. There'd been prior payoffs to necessary air-traffic control along the way, whoever and wherever that might be, with an assortment of Osaka samurai in place at ground control. Factoring in brief layovers at refueling stops, and figure them streaking above the Pacific at top or near top speed, Bolan guessed it would be at best a good fifteen-hour flight. It all depended, though, on a number of factors—weather, for one, as well as possible interception by U.S., even Russian fighter jets in the South China Sea and Indian Ocean. For damn sure, they wouldn't be cutting directly across

China, a country as historically paranoid and xenophobic as Stalin's Russia. And if Harisomo was worried about being intercepted by some F-16s, maybe over Subic Bay, then he sure as hell hadn't looked the least bit concerned to Bolan.

Osaka, Bolan had already seen, wasn't motivated by logic or even fear of discovery or reprisal. No, the new would-be shogun and his samurai were guided solely by rage and vengeance. It was a dangerous combination, but it was the same time bomb the Executioner felt ticking away in his own gut. And he couldn't help but wonder how many others in top positions at Osaka Worldwide and beyond, cloaking themselves in legitimacy, might be involved in the Osaka nuclear conspiracy.

Bolan went through a quick assessment of the numbers and hardware he'd seen before boarding the Firehawk. There were thirty or so Iraqis and what he supposed was a six-man team of North Korean physicists on one of the two other superjets. Figure fifteen samurai, outfitted in traditional black *gi*, toting long and short swords. All of them were bolstered with firepower, ranging from M-16s with attached M-203 grenade launchers to Ingrams and Uzis. A few samurai had holstered side arms, and the Executioner had spotted two MM-1 Multiround Projectile Launchers. All of it was the exact same kind of hardware he'd seen used in the slaughter in the streets of Chicago. He couldn't help but wonder how many of the ninja killers aboard the jets had been responsible for the deaths of countless innocents, dozens of lawmen in America. How many lives shattered and ruined forever? How many more lives about to be potentially destroyed if Osaka's lethal cargo reached the hands of the Iraqis?

However the flight panned out, the Executioner was determined to be ready when they touched down in Iraq. It helped Bolan to focus on the task at hand knowing that his own personal Armageddon wasn't imminent. He was almost one hundred percent certain Harisomo wouldn't make a killing move on his head until the deal was finalized on Iraqi soil.

In a face-to-face with Saddam Hussein.

The Executioner kept feeling the stares of samurai behind him, boring into his head. Also aft, the two Indians had been ordered to take their places by Harisomo.

For some time the scar-faced samurai had been in the cockpit with his three-man aircrew, door closed. Bolan didn't think he would have to worry about a sword spearing through the back of his seat, with or without Harisomo present, but he kept his senses on full alert, ready to strike back in the blink of any eye. Just in case.

A firefight at thirty thousand feet, though, would prove suicidal for all concerned.

By all and every means available, the Executioner grimly intended to reach his destination. When they would land in Iraq, he had no idea, couldn't even measure time. Before boarding the Firehawk, Harisomo had ordered Bolan to remove his watch. Why, the soldier couldn't be certain, but he figured Harisomo was playing some psy-war with him instead of indulging in petty larceny. Leave the American stuck and steaming for long, timeless hours in the air to sweat out his inevitable fate.

Finally Harisomo emerged from the cockpit.

Bolan met the samurai's gaze as the Japanese stood in the aisle. Hate-filled eyes sought out the Executioner.

"You can relax, Powers-*san*. The Iraqis are in another Firehawk. And you need not worry about my claiming your head. At least not now. If you wish, you need not even remain in your assigned seat." Harisomo nodded at an empty seat, across the aisle, which faced aft.

"Most hospitable, Harisomo-*san*. I'll keep it in mind."

"Well, keep this in mind, also. I have seen the hatred the Iraqis have for you. Exactly what happened in Beirut, I do not know, nor care to know. But I will not allow them to kill you. That privilege will be mine alone."

"I'll keep that in mind, as well."

And Bolan would. It could prove to be his moment of opportunity, with the Japanese and Iraqis bitterly arguing over who was to have "the honor" of taking their hated enemy's head. While they debated over who was owed his blood more, Bolan would strike. Maybe.

Harisomo chuckled. "You are a fool. You are weak just like all of you Westerners. Even when you win in war, you lose, you set yourselves up for future disaster. Your country's single greatest mistake, its foolishness, its lack of warrior character, showed when you did not go all the way to Baghdad during your Gulf War. Had your tanks and aircraft reduced that city to smoldering ash, had your soldiers been brave enough to engage in hand-to-hand street fighting to dig out, then execute Saddam, you would not be facing this crossroads of destiny. Saddam was beaten, but not defeated.

"Your lack of good judgment, your inability to see the way, will come back to haunt you. Does it not strike you as strange, that even after you defeated Japan and Germany in World War II, that both our respective countries have emerged from the ashes to become the leading titans in the world's economy? Instead of completely crushing us, subjugating us, you helped us rebuild. What manner of conqueror does that to a vanquished enemy?"

Bolan paused while Harisomo gloated. There was steel in Bolan's voice as he told Harisomo, "Something strikes me as even more strange, Harisomo. You and Osaka and your ninja killers all talk about honor and respect. Something you fail to understand is that those virtues cut both ways. To get you have to give. You act as if you're entitled to tribute, that honor and respect should be thrown all over you just because you think you've had a tough time of it.

Those Western soldiers you mentioned, too many of whom clearly sacrificed their lives against a defined wrong, they displayed true honor in also doing their damnedest to not kill innocents. Their duty was real.''

"There is nothing honorable when your enemy is beneath your boot heel and you allow him to live to kill you another day. It is weakness.''

"That's the thing that obviously escapes you. Sometimes true honor appears weak. Only because real honor allows for other men to judge themselves by their own actions. The code of Bushido even comes complete with the virtues of compassion, even forgiveness—under certain circumstances.''

"There is no comparison between us and you.''

"You're right about that. There is no comparison.''

Harisomo clenched his jaw. For a dangerous moment Bolan was tensed to make his move, certain Harisomo would draw his sword.

"You think you're the real thing, then draw it,'' Bolan taunted.

Harisomo's eyes burned with fierce hate for another stretched second, then he shook his head. "No. In time. You will know when.''

As Harisomo lingered for a moment before striding on, Bolan kept himself poised for the samurai to strike. He had issued the challenge, but was certain Harisomo wouldn't strike. Not yet. The man wanted him to sweat it out, ponder his fate, Bolan believed.

The samurai was holding hard to that moment when he could claim his trophy. Bolan was sure the man wanted to do it, or make the attempt, but before Saddam's eyes. It would be a display of his power, the crowning achievement for Osaka's top ninja assassin. Of course, if Bolan mentioned Miji, he strongly suspected the moment would erupt. But he wasn't looking to antagonize Harisomo into the ultimate moment of truth. Not yet.

The Executioner decided it might be best to take that seat across the aisle, after all, to keep his back to the wall, eyes on the enemy.

THE HOURS DRAGGED BY. For an endless stretch, they had been flying due west, gaining time, soaring with the sun to their backs. When they hit a break in the cloud cover, Bolan found they were streaking, maybe twenty thousand feet, over an infinite expanse of velvet blue sea. What appeared to be giant coral rings began to break up the ocean floor. Islands, somewhere in the Indian Ocean, the warrior supposed.

From his aft seat, the wiry, swarthy Colonel Puhjdani, looking out the window, confirmed they were over the Maldive Islands.

Perhaps an hour earlier they had landed for a brief refueling stop on a remote island where a landing strip had been cut out of the jungle. Obviously Harisomo's main concern was keeping the Firehawk fuel tanks topped. Bolan's guess would be the speedy birds, with their loads and pushing top cruising speed at high altitude, were eating up fuel at a hungry pace.

The Indian colonel, and another dark, hawk-faced man Harisomo had addressed as Captain Sanji had both informed the samurai their flight was secured. They knew exactly where all the air and warship ports of call were located. As long as their radar scramblers were operating, there should be no problem clearing any airspace monitored by the Americans or the British. Too much ocean, too many ships, too much air traffic for anyone to be concerned with three private jets, the Indian colonel announced.

Following that reassurance, there was a brief but heated exchange between the Indians and Harisomo, concerning money. The Indians didn't think they were getting enough for their part in the deal. Harisomo, in his usual angry way that always held the threat of sudden violence, told the Indians the money matter had already been settled.

Apparently it hadn't, at least not in the minds of the Indians.

From his new seat facing aft, Bolan watched. The soldier sensed Harisomo was going to head off any discussion about money, quickly and in his own way. Murder instantly flared to life in Harisomo's eyes when the Indian colonel said, "You are getting, what, two billion of Saddam's plundered oil money for this delivery? We are getting a mere two million. A pittance. We played no small part in this shipment."

"You are getting paid in American dollars, not worthless rupees," Harisomo replied.

Bolan watched the scar on the samurai's face start to pulse with simmering fury.

"Without us," Captain Sanji said, "your airspace off the coast of India would never have been secured."

"What's more, we are the ones who erected the refueling site near Bombay," Puhjdani injected. "But you seem to have chosen to strike out on your own and build your own refueling depots. This was not my understanding of how our flight was to go. It would appear to us you are not acting in good faith. Do not forget, we still have six of our own Indian nuclear physicists to pick up and fly with your team of North Koreans to Saddam."

Harisomo's gaze narrowed. "There has been a change in plans. We won't be needing your landing site."

"What?" Puhjdani snarled.

Bolan watched as the colonel's hand slid toward his holstered pistol.

"This is an outrage!" Sanji rasped.

"You will fly with us into Iraq," Harisomo said. "Once the deal is finished, we will return you to this port of call you erected for us. We have plenty of fuel. Once my money is secured, then you shall be paid."

"No. This is not the way it was supposed to be," Puhjdani shouted, trembling with suppressed rage.

"You are whining, Colonel."

"Whining!"

"Take caution in your tone."

"You have not even seen fit to show us our money yet! Now it would seem you do not even have it."

Harisomo's voice was cold, controlled. "Are you telling me you do not wish to fly with us to Iraq?"

"Precisely," Puhjdani said. "I have been flown halfway around the world, fulfilling my end of our deal, risking everything. I demand you honor your end of our bargain this second."

"Very well."

Bolan knew it was coming as soon as Harisomo dropped a hand over the hilt of his sword. In one swift motion Harisomo drew the blade and leaped to his feet. For a critical microsecond the Indians sat, frozen in disbelief. Before either man could even open his mouth, the sword flashed. If there was any doubt in Bolan's mind about Harisomo's fearsome skill with the weapon, it vanished in the blink of an eye.

Two eye blinks actually.

Two heads were lopped off with the same lightning stroke, a blinding sweep of steel driving so easily through flesh and bone it looked no harder than slicing through a thin piece of cheese.

Puhjdani's head spun through the air, thudded to the plush carpet and rolled several feet down the aisle, while Sanji's expression of naked fear thunked into his lap. The Indian captain's bulging eyes stared up at the geyser of blood jetting from the stump of his neck. Both headless corpses sat perfectly upright, arms twitching in dying nervous spasms.

None of the other samurai had appeared to even flinch over the decapitating blows.

Harisomo turned and pinned Bolan with wild eyes, the samurai clearly still seized by feverish bloodlust. The samurai tapped the chest of Puhjdani, as if warning Bolan his time would also soon come.

# CHAPTER NINETEEN

*Iraq*

The nightmare deal of the century was going down.

From his window Bolan watched as the Firehawk descended for what appeared to be a long ribbon of asphalt, cutting arrow straight between what looked like two walled cities. Whether it was a runway or a highway, Bolan didn't know, couldn't tell. But there was company waiting down there, including two Soviet-made heavy-lift choppers, possibly Mil Mi-10s, maybe superlift Halos needed to haul off the nuclear payload. Even with those deep shadows of dusk stretching over the jagged hills of the lunar landscape in this part of Iraq, Bolan counted at least a half-dozen vehicles, and twice as many stick figures that quickly grew into armed men. Headlights on, jeeps and transport trucks basked the runway in a heavy glow, with flares lining the landing strip on both sides to guide the aircraft in. For the past hour Harisomo had been in the cockpit, making final preparations, no doubt.

Harisomo reappeared and took his seat aft. No one buckled up. Somehow even that made sense to Bolan. If they went skipping off the runway or flipped end over end on a disastrous landing, with the deadly cargo they carried...well, spreading a radioactive superhazard over half the Iraqi countryside would be the last thing any of them would have to worry about.

They touched down, bounced, then Bolan braced himself to ride out the long taxi. Just before the Firehawk stopped, Harisomo and his samurai were up and moving for the door. Harisomo ordered Bolan on his feet.

The three-man flight crew was ordered off the jet first. Harisomo told his samurai to lock and load, safeties off their weapons. It paid to be cautious. Saddam was Saddam, after all.

The door opened, and Bolan was marched down the ramp, into the stifling heat. The Iraqis, the respective flight crews and the North Koreans disgorged from the two other Firehawks.

"Stay right here," Harisomo ordered Bolan. "In two minutes I will send for you. I suggest you make your peace with God."

As the Japanese strode off, the Executioner found himself flanked by two samurai. One man wielded an Uzi subgun with plenty of clips in his obi, while the other killer cradled an MM-1, an M-16 slung over one shoulder. It was just the kind of firepower Bolan needed. Maybe, he thought, a divine wind had blown his way, after all.

Adrenaline racing, Bolan watched the large group move into a no-man's-land off the runway. He took in his surroundings, spotting to the west the domed minarets of two mosques rising from the shadows. Recalling what he'd seen from the air, the soldier knew the Russian choppers were hidden now from view, beyond the mosques. On his left flank he noted a large lion statue, beyond which stretched some ruins leading into the walled city. The Executioner was planning ahead, already knowing what he was going to do, what he had to do. Strike. Cover. Hit and run. Take them as they came.

First he had to seize the moment. The doomsday numbers were ticking down hard.

The Executioner peered into the large group. Enemy range was thirty yards. Cannibals all nice and packed. A tall Iraqi in a black beret and the dark green uniform of the Republican Guard rolled up to meet Harisomo. Meanwhile Bolan saw a few of the Iraqis, including Abriz, actually fall to their knees to kiss the ground. The Executioner thought he glimpsed disgust on Harisomo's face over this display, but Bolan's only concern was the moment when the samurai would call for his head.

Bolan listened as Harisomo greeted the six-man contingent of Iraqi soldiers.

"Colonel Barak, a pleasure once again. I trust President Hussein is on hand."

Barak bowed. "Indeed."

One of the soldiers got on a hand-held radio. Obviously Bolan was a mere few minutes away from laying eyes on the most infamous megalomaniac since Hitler—minutes he didn't have. While the Iraqis embraced and the Republican Guard congratulated Abriz and Zabir on their success, Harisomo drew his sword.

"I have something I would like to present President Hussein," Bolan heard Harisomo say to Barak.

Bolan caught the hard looks thrown his way.

There it was. The moment of truth.

In the distance Bolan spotted a rolling wall of uniformed men, marching hard for the aircraft. As they closed, became starkly outlined in the glow of flares and vehicle headlights, Bolan saw the infamous black beret, recognized the mustache, that world-renowned dark uniform loosely fit on a narrow-shouldered, potbellied frame.

Saddam Hussein.

"Bring me the American!" Harisomo bellowed.

It was now or never, Bolan knew. If he was led into the large group, it was over. It would be perfect to wait until Saddam was right there among the group, but the Executioner couldn't wait any longer.

With the Iraqis embroiled in ongoing congratulations, Bolan seized the moment. The samurai with the Uzi lowered his weapon and reached out to touch Bolan.

The Executioner exploded, delivering sudden death in the span of two heartbeats. Bolan crushed the man's windpipe with a single blow from the side of his hand. Following up with the same lightning speed, he speared an elbow into the other samurai's nose, drilling cartilage and lethal fragments of bone into the man's brain. It took a long moment for the enemy in no-man's-land to register what was happening. But no sooner were Bolan's first two victims crunching to the hard-packed soil than the big American was grabbing up the Uzi.

Judgment day took them by surprise.

The Executioner's first wave of subgun fire got their full and undivided attention. Downrange at least a half dozen of the enemy were toppling under the raking stream of the 9 mm lead, chopped up, screaming, into bloody rags.

It didn't take long, though, for return fire to come tracking for Bolan. With all those enemy numbers packed tight together, it was difficult for him to tell who he was dropping during his initial onslaught. Panic set in right away from the killing ground, and Iraqis, mostly, were nose-diving out of the line of Bolan's sweeping fire or bowling over samurai.

From somewhere in the scrambling mass, Bolan heard Harisomo's roar, "Don't fire at the American! You will hit the aircraft! Move out!"

Bolan's position near the Firehawk bought him a few more precious seconds, allowed him the critical moment to snatch up four spare clips for the Uzi, tuck them in his waistband, haul in the MM-1 and get moving for cover. Beyond his gun sights he glimpsed Saddam's phalanx ushering him back toward to the edge of the low-lying stone buildings. Evac. Dammit.

No matter what it took, Bolan intended to score the world's biggest kill of a tyrant to date. Firing the Uzi on the run, he secured cover near the lion statue.

Then three figures stumbled out of the duststorm. Even at a distance, the Executioner recognized Abriz and the man he believed was Zabir. It was too good an opportunity to pass up. Having captured Abriz in Beirut, lost him in Chicago, then chased him more than halfway around the world, nearly encircling the earth to bring the Iraqi down, Bolan knew he might not get another chance. With the enemy in disarray, Bolan stole a few more critical heartbeats. But the lull would be brief, he knew, before even more savage return fire sought him out.

For some unknown reason, Abriz froze. Another split second of hesitation allowed Zabir to bump into him, then Abriz lunged for a nearby discarded M-16.

Slinging the Uzi, Bolan lifted the MM-1 in a rock-steady double-fisted grip. He locked on and triggered the 40 mm warhead, zeroing in for Abriz, a streaking magnet of death.

The Iraqi terrorist leader's mouth opened, but the scream was lost as the missile slammed him, dead center in the chest.

Abriz and ten other terrorists were instantly vaporized inside the whooshing fireball. It was overkill, to be sure, but Bolan wanted the man out of the picture.

Gone with no doubt to spare.

The cleansing flames of a warrior on a righteous rampage continued to sweep up still more enemy numbers as the Executioner pounded their ranks with another thundering HE warhead. One more flesh-consuming ball of fire from the MM-1, and Bolan rolled back the samurai charge on his flank.

Armed with the Uzi and MM-1, Bolan plunged past the crumbled ruins, on a grim hunt for Saddam Hussein.

Now that he had started the killhunt, Bolan knew there was only one way to finish it. It was every man for himself, with only the quickest, mean-est and most determined warrior to prevail. And get-ting stranded in Iraq was the last of his concerns.

No one was going home.

Only moments earlier Bolan had heard Hariso-mo's voice in the distance, raging for whatever was left of his samurai to find the American. So Hari-somo had survived the initial blitz.

So be it.

Hugging the facades of the stone dwellings, fresh clip in his Uzi, Bolan swiftly moved on, his death-sights fixed on the mosques to the west. There he spotted the billowing dust storm, heard the whapping bleat of the Russian transport choppers. Checking his rear and flanks, Bolan found Iraqis huddled in doorways or creeping for the safety of their respective abodes. War had come to their ancient city, and it was obvious to the Executioner they wanted no part of the kill-or-be-killed scenario. Innocents here, Bolan strongly supposed, were not about to interfere. Saddam's cruelty, atrocities committed against his own people, especially the Kurds, was enough for all innocents concerned to hear no evil, speak no evil.

The choppers loomed above the mosques.

Bolan laid down the Uzi and hit a combat crouch beside a doorway. He took the MM-1 by its pistol grip, lifting the squat twenty pounds of rocket launcher. Less than a hundred yards from the evacuating choppers, the soldier was well within the weapon's effective range. Nine HE rounds remained in the 12-round rotating chamber. If he had to, he would expend every last round to bring down those choppers in a blaze of fireballs.

The Executioner sighted on the lead chopper, locked on and felt his finger start to tighten on the trigger. One deep breath steadied his aim.

And they came barreling around the corner, dead ahead.

Three samurai ran directly in Bolan's deathsights, their subguns swinging his way. The Executioner adjusted his aim, lowered the rocket launcher and belched a warhead at the samurai trio. He was forced to hit the ground as scorching lead bit off stone fragments beside his face.

The concussive roar sounded downrange, taking

shredded stick figures to the sky on a blinding wave of rolling fire.

Looking up, Bolan found the choppers veering away, shrinking rapidly to the west. Deal of a lifetime or not, he could see it was obvious the Iraqis were concerned only for the safety of their leader. At the first sign of a problem, they had bolted.

On his feet, the Executioner was about to charge off in pursuit for one final shot at the choppers, hauling in his Uzi, when he instinctively turned to check his rear, sensing sudden movement from behind.

He was just in time to see steel arching for his neck.

Reacting instantly, Bolan threw up the Uzi. At the last split second before razor-sharp steel would have sliced his head clean off at the shoulders, the Executioner deflected the blade with the subgun, taking the jarring impact to the marrow of his bones. He was knocked off balance, but not hard enough that he couldn't duck the next sweeping blow for his head. Before he even made out the face of his attacker, instinct told the Executioner he was face-to-face with Harisomo.

The Japanese assassin's decapitating attempt bit deep into the stone wall beside Bolan. Pure rage and hate stared back at the Executioner. There would be no technique, no style here.

Every move was straight ahead, meant to kill in the blink of an eye.

The Executioner swung up the Uzi to try to disembowel his opponent with a quick burst, but the scar-faced samurai thrust out a hand, obviously anticipating the lethal move. Before he knew it, Bolan was locked in a death grapple, the Uzi forced to the side, jumping and flaming in his hand. With his other fist the soldier grabbed Harisomo's sword hand. Fury felt like a living force, magnetizing Bolan to Harisomo as they spun, a human whirlwind. A heartbeat later they were crashing through a flimsy wooden door, pounding onto stone flooring. Still locked on, the soldier hauled Harisomo to his feet. The samurai speared a knee into Bolan's gut, but the Executioner tightened his stomach muscles at the last second, absorbing the impact without having precious wind driven from his lungs.

Bolan turned up the bloody heat, smashing Harisomo's nose to a squelching spray with two vicious head-butts. Somehow the Japanese found reserves of ferocity, driving a knee into the soldier's solar plexus. This time there was enough force behind the blow to punch some wind from Bolan's lungs. The Uzi dropped from Bolan's hand.

The sound of the weapon clattering to the floor propelled a fresh wave of urgency through the Executioner. With all the might he possessed, he grabbed his enemy's shirtfront, then lifted and hurled him across the room, where Harisomo hammered into the far wall.

Through the ringing in his ears, the Executioner made out the distant sounds of autofire from somewhere down the street, closing fast.

He knew enemy reinforcements could surge through the door at any second. It was time to finish Harisomo. Bolan swept on for his Uzi.

Across the room Harisomo got to one knee and was drawing his short sword.

After all the innocent blood the Executioner knew this man had shed, there was no way Bolan would allow the samurai to go out his way. There would be no seppuku, the warrior's way of honor in death, for Harisomo.

Still the man managed to drive the blade into his stomach. But before the samurai managed the final cutting thrust, Bolan loosed a burst from the Uzi, the steady stream of slugs pinning the samurai to the wall.

Before the echo of killing shots faded and Harisomo slid to the floor, a boneless sack, Bolan spotted shadows stretching across the doorway.

A voice called out, "Mr. Powers, I am Tanawa Yakata, the pilot of your Firehawk. I am here to help you. The others, they are either dead or dying. I am with my copilot, Kyoto Nagashina, and our radioman, Owara Asakura."

Bolan wasn't about to trust any truce, peace offering or insinuations of help. But there was something in the man's voice that sounded honest. Not to mention he needed help to get out of Iraq, back to Japan.

"Skip the formalities," Bolan said, ramming a fresh clip into his Uzi. "Throw down your weapons and step inside. Hands up. I'll decide if you're sincere or not.''

Subguns clattered into the doorway. One by one they stepped inside, hands held high. Bolan recognized the flight crew of his Firehawk.

"Please, Mr. Powers, there is not much time. We can get you safely back to Japan. Our only honor anymore is our word to you. You must trust us.''

"Looks like I'm going to have to do just that.''

Before he left, Bolan claimed Harisomo's scabbard, then retrieved the cherished sword of the legendary Yokitomo.

If for nothing else than to return to Japan to deliver to Osaka his own moment of truth.

The warrior way.

*Japan*

MIJI OSAKA FOUND her father, alone in the Zen garden. It was the dead of night. A sea of stars and a full moon glittered from a velvet heaven, adding to the illumination of the lantern her father carried. She wondered how long he had been standing there, staring at the perfectly raked rows of white pebbles. Staring, it seemed, at nothing. There was the strangest expression on her father's face, and the look frightened her.

Venturing a few steps closer to him, she clearly saw the naked torment on his face. And her father was drenched in sweat. The fever.

Still, observing him from a safe distance, she was amazed that he showed no outward signs of pain or discomfort, no grimace, no clenching of teeth.

Suddenly the pain faded in his eyes, gone the way of a fleeting wisp of smoke. She watched as a look of odd, childlike innocence, a serenity, molded his features. It was as if, she thought, her father had just come to terms with some great and awful truth. For a second she was ashamed of herself for intruding on her father's privacy.

No matter what she was seeing right then, she knew the Osaka empire was in dire trouble.

First a warning had come out of Tokyo from one of their sources close to the Yakuza. Sometime tomorrow the gangsters, it was rumored, were going to attack them. It didn't bolster her confidence knowing the castle was now only protected by a mere skeleton force of fifteen samurai.

Worse, there had been no word from Harisomo, no radio message. Via satellite linkup, even from thousands of miles away Harisomo could raise them from the Firehawks. And even though she knew her father had ordered no radio contact with the castle until Harisomo was safely returning to Japan, for fear of their signals being intercepted, something was wrong—she could feel it. It flickered through her mind that if something disastrous happened in Iraq to disrupt, possibly even shatter, her father's ultimate moment of triumph, then Michael Powers, the traitor, had something to do with it. Rage burned in her heart for a long moment as she thought of how easily she had given herself to the American. Like some schoolgirl with a crush. Like that whore she had always wanted to be, but could never allow herself to become because of her heritage, tradition.

Her heart grew heavy the longer she watched her father, standing, unmoving, looking so lonely, dressed in his formal samurai dress. Even with his long and short swords firmly secured around his waist, she wasn't sure he was ready to fight.

Agony, and fear of tomorrow, gripped her heart. If she didn't know better, she would have sworn her father looked defeated, on the verge of despair.

It would appear she might have to take matters into her own hands, solidify the force at the castle to repel, then crush any attempted Yakuza storm.

The worst possible thought of all then consumed her mind.

If it was over, if her father was planning his own ritual suicide, then she would inherit the kingdom.

By herself. Alone. The last known living Osaka.

As if sensing her presence, her father suddenly sought her out in the shadows. A gentle smile stretched his lips.

"Miji. My dearest Miji. Come here. Allow your father to hold you."

With wooden legs she went to her father, fell into his embrace. In his arms now, she could feel the power and the awful heat radiating from inside his body. Never had her father shown her this depth of tender feeling. Indeed, ever since she was a child, he had almost always treated her with a distant coolness, that reserve and the measure of others a man used when dealing with samurai.

Never like a daughter.

It was all she could do to choke back the tears.

Why did she suddenly feel this would be the last night of the Osaka empire, that they were on the eve of their total annihilation? Was it something she had seen in her father's eyes, some warning that was telling her he had seen the future?

"I was just thinking of your brothers, your mother. Their spirit is here, Miji. Right here. I just saw them. They said they are waiting for us."

Hearing the faintest cracking of emotion in her father's voice, she squeezed her eyes shut, fought back the tears. It was worse than she could have imagined. For years she had dreaded this moment.

The fever had finally eaten up her father's mind.

He was insane.

*Over the Indian Ocean*

FOUR HOURS OUT OF IRAQ, somewhere over the Indian Ocean, they went in for a landing at one of the fuel depots. And damn near on fumes.

Bolan moved out of the cockpit, having already taken in the lit runway. Whether it was one of the two refuel sites they previously used, he couldn't be sure, didn't ask. But it looked the same, a long, narrow runway cut through the jungle foliage of a remote island, east of the Maldives. So far so good.

Before taking his seat, Uzi subgun in hand, Bolan looked back at Yakata. "Four, you said."

The pilot nodded. "A skeleton crew."

The SOS had just gone out, radio contact established with the ground force. Hopefully the cover story Yakata had given the ground force about the other two Firehawks being forced to land at the Bombay depot for emergency maintenance would hold up. Bolan wanted the four-man samurai force on the ground, at the ramp and in his face, when he emerged. Yakata informed him it would go down exactly as he wanted—quick and ugly.

"From here, how much longer to Japan?"

"Twelve hours, if we push it, with luck," Yakata said. "Sometime late tomorrow morning, noon, at worst."

"Our luck damn well better hold."

The warning was not lost on Yakata. "Please, Mr. Powers. I have explained. This was to be our last mission to Iraq. What Osaka has done, it is wrong, a great evil. We knew about you."

"Yeah. Bad news travels fast."

"And at the breath of the same divine wind now guiding us. Either way, had you not been there in Iraq, we would have acted in the same warrior manner you displayed. We would have succeeded in defeating Harisomo and leaving intact with their nuclear poison, or we would have died in the attempt. We will get you back to Japan.''

"One last thing," Bolan said. "I assume you can contact Osaka once we reach Japanese airspace?''

"We can do it from as far away as two thousand miles, if you wish.''

"No. Once we're near the coast, I want you to send a message to whoever is at the other end. I want the message to get to Harry Osaka. The message is, 'A divine wind from the West will be delivering a moment of truth to the house of Osaka.'''

"Understood.''

Moments later they hit a hard landing, then rolled to a stop. On his feet, Bolan rammed a fresh clip into his Uzi, hearing Yakata say that the four-man crew was converging on the Firehawk armed with submachine guns.

Bolan opened the hatchway and cut loose.

The four-man samurai force never knew what hit them.

*Japan*

ARATA MITISUMA and his thirty-man assassin squad disgorged from six limousines and two Cadillacs. The Yakuza boss, wielding his own Ingram submachine gun, listened as his soldiers rammed clips into their own SMGs or assault rifles and chambered the first rounds.

It was close to noon. The sun now blazed from a

cloudless sky, basking the castle in glittering rays, the gables of the famed Osaka fortress rising to the northern distance. The Osaka legend, Mitisuma thought, was about to come to an abrupt end.

First they would have to move up the two twisting paths between a variety of trees, with other tangled brush off the sides of the trails obscuring their view of the wall around the moat. They'd cross in two teams over the twin drawbridges and from there, race across the courtyard into the castle. His orders were explicit. Nothing was to be left breathing. And the head of Osaka belonged to him and him alone. Of course, Mako Nagachi had been promised the daughter. Nagachi was, after all, Mitisuma's top and most trusted lieutenant, worthy of such an honor.

The Osakas had been a force in Japan for too long. The end would come in shame, dishonor and blood for all who dwelled in the castle.

Mitisuma put his mind to this task, for victory hadn't been assured yet. His only pleasure would come when he cut off Osaka's head. Beyond that he would let others carve his legend in samurai folklore.

He sifted through his intelligence gathering one last time. During the night Mitisuma had sent soldiers through the empty maze of streets of the castle town on recon. Samurai quarters, villas and gardens were vacant, but he had expected as much. What he didn't expect was the report that the castle appeared deserted at first. Then his recon force said they eventually spotted two sentries, moving just outside the front gates.

Mitisuma had already determined there would be no night strike. He knew all too well the dark powers of ninja assassins who could cloak themselves with the night and strike out of nowhere. By daylight the boss figured he stood a much better chance. Full frontal assault. No ninja boiling up out of the blackness. No sudden flashes of steel.

He gave the order, and his force moved out. Maybe it was his paranoia, or natural instinct honed razor sharp for danger. Whatever it was, something suddenly felt wrong as soon as he led his own team deep into the shadows of the trail. He thought he saw the foliage overhead move.

Then he was certain of it.

They dropped out of the sky. Before they even got off the first rounds from their submachine guns, Mitisuma witnessed that fearsome steel flashing, cutting into necks, sending severed heads flying through the air. Since the ninja were garbed in the dark gray khaki for daylight attack, he hadn't seen them at first glance.

Mitisuma held back on the trigger of his Ingram, spraying the woods in all directions as darting shadows converged on his men.

For a moment he couldn't believe what he was seeing: steel was taking on and winning against automatic weapons. What foolishness was this? Swords against bullets?

Mitisuma couldn't deny what he saw. It was madness, but if he didn't do something quickly, he would be defeated before the battle even began.

The Yakuza boss got lucky with a long burst that kicked two ninja into the brush. Then he raced up the trail, gripped in a feverish bloodlust to kill Osaka. Even if the ninja tracked him down, Mitisuma would see Osaka dead first.

THEY WERE WITHIN a five-mile sighting of the Osaka castle, closing hard and low. It was high noon by Bolan's best guesstimate. Just outside the cockpit doorway, the Executioner gave the flight crew a long look, knew his gratitude wasn't lost on them. And Bolan's message had been received, right at the Osaka castle.

"I trust you found the parachute in the back, Mr. Powers?" Yakata said.

"I'm looking right at it."

"Good luck. We will take it from here, I assure you."

"You've honored your word. I have no doubt you'll make it to Narita."

"An emergency landing, yes, then we will inform the proper authorities."

Bolan had already given Yakata Brognola's emergency number to call. After agreeing the danger of landing at Osaka's private airport was too great, the contingency plan was laid to send out the SOS to Narita traffic control. The Executioner trusted these men to fulfill their duty. He had no doubt the nuclear cargo would fall into the right hands.

"You have the number, and I urge you to use it. My man in the States will know what to do," Bolan said.

The Executioner quickly shrugged on the chute's pack.

## CHAPTER TWENTY

Bolan was falling hard and fast, angling in on the courtyard from the east. As he plunged for the castle, the Executioner found a raging battle waiting at the end of his drop. Men with automatic weapons and gray-cloaked ninja fighting one another in the courtyard with all the fury of a samurai who knew there was no tomorrow, only honor in the now of death.

East, Bolan glimpsed the luxury cars, the bodies sprawled on the trail leading to the walls of the fortress, and realized he was dropping into a full-scale war between the Yakuza and Osaka's last stand of samurai.

Right before he landed, Bolan spotted the Shinto shrine, looming above the tree line, two hundred yards or so west of the castle. A lone figure was slowly moving into the structure. Even at a distance, the soldier recognized the unmistakable shape and gait of Harry Osaka.

First things first, though. Bolan needed to crush any gunman or sword-wielding ninja who might pick up his trail to the shrine.

That was all provided, of course, he took care of grim business at the castle.

Using the risers, and maybe with a little help from a divine wind at his back, Bolan came in from behind the two battling groups.

The Executioner hit the ground hard at the end of his six-hundred-foot combat drop, took the jarring impact on a roll as soon as his feet touched the courtyard. The pack was off and the chute was billowing behind him when he came up, holding back on the Uzi's trigger. He caught the first wave of enemy near the steps by deadly surprise. A half-dozen gangsters and several ninja were swept up in the relentless wave of 9 mm flesh-shredders.

Bolan fired on the run, expended the clip, then rammed home a fresh magazine. Shadows were now retreating into the castle.

Uzi poised, the soldier barreled through the front door, primed to drop anything that rolled into his sights.

They were battling one another in the hallway. Neither side was prepared to yield the first inch of real estate. Ninja steel flashed and took heads while Yakuza submachine guns stammered and flamed all over the hallway, at point-blank range. Two gangsters wheeled on Bolan as he surged through the doorway.

The lone warrior helped both sides eliminate each other.

The Executioner ventilated flesh with a long

sweeping burst that kicked ninja and gangster alike through sliding doors, hurling them down the hall.

One of the gangsters was crawling along the floor, trailing a slick pool of crimson.

"Nagachi!"

Combat senses on full alert, Bolan ventured down the hall. He was about to put the gangster out of his misery forever, when a figure with a face like a man-eating shark whirled from the war room. A finger of lead was blazing for Bolan's face, but the Executioner darted to one side, nose-diving through a sliding door. As he got up on a knee, Bolan stroked the trigger, ripping the door downrange with a long burst, catching sight of the shark-faced gangster spinning, shredded to crimson rags.

Looking up and down, checking his flanks, Bolan was back in the hall, just in time to spot a ninja drop from the ceiling to impale the wounded gangster to the flooring. As the ninja drove the sword through the gangster's back, the soldier ventilated the silent killer with a 3-round burst.

The Uzi clicked dry.

Bolan sensed them coming. With no time to reload, he drew Harisomo's sword. Senses electrified, Bolan caught the first ninja, falling straight from above. Stepping back, the Executioner sliced the ninja's midriff open to an eruption of blood and innards. Moving on, he glimpsed another hooded shadow pop out of a hidden slat in the wall. A lightning stroke took off the ninja's head.

Quickly searching for more attackers and finding none, Bolan rammed a fresh clip into his Uzi.

He was about to venture into the war room when Miji Osaka came up on his rear, out of nowhere.

Whirling, Bolan ducked, feeling the slipstream of wind as the blade swept past his head.

''You bastard!''

Bolan flung himself back as Miji went for a disemboweling swipe. When she missed the second time, he ended it.

Whether it was adrenaline, or feeling a strange elation-exhaustion from an endless flight, Bolan wasn't sure. Whatever it was, the sword of Yokitomo felt as light as a feather in his hand, as if it indeed possessed a life of its own.

Bolan impaled Miji's heart with one driving thrust of steel.

When she crumpled, Bolan stood utterly still, listening to the silence of death all around him.

With no regrets Bolan left the crumbling empire in search of its king.

IT WAS TIME TO GO.

Death was only moments away.

Harikami Osaka stood in the middle of the main sanctuary, his sword low by his side.

He had seen the Firehawk, then the lone figure parachute from the sky. He didn't need to see the man to know who it was.

The American. Powers. The warrior from his dreams.

Osaka waited. Minutes earlier he heard the distant rattle of autofire cease from the direction of the castle. The fever told him they were all dead. His ninja. The Yakuza. His daughter.

Osaka wanted to die right. The end of his life had to be faced as he had lived. Strong. Unflinching. Unyielding.

With honor.

Even still, as he stood there, alone in the silence, burning up with fever, he heard the voice reaching from somewhere deep inside his soul. He wanted to deny the voice, but he couldn't help but listen. The voice wanted to tell him he was wrong, that it was over, that all that he wanted and hoped for would never be. Was never meant to be.

That it was right for him to die.

Right before he steeled himself to face his fate, the faint voice asked God to have mercy on his soul.

Osaka heard the flooring creak beyond the sanctuary. Before he even saw the man appear in the doorway, he knew it was Powers.

Osaka took up his sword.

SLOWLY THE EXECUTIONER walked into the main sanctuary, the sword of Yokitomo by his side. He found Osaka, waiting for him.

A strange smile ghosted the man's lips. In that

fleeting second Bolan knew Osaka had been expecting, indeed, longing for this moment.

The Uzi was slung across Bolan's shoulder. He could have shot Osaka where he stood, but he couldn't do that. It would be cold-blooded, as the old man had only his sword with which to defend himself.

If Bolan didn't let Harisomo have an honorable death because he committed atrocities, then Osaka should be denied the same. He ordered the atrocities, after all.

No killers, silent or otherwise, had trailed Bolan to the Shinto shrine. A quick search of the castle revealed no one had been left alive.

It was just himself and the man who wanted to be shogun of a new imperial Japan.

Osaka came at Bolan with sudden fury. The soldier blocked the man's first attempt to take his head. Sparks flew as steel smashed together. Osaka left no opening, swinging the sword again and again, going for either decapitation or disembowelment. Bolan surged on, banging away each lightning swipe, then hurling steel at Osaka's head. The man displayed his years of training, parrying each killing intent of the Executioner's blade, as if he had prepared for decades for this moment.

Suddenly Osaka took a step back, lashing out with a long swipe at Bolan's neck. The Executioner hammered his blade into Osaka's sword, throwing his opponent's weapon off its mark. For some strange reason, Bolan saw Osaka hesitate for a critical split second.

It was just long enough for Bolan to drive his sword straight and deep through Osaka's stomach. A quick sideways wrench, slicing up at an angle, through vital organs, and Bolan watched the pain burst, then fade in Osaka's eyes. The Executioner slid his sword clear of flesh, and Osaka plunged on his back.

Utter silence filled Bolan's ears. The sword lowered by his side, he finally heard the soft spatter of blood on wood.

For several heartbeats, unmoving, his pulse still pounding in his ears, Bolan was struck by how peaceful Osaka looked in death.

Everything was gone with death, an empire in ruins, with others left scrambling to sift through the ashes.

The Executioner dropped the sword, turned and walked away.

The final moment of truth had come to pass.

**A violent struggle for survival
in a post-holocaust world**

# JAMES AXLER

# DEATH LANDS ®

## Watersleep

In the altered reality of the Deathlands, America's coastal waters
haven't escaped the ravages of the nukecaust, but the awesome
power of the oceans still rules there. It's a power that will let
Ryan Cawdor, first among post-holocaust survivors, ride the crest
of victory—or consign his woman to the raging depths.

---

**Don't miss out on the action in these titles featuring
THE EXECUTIONER®, STONY MAN™ and SUPERBOLAN®!**

## The Red Dragon Trilogy

| | | | |
|---|---|---|---|
| #64210 | FIRE LASH | $3.75 U.S. | ☐ |
| | | $4.25 CAN. | ☐ |
| #64211 | STEEL CLAWS | $3.75 U.S. | ☐ |
| | | $4.25 CAN. | ☐ |
| #64212 | RIDE THE BEAST | $3.75 U.S. | ☐ |
| | | $4.25 CAN. | ☐ |

## Stony Man™

| | | | |
|---|---|---|---|
| #61910 | FLASHBACK | $5.50 U.S. | ☐ |
| | | $6.50 CAN. | ☐ |
| #61911 | ASIAN STORM | $5.50 U.S. | ☐ |
| | | $6.50 CAN. | ☐ |
| #61912 | BLOOD STAR | $5.50 U.S. | ☐ |
| | | $6.50 CAN. | ☐ |

## SuperBolan®

| | | | |
|---|---|---|---|
| #61452 | DAY OF THE VULTURE | $5.50 U.S. | ☐ |
| | | $6.50 CAN. | ☐ |
| #61453 | FLAMES OF WRATH | $5.50 U.S. | ☐ |
| | | $6.50 CAN. | ☐ |
| #61454 | HIGH AGGRESSION | $5.50 U.S. | ☐ |
| | | $6.50 CAN. | ☐ |

### (limited quantities available on certain titles)

| | |
|---|---|
| **TOTAL AMOUNT** | $ |
| **POSTAGE & HANDLING** | $ |
| ($1.00 for one book, 50¢ for each additional) | |
| **APPLICABLE TAXES\*** | $ |
| **TOTAL PAYABLE** | $ |
| (check or money order—please do not send cash) | |

To order, complete this form and send it, along with a check or money order for the total above, payable to Gold Eagle Books, to: **In the U.S.:** 3010 Walden Avenue, P.O. Box 9077, Buffalo, NY 14269-9077; **In Canada:** P.O. Box 636, Fort Erie, Ontario, L2A 5X3.

Name:_____

Address:_____ City:_____

State/Prov.:_____ Zip/Postal Code: _____

\*New York residents remit applicable sales taxes.
Canadian residents remit applicable GST and provincial taxes.

GEBACK18

# Don't miss out on the action in these titles!